MELISSA MAYHUE

A Highlander's Homecoming

POCKET BOOKS

New York   London   Toronto   Sydney

Pocket Books
A Division of Simon & Schuster, Inc.
1230 Avenue of the Americas
New York, NY 10020

First Pocket Books paperback edition February 2010

POCKET and colophon are registered trademarks
of Simon & Schuster, Inc.

For information about special discounts for bulk purchases, please contact Simon & Schuster Special Sales at 1-866-506-1949 or business@simonandschuster.com.

The Simon & Schuster Speakers Bureau can bring authors to your live event. For more information or to book an event contact the Simon & Schuster Speakers Bureau at 1-866-248-3049 or visit our website at www.simonspeakers.com.

Cover art by Alan Ayers
Cover design by Min Choi

Manufactured in the United States of America

10 9 8 7 6 5 4 3 2 1

ISBN 978-1-4391-4425-1
ISBN 978-1-4391-5602-5 (ebook)

This book is for all the wonderful readers who take the time to send an email, write a letter, or come to the book signings. You all mean so much to me. It's your love of these characters and this world that keeps me going on the days the words just don't want to come.

Thank you for your support!

Acknowledgments

My thanks to my family, as always, for their continued support and love.

A big shout-out to the talented Nicholas Mayhue for the beautiful design work on the Mark of the Guardian.

Thanks to my critique partners, the talented Kirsten Richard and Rena Marks.

My thanks to The Knight Agency and, most especially there, my own Elaine Spencer.

As always, hugs to my ever-wonderful editor, Megan McKeever, who never fails to help me make these books even better. You're a joy to work with . . . even when you want me to hurry up!

A Highlander's
Homecoming

Prologue

WESTERN HIGHLANDS
SCOTLAND
1272

Thundering hooves echoed through the dark, misty Scottish night.

Robert MacQuarrie leaned into his massive black destrier, urging his mount to give him all the speed the animal could muster.

He rode like a madman, without care or caution, his only thought to reach Merlegh Hall before it was too late.

Before his friend Thomas MacGahan took his last gasping breath.

Thomas was more than a mere friend. If not for him, Robert would have died in battle on the point of a Saracen spear. A spear Thomas had taken in his stead and lived to tell about it.

He owed his life to Thomas.

Robert kicked the sides of the wild beast he rode, demanding more.

Faster.

"He calls for you, MacQuarrie. To be at his side when his spirit departs his poor broken body. To carry out his last request."

The watery blue eyes of the old shepherd who'd brought Robert the message haunted his memory now.

"I dinna believe he'll last through the night. You maun ride hard, lad, if yer to fulfill his final wishes."

Robert had just left an audience with his king, Alexander, when the messenger had arrived. In two days' time, he was to accompany Alexander to the wedding of a fellow King's Guard, Connor MacKiernan. Learning his friend Connor had found a woman to settle his wandering ways, Robert had left the king's chambers with a full heart. Though there was the little matter of the rumored threats against Connor's safety that concerned Alexander, it should be nothing too serious. Certainly nothing that he and Connor couldn't handle together. They were, after all, two of Alexander's finest.

Robert had been on his way to find a celebratory libation or two when the exhausted shepherd had entered his life, sending him on this urgent mission.

For Thomas to die in such a fashion simply wasn't fair.

Not that Robbie considered himself a man to waste undue thoughts as to the fairness of life. The things he'd seen, the places he'd been had taught him well the lesson that there was little in the way of fairness in this world.

But this, the loss of a warrior like Thomas to such a cruel twist of fate, brought a cry of foul to Robert's lips.

Thomas, who'd survived more battles than most men ever fought, laid low by a sharp turn in a muddy track at mountain's edge.

The warrior and his horse had tumbled over the precipice, the great beast landing on top of Thomas on a ledge below. Now, instead of a quick death on a glorious battlefield, Thomas faced the slow agony of drowning in his own fluids.

Ahead of him, the flicker of light caught Robert's attention.

Torches. He'd reached his destination at last.

The faces surrounding him as he made his way into the hall were a blur, his thoughts focused on one man only.

A woman—a redhead, of all the foul luck—approached, the keys dangling from her waist announcing her position as Merlegh's chatelaine.

"Come with me. He awaits you."

Following the woman's steps, he hurried through the dark hallways. If the shepherd's warning hadn't been enough to convince him of the seriousness of Thomas's condition, the grim faces he saw here certainly did. The expressions of those he passed and that of the chatelaine. A redhead. Always a bad sign for him.

After what seemed an eternity, he entered his friend's room.

"Robbie? Is that you?" Thomas lay in the center of a great bed, his voice weak as he asked the question.

Shock coursed through Robert. Though his friend was little more than a decade his senior, the man lying in that bed looked to be ancient, his face ashen and drawn with his pain. Only his piercing blue gaze remained the same. A cough wracked his body, sending small flecks of blood to decorate his lips and the linen bedding where he lay.

Robert shook himself to action, crossing to Thomas's side. "Aye, my friend. I've come as fast as I could."

"I've a boon to ask of you." Thomas paused, a strange gurgling sound coming from his chest as he strained to fill his lungs with air.

"Anything you ask. My debt to you is without bounds." Robert fought the urge to take his friend's hand. He recognized the signs of Thomas's coming end all too well.

"I've a daughter," Thomas rasped. "You must give me yer oath to protect her. When you carry word of my death, my father will be—" His words dissolved in another struggle to breathe.

"You need say no more, my friend. I will go to yer family and see to yer daughter."

Thomas reached out, his hand wavering unsteadily in the space between them until his fingers clutched at Robert's wrist. "It's no that my father is an evil man. It's just that Isabella is . . ." he struggled as if trying to find the words he wanted. "She is different, as was her mother. She's but an innocent child, and with me gone she will need protection and guidance. It willna be easy. Your oath, Robbie. I must hear yer oath."

"I'll see to yer daughter's safety. I swear it. On my honor. On my life."

"Then it is done." Thomas's fingers slipped from Robert's wrist. "Go now. Leave me in peace to meet my saints."

A strange tightening of Robert's throat prevented his speaking. He bowed his head respectfully and turned, leaving his friend for the last time.

Fighting for the emotional distance he regularly wore as part of his persona, he mounted his barely rested horse and set out for his return to Alexander's court.

As close as they'd been, he'd never known that Thomas had a child. And what had he meant by saying she was different? What would he do with a girl child? He was a warrior. A good one, too. A knight to King Alexander III of Scotland. A family had no part in his plans. Someday, certainly, but not now.

Apparently his plans would have to change.

MacQuarrie Keep had been a fine place for him growing up, and though he would not return to his family home to live, he felt certain the child would be welcomed there.

With something of a plan formed, he pushed all thoughts from his mind. None of them mattered for the moment. When he finished the task his king had assigned him, nothing save death would keep him from his oath to see to the safety of Isabella MacGahan.

Chapter 1

~◦~

*A*s it turned out, death was exactly what had kept Robert from fulfilling his oath to protect Isabella MacGahan. Or more precisely, the death he would have suffered had Connor MacKiernan's bride not whisked him more than seven hundred years into the future through the use of her Faerie Magic.

The battle they'd fought to overpower those who had sought to murder Connor and Cate had been hard won. Robert had paid with a sword to his rib cage that would have ended his life had he not had the expert medical care afforded him in this new time.

That had been almost ten years ago, and though he found this new world to be very much to his liking, his failure to carry out his oath to Thomas had haunted him since that day.

Leaning against the doorjamb next to his friend Connor, Robert pushed away the memories of his past as he scanned the people in this room. His new clan surrounded him here. MacKiernan, Coryell, Navarro—all as much a part of him now as if the blood of the MacQuarries ran through their veins. A good thing since he'd likely never have the family he'd imagined in his youth.

A fierce loyalty to each and every one of the people in the room surged up in his breast as he forced himself to concentrate on the urgent matters at hand.

"You don't know them like I do. They'll find me." Leah Noble spoke up from the corner of the massive living room in Connor's home. The teenager sank back into her chair, arms crossed defensively in front of her, almost as if she hoped to make herself invisible.

As a Faerie descendant, Leah carried the gift of the Fae Magic. That gift had made her the target of the evil Nuadians, renegade Fae exiled to the Mortal World. They'd held her prisoner for over a month, subjecting her to things no young woman should endure. She and her older sister, Destiny, had gone through hell before Jesse Coryell, with Robert's help, had rescued them.

Now they were both here in Connor's living room surrounded by those who would do everything in their power to change the women's lives for the better. And considering how many of those present were also of Fae heritage, that *power* was considerable.

Destiny reached out a hand and Jesse captured it, pulling her to sit on the arm of his chair, close to him.

Robert smiled to himself at the seemingly uncon-
scious action. Anyone with eyes could see that his friend
Jesse had found his Soulmate.

"We'll no let that happen, lass. Dinna you worry
yerself about it." Though Connor spoke with absolute
confidence, his expression betrayed the concern they all
felt.

Leah shook her head, her serious brown eyes
haunted in her fear. "You don't understand. You have
no idea what they're like. They're Faeries, for God's
sake. I'll never be safe from them."

"No all Fae are evil, Leah." Mairi, Connor's sister,
spoke from her spot on the sofa next to her husband,
Ramos Navarro. "And we do know what you fear.
We've dealt with these renegades ourselves."

Leah rejected their comments with a shake of her
head but didn't answer, tears dripping down her cheeks.

Destiny dropped Jesse's hand and crossed to kneel at
her sister's side. "We'll think of something. I promise.
That's why we're all here."

"There's nowhere I'll be safe," Leah whispered,
clutching at Destiny's hand. "I can't go back to them,
Desi. I can't."

"You'll stay here." Connor spoke again, taking
charge as he was wont to do. As if by the power of his
sheer will he could eliminate the young woman's fear.

"That won't be enough to keep her safe." Ramos
turned to look up at his brother-in-law. "She's right.
Adira won't give up. They'll find her and then every
female in this family will be at risk. We have to find a
more secure spot."

Robert silently agreed. If anyone in this room should

know what the Nuadians were capable of it would be Ramos. After all, he'd been raised by the devil's spawn.

"I believe I may have a solution." Pol, High Prince of the Realm of Faerie, long-distant ancestor of many in this room, rose to his feet. He turned his gaze toward Leah, his eyes sad. "If our young guest is agreeable to my suggestion, that is."

Leah straightened in her seat, her face a mask of false bravado. "I'll do anything that keeps me away from that woman. What's your plan?"

"If the Nuadians' new strength prevents Leah from living out her life without fear, perhaps we err in looking for a *where* to take her. Perhaps we should consider a *when.*"

Of course! Leave it to the Prince to point out the obvious. The solution that none of them would ever consider on their own.

"I suppose it could be done," Cate said thoughtfully. "We'd need to choose the spot carefully. Send her to someone we could trust."

"But we couldn't send her alone." Mairi added her voice, betraying her growing excitement to anyone who knew her as well as Robert did.

"Send her where?" Destiny's face had taken on an ashen look of panicked suspicion that spilled over into her voice. "What's going on here that I'm not getting?"

"Not where," Jesse explained. "When. They're talking about sending Leah back in time."

"That's crazy."

Robert fought the urge to shake his head. After all the woman had been through, how could she still doubt?

How could she not, he reminded himself. The knowledge that Faeries and magic existed was difficult to work your mind around in the beginning. He'd had his own time to get used to the idea. Destiny would need hers as well.

"You could really do that?" Leah sat up straight, interest lighting her eyes.

"Yes," Jesse answered. "They can. But you'd need to understand, once you're there, there's no guarantee they could ever get you back."

"Like you think I'd ever want to come back?" Leah scooted forward in her chair. "I'd spend my life in the Stone Age if it meant I could be safe from . . . from them."

"I promise it's not the Stone Age we're considering." Cate smiled at the young woman. "But it would be a very, very different life for you."

"Anywhere." Determination radiated around Leah. "How soon can I go?"

"As quickly as we can make a few preparations," Cate answered.

"And decide who's to accompany you," Mairi added.

"I'll go." Jesse rose from his chair and crossed to where Destiny knelt next to Leah's chair.

Robert's spine stiffened. Jesse felt as much brother as friend to Robert after all these years. There was no way he could allow Jesse to take this kind of risk. Not now that he'd discovered the one woman fate had intended for him.

Before he could voice his opinion, Leah rejected the offer herself.

"Not you." She shook her head, her hand fisted on the arm of the chair. "I didn't go through all that agony to save your life just so you could abandon my sister. You need to take care of her."

"She already knows that I have every intention of doing exactly that," his friend responded indignantly.

This time Robert made no attempt to school his expression. If there was a single soul in the room who couldn't see how Jesse felt about Destiny by now, they were too far beyond blind for help. They were lost in the land of stupid.

Those two might need a lot of things going forward, but time apart wasn't one of them. In fact, there was no one sitting in this room who could afford to take the risk of being left behind in time.

Except him. Were he to go, there would be no one left behind to worry over his return. No loving wife. No passel of children clamoring for a spot in his lap each evening.

He pushed the thought away. His was a good life, filled with trusted friends and blessed opportunity. That he seemed destined to live out this lifetime without finding his own Soulmate was out of his control. Had these people not become a part of his life, he would never even have known that he was supposed to have a Soulmate. He would have simply traveled his life's journey alone, accepting what came to him.

He wouldn't waste his days filled with envy for what his friends had found. Perhaps in another lifetime he would cross paths with the one meant for him. For this life, he would simply have to content himself with filling that empty spot in his heart by being the friend, the uncle. He was a warrior. Certainly he could be strong enough to face life alone.

Besides, this could well be his one and only opportunity to redeem himself. A last chance to keep his promise to a dying friend.

As far as the risk was concerned? He scoffed at the idea. He lived on the thrills that came from risk. This situation was a gift, pure and simple.

Taking a step forward, he broke the silence that had fallen in the room.

"I'll do it. I'm the one to go with the lass."

"Yer sure about this?" Connor questioned, his ice blue eyes intent as they turned in Robert's direction.

"Even knowing we can't guarantee getting you back here?" Cate added, her pretty brow wrinkled with concern.

Robert shrugged. His going only made sense. He'd sworn an oath. What happened to him was of little consequence as long as he was able to keep his word. "I've a small matter left undone by my abrupt departure. It would be good to get it off my conscience after all this time."

The one nagging failure of his life. Bad enough to have failed a friend. Inexcusable to have failed a helpless child. Though he would never have children of his own, there was one small girl waiting for him to rescue her, seven hundred years in his past. At long last he'd keep that vow.

Across the room, Jesse chose this moment to announce his intention to marry the woman who gazed adoringly up into his eyes. Right there in front of all of them.

About time the man publicly acknowledged what they all could see.

Robert smiled and shook his head, turning from the celebration erupting around him and heading out toward the silence of the well-shaded grounds surrounding the renovated Scottish castle.

Though he shared his friend's joy, he needed to step away from it for a moment. Not that he envied his friend. Not that the couple's happiness highlighted the empty place by his own side. The empty place in his heart. He was too strong for such womanly feelings as that. No, it was simply that he needed the quiet and solitude to think. He needed time alone. Time to carefully plan.

There actually were any number of details to take care of before he left. Charlie, his bright-eyed Boston terrier came to mind. He knew Connor would see to picking the dog up from boarding and take it to his home where Charlie would be cared for and well loved. That was no worry. Though the idea he might never see his adoring pup again—that was a bit harder to stomach.

There were other arrangements to make as well. Legal paperwork of some sort would be required. He should set up a power of attorney, turning all his property over to someone.

Just in case.

If all went well, he'd do what needed to be done and then the magic would bring him home. The problem with using Faerie Magic was that it didn't always do the expected, and Robert knew going into this he could well be giving up the life he'd come to love.

When a woman with Cate's considerable Faerie Magic told you she might not be able to get you back home, you'd be well advised to take her seriously. If this was going to end up being a one-way trip, he'd best make sure someone here would have access to his belongings. None of his wonderful toys, not the vehicles or the machinery he'd collected—none of it would do him any good where he was going.

When he was going, he corrected himself. The Highlands of Scotland in 1272. The exact same time he'd left behind all those years ago. As long as they'd determined to hide Leah in the past, he could think of no better time than the one he'd left. It would suit both their needs. He'd be able to fulfill his vow to Thomas, and there were many people in that time they could trust to keep Leah safe.

The Nuadians had vowed to hunt her down, no matter where she went. No one in the room he'd just left doubted for a moment they would do exactly that. But as everyone sitting in that living room had reasoned, while the Nuadians might well track Leah down wherever she hid in this world, they'd have no chance at all of finding her in a completely different time.

He would accompany Leah on her unimaginable journey to thirteenth-century Scotland. He'd see her safely settled.

And then?

Then he'd be free to fulfill the oath he'd made over seven hundred years ago. He'd find Thomas's daughter, Isabella, and take her to his own family's home, where she would be cared for properly.

"Mr. MacQuarrie?"

Robert looked over his shoulder to find Leah picking her way across the damp lawn toward him. Though the young woman herself was almost hidden in the baggy jeans and heavy sweater she wore, she couldn't hide what she most wanted to remove from her identity. Whether it was the long golden hair tossed by the breeze or simply the way she carried herself, there was no denying her Faerie heritage.

If he ever had been blessed with a daughter, he would have wished for one as brave as this girl.

"Robert, lass. Call me Robert. Is there something you need of me?"

She nodded, her eyes fixed on her feet even as the color rose in her cheeks.

"Everyone back there's pretty excited about planning a wedding. I didn't want to interrupt them." She lifted her gaze to meet his steadily. "But I have so many questions. Can you tell me where we'll go? What it will be like?"

"I can try," he answered as he led the way to two garden benches separated by a small table.

When he reached toward her, she flinched, a haunted expression fleeting across her face.

How could he have been so thoughtless? Considering what the lass had been through, he shouldn't be surprised she could bear no man's touch. The filthy Nuadian bastards had kidnapped Leah and held her captive, poked her with needles as they drained her blood to increase their own powers, and all but raped her.

Stepping back a respectful pace, he waited for her to choose one seat before he took the other.

"You've no changed yer mind about going, have you?" Was that the root of her questions?

Her eyes rounded and she shook her head vehemently, her fingers playing over the stone hanging from her neck. "Oh no, not at all. I want to go. We can't leave soon enough as far as I'm concerned." She shrugged and looked out over the expanse of garden. "I just . . . I just want to have some idea of what I'll be facing when I get there. I mean, it's not like we're talking about a trip across the country. I remember from my literature class last year that the language used in medieval Britain was entirely different from what's spoken today. How are we even going to communicate with people?"

Robert nodded thoughtfully. That one had concerned him, too, when he'd first come forward in time. "You'll have no problem, lass. I canna explain how, but the Faerie Magic takes it all into account. What you'll speak, what you'll understand when you arrive in that time—it will all be the same to yer ears and to those around you. The only difference you'll note is that some of yer words are unknown to them, so they'll likely find yer speech patterns to be strange."

"What kinds of words?" Leah leaned toward him, her thirst for knowledge lighting a fire in her eyes.

"Words for those things they've no understanding of. Cars, for example. Or airplanes. Do you get my meaning?"

She nodded thoughtfully, wisps of gold hair falling over her shoulder. "So I don't need to worry about learning a new language. Do you have any idea where we'll go?"

It was Robert's turn to nod slowly. He'd been giving this some thought since the moment he'd volunteered to accompany Leah. "We'll head for the MacQuarrie

Keep. I'm thinking you'd be safe there, with my own family."

His parents would welcome her into their home even though he wouldn't be able to stay there himself. Not under the same roof with that redheaded bitch his brother had married. MacQuarrie Keep stopped being his home the day Elizabeth moved in.

When Leah's brow furrowed, he held up a hand to forestall the questions he saw running through her mind. "It's where I came from, lass. *When* I came from, to be more accurate. Just over nine years ago, Jesse's sister, Cate, used her powers to bring me forward in time to save my life. It's too long a story for now, but I'm sure you'll hear the whole of it as we prepare for our journey."

Too long and too painful for him to recount to the lass. Likely the women of the house would fill her in later.

Leah chewed on her bottom lip for a moment before making eye contact again. "Is that why you said you'd go back with me? Because you feel like you have a debt to them? I'd hate to think you're disrupting your whole life because you feel like you have to."

He shook his head. It was a debt that was driving him, all right, but not the one the girl feared.

"Dinna you fret yerself over this, lass. Accompanying you is but a piece of my reason for returning. I've my own purposes to be met in going back."

Purposes long past due.

Chapter 2

"You should feel no more than a sensation of movement against your skin." Dallyn Aí Lyre, High General of the Realm of Faerie, fastened a strange metal band around Robert's arm before backing away to resume his position in the circle of men surrounding Robert.

Robert looked around the glen to the faces of the men he knew so well, words failing him at this moment of honor.

And honor it truly was.

Not an hour ago, Jesse had insisted Robert leave the preparations for his trip and join him on a small adventure. The adventure had begun at an ancient circle of standing stones on the property Jesse had recently purchased.

To Robert's amazement, as Jesse ran his hand over one of the stones, its face changed and they seemed to be looking through an open door into another world. A world Robert had never expected to see with his own two eyes.

Wyddecol. The Realm of Faerie.

When they had crossed through the portal, Robert's second surprise was the five men who were waiting to greet them. Dallyn, Pol, Ramos, Connor, and even Ian McCullough, all those men closest to him who had ties to the world of Fae.

"You have honored us with your friendship and your unquestioning service to our people." Pol had stepped forward as the others formed a large circle around Robert. "Now you willingly take on the duties of a Guardian of the Realm in accompanying one of our daughters on a perilous journey. As such, we wish to recognize your service and name you as one of the Guardians."

Robert had never considered this could happen to him. Guardian was an elite title held only by Fae descendants.

"I . . . I don't know what to say."

"Say you'll accept," Jesse said, a grin covering his face. "And strip out of that shirt."

All of that had led up to this moment, the moment when Dallyn placed the large bracelet-like band around Robert's bicep before rejoining the others in the circle. Each of the men in the circle bowed his head and a hush fell over the group as Pol spoke once again.

"You undertake this sacred pledge of your own free will?"

"I do." Robert nodded, still in awe of the honor his friends offered.

"So be it. Know, then, that Guardians serve as instruments of the Magic, to repair that which was torn asunder. Grant that the power to reunite the broken Soul Pairings might reside in us that we might bring harmony and peace to the divided worlds. Until that day, we protect those unable to protect themselves, bending only to the will of the Magic."

Pol's words echoed eerily through the glen, and as the last sound died away, a strange humming noise filled the silence, resonating around Robert like voices heard from very far away.

As the tenor of the sound increased, he felt the first sensations against his skin, underneath the band Dallyn had placed there. Small, wispy movements, like grass blowing in the wind, tickled his arm. The feeling grew, building to a crescendo in time to the vibration of the voices until the pitch became almost too high to hear.

It was then the power of the Faerie Magic flooded Robert's body, passing through him in a burst of energy, leaving him weak in the knees and gasping for breath.

The men around him broke into cheers, clapping their hands and slapping him on the back. Dallyn removed the large metal band and Robert felt the shock of recognition at what he saw on his skin where the bracelet had been. A tattoolike mark, exactly like the one adorning the arms of each man in the circle.

The Mark of the Guardian.

Pol stepped forward once again and they all fell silent.

"All of Wyddecol will recognize you by your Mark as one of our own. Welcome to the brotherhood, Guardian."

Chapter 3

"There's one more thing I want you to keep in mind, Robbie." Cate MacKiernan lifted her hand to his stirrup, casting a quick look to the woman at her side, Mairi MacKiernan Navarro. Cate spoke quietly, her words clearly intended only for the three of them.

Moments from now, these two women, Faerie descendants both, would be the ones to send him and Leah hurtling through time.

They'd come to this relatively secluded clearing not far from the ruins of where his family keep had stood in the thirteenth century. He and Leah, dressed in authentic garb for where they were bound, sat on horseback, waiting for the moment they would travel into the multicolored lights of the Faerie Magic.

Robert cocked an eyebrow and leaned down toward the two women, waiting for whatever they wanted to tell him. He knew there was no rushing them. Cate would finish in her own good time. From the looks she and Mairi exchanged, this clearly concerned something the two of them had already discussed.

"You do understand that there are no guarantees for how the Faerie Magic works, right?" Cate glanced to Mairi once more.

"And you realize we've little control over the process if the Magic itself takes over," Mairi added as her fingers worried at her long blond braid. "It's no at all a scientific process."

Robert nodded, watching both of them closely. He knew them too well. There was more. He could feel it in his bones. "I never thought it was. And?"

Cate needlessly cleared her throat. "You're going back to a time when you're not supposed to exist. If the Magic seeks to equalize what should be with what is, you could be in real trouble. There's a chance that because of your unique situation you could be in even more danger than anyone else who might go back."

"Mairi survived the same herself, did she no?" This woman standing in front of him had returned to a time where she wasn't supposed to exist, either, and she'd come back from it unharmed.

Cate glanced to Mairi, who avoided his gaze, instead looking down at the braid she held in her hand. Nerves? That wasn't a sign he liked to see from women as powerful as these two.

"It's not quite the same, Robbie." Cate shook her head and took a deep breath before continuing. "When we pulled Mairi from the past, we did so under the assumption that she *would* be killed. Nothing had actually happened to her yet. You had already received a mortal wound. There was no doubt as to what your fate would have been if we'd left you behind. It was only by bringing you to our time, by getting you immediate medical attention that didn't even exist in your time, that your life was saved."

Mairi stopped twisting the end of her braid long enough to add, "We just can't be sure what will happen. You know how Pol always says we can't change history, only alter the circumstances? Well, yer being alive in that time is no what history had in store for you. If you want, Robbie, there's still time to change your mind about going. One of the others can take Leah back."

Robert snorted his derision, smiling down at the women in an attempt to reassure them. "If that's the problem, then we're simply looking at it all wrong. Instead let's choose to think of my being there as a small alteration of history's course, no an attempt to change it. How's that work for you? There'll be no changes in our plans at this late date. My decision's firm. I'm the one who's going, so let's get on with it."

Robert gritted his teeth against his irritation. Wasn't that just a lovely bit of news they'd saved up for him? Not only was he staring down the possibility of never being able to return to the time he'd come to love and think of as his own, but now he'd also need to keep an eye out for the Magic trying to eliminate him entirely from the spot where he was headed. So bloody typical of the damned Fae. Their magic was as fickle as a red-headed woman.

No matter. He didn't need a lot of time. Just enough to settle Leah and to keep his promise to Thomas.

Surely he could manage to stay alive long enough to accomplish two simple tasks.

"Okay, then," Cate said loudly as she and Mairi backed away from the horses and toward the trees where Cate's young daughter, Rosie, waited. "You have Leah's envelope with directions to Dun Ard, right?"

"I don't need it," Leah interrupted. "I told you not to bother. I don't want anything to do with *any* Faeries. Not ever again."

Cate's eyebrow rose in a perfect imitation of her husband. "Right. But you do have it, don't you, Robbie? Just in case?"

He nodded his reassurance to the woman. Leah might not ever have any need of contacting the MacKiernans, but just in case she did, he planned to leave the envelope, wrapped in its linen disguise, in his mother's care for the lass.

"I guess that covers about everything." Cate ran a hand over the back of her neck, as if stretching out her muscles before exercising. "Both of you need to keep in mind that the most powerful moments for the Magic are when you first feel it beginning to work. Concentrate on when and where you want to go. Clear your minds of everything else but what you want most."

"Because it's what you want most that the Magic will act on," Mairi added.

Or, more likely, what the Faerie Magic itself wanted most.

Robert pushed away the negative thoughts, concentrating on his family estate as it had been in 1272, not the ruin of tumbled stones it was now.

A gentle breeze wafted through the glen, carrying it

with it the sounds of birds in the trees above them. No other sound disturbed the silence as they waited.

And waited.

"Shouldn't something be happening?" Leah hissed his direction, her eyes round with apprehension.

Robert shrugged, wondering the same himself. Unable to answer her excellent question, he turned to the experts.

"Ladies?"

"I know, I know. It's just that nothing's coming." Cate grabbed up Mairi's hand and they both closed their eyes. "I don't understand," she said after a moment. "I'm not feeling anything."

"Let me help, Mommy!" Rosie jumped to her feet and ran to join her mother and Mairi. With one last wave in Robert's direction, the little girl lifted her arms to join hands with her mother and aunt, becoming a part of their circle. "Be safe, Uncle Robbie. See you soon!" she called, a wide grin breaking over her face.

Returning Rosie's infectious smile, he only hoped the child was right. For an instant, their gazes locked.

As sometimes happened when his eyes met those of the child, his thoughts skipped away to another young lass. Isabella MacGahan. She would be only a year or two younger than Rosie. He'd never seen Thomas's daughter, but he had always pictured her in his imagination to be very much like Rosie: a small, blonde bundle of smiles and giggles with gangly arms and a wild imagination.

He had long ago lost any hope that he would have children of his own. No matter how much he might want it, finding his Soulmate was surely not his destiny in this lifetime. And even though his deepest desire would not be fulfilled, his life was still good. He had been given a second chance, one that included true friends who had accepted him as one of their family. A family he would do anything for. A family he wouldn't hesitate to give his life for.

At this very moment, sitting here in this peaceful clearing, all he truly wanted in life was to deliver Leah to the safety of his family and to see to it that Isabella MacGahan got the life she deserved.

Was that so much to ask?

A strange tingle webbed its way around the lines of the mark on Robert's arm and he realized with a start the Magic had already begun to work while he was lost in his thoughts. Both he and Leah were already encased in a large sphere of wavering emerald with a growing multitude of brilliantly colored sparkles shooting around them like crazed comets in an eerily green night sky.

Leah reached out to him. Without thought, he grasped her hand, just as the myriad colors gyrating around them hit the peak of their frenzy and merged, turning their world to black and hitting them with a force that felt like it sucked them into a dark, invisible vortex.

Chapter 4

As quickly as the black had descended, it disappeared, evaporating around them into a fine green mist.

Robert shook his head, trying to rid himself of the sense-mangling aftereffects of the time travel. The last time he'd done this, he'd passed out before arriving in the future and slept for days after, so he'd completely missed the entire experience.

And what an experience! It had felt like a thrill ride, similar to nothing he'd ever gone through save for possibly the rush of parachuting out of an airplane.

The mark on his arm felt almost alive, crawling with invisible movement so that he finally gave in to the urge to scratch it.

Beside him, Leah's whimper drew him from the dregs of his adrenaline high. When she tugged at the hand he still held, he let go immediately.

"Are you no well, lass?" He realized it was a stupid question the minute the words passed his lips.

She sat her mount, her arms clasped around her middle as she bent forward, her eyes closed. After a deep breath she looked up, her face pale.

"I'm dying here," she groaned. "Why didn't somebody warn me there was actual movement? I feel like my stomach is getting ready to spew out my ears."

Robert grinned sympathetically. The poor lass had the motion sickness just as her older sister did. "It'll pass soon. Do you feel up to going on or do you want to wait a bit?"

"Go," she muttered, gripping her reins so tightly the gentle horse carrying her whinnied in protest.

"Give Nelly her head, then, lass. Dinna hold her so firmly. She'll take good care of you." It was why he'd chosen this particular animal for Leah. She didn't need any riding skill at all with this old girl. The horse would do her well for years to come.

Leah nodded, and after a deep breath as if to steady herself, she gave the reins some slack and they headed out.

Robert took a deep breath of his own, his nervous excitement building at seeing his family again.

There had been a great discussion about taking Leah to Connor's family farther north, but the moment she realized the MacKiernans and MacAlisters were Faerie descendants, she put her foot down. The poor lass had suffered enough at the hands of the Nuadian Fae to sour her on the entire Faerie race. She'd pleaded to be sent someplace where there were no Faeries at all, good or bad, as if in avoiding them she could deny her own heritage. Nothing but pure Mortals would do for her, so here they were, in another time, on their way to MacQuarrie Keep.

Leah's stubborn resistance had worked itself right into his original idea of when and where they should go, making his plan to return to his own time, to his family's keep the best solution.

Once they'd decided on their destination, they'd picked their starting spot well. Within minutes he and Leah emerged from the trees and onto the hard-packed path that led to his family home. A few minutes more and the castle itself loomed ahead.

Funny how the memory played tricks on you. Robert would have sworn it an impossible task for the trees to have been cut back so far from the castle walls since he'd been here last. Though he had lived almost ten years since he'd laid eyes on MacQuarrie Keep, he'd been home for a quick, uncomfortable visit no more than three months before he'd left this time. He'd carried the memory of that visit and his family home buried deep in his heart for almost a decade.

As a child, he had never imagined he would live anywhere other than this very place. The people and the land were as much a part of him as breathing had been. He'd seen the straight path of his life stretching out ahead of him. A wife and children who would join him here, making him as happy as his parents had always been.

But that dream had shattered in his sixteenth year when he'd met Elizabeth Hawthorne. Her father had traveled here on the king's business, bringing his daughter along. Two years his elder, she'd flirted her way into his heart only to break that heart when she'd suddenly married his brother.

Robert had ridden out these gates the day after Richard's wedding without a look back, pledging his service at Alexander's court. Only by the grace of men like Thomas MacGahan and Connor MacKiernan had he been accepted into their ranks and trained. Only through their friendship had he managed to live with the loss of his childhood dreams.

But neither those hateful memories nor the ones from his last visit to his mother and father meshed with what he saw now.

It all seemed different to him as he stared at the closed gate ahead of them. That was fair odd, too. His father had rarely kept the portcullis set. His eyes scanned up, quickly assessing other changes to his home. It appeared the parapet had been strengthened along the wall walk.

"They do say the memory goes first," he muttered out loud. Of course, those types of structural changes would be virtually impossible to make quickly. Work of that nature would have taken years, not months.

"Hearing," Leah corrected, her gaze fixed ahead of her, appearing to miss nothing as she soaked in what would be her new home. "I'm pretty sure I read that it's the hearing that goes first."

A movement ahead of them caught his attention and the muscles in Robert's back tensed. His warrior senses on full alert, he grabbed Leah's reins, forcing her mount to a stop. "Stay behind me."

"Why do I have to—"

"Dinna question me," he interrupted. "Do as I say. Now."

He was sure those arrow loops along the parapet were new. As were the tips of the arrows peeking out the holes.

All aimed directly at him and Leah.

"Who goes there?" a man's voice demanded from the corner of the wall walk. "State yer business or be on yer way."

Biting back his irritation at being challenged to enter his own home, Robert paused before responding. The guard must be new not to recognize him.

"Sir Robert MacQuarrie, younger son to Hugh, laird of the MacQuarrie." The title came haltingly to his tongue, it had been so long since he'd had need of it. Neither knights nor lairds played any part in his new life.

"The MacQuarrie heir, are you? Och, aye, of course you are," the guard yelled down. "And meself? I'm the king of France, I am."

Laughter filtered into the air, wafting down from the wall walk, and Robert felt his anger grow. He hadn't claimed to be the heir. Everyone knew that would be his older brother, Richard, so the comment didn't bear his response. Whoever the new guard was, the man needed a few lessons in proper behavior, and at the moment, Robert began to feel just irritated enough that he might be the perfect instructor.

"King of France, my arse," he muttered before yelling back the only reasonable response. "Do yer job, you slackard. I'd have you bring the MacQuarrie himself to settle this."

Time lengthened as they waited until at last the chains holding the portcullis groaned and the gate began its slow ascent, allowing them access. The tunnel through the wall of rock seemed longer and darker than he remembered, though common sense told him it was the same ten feet it had always been. He hated small, dark places. With a quick glance back to assure himself Leah followed closely, Robert fixed his eyes on the arch of light ahead of them that opened into the inner courtyard of his family's castle.

Four guards, spears at the ready, stepped out to block their path as they came through the archway.

"Stay yer mounts," one of them ordered. "You'll wait here for his lairdship. And keep yer hands where we can see them."

Robert glared at the man, a look well calculated to cause discomfort. Only when the guard dropped his gaze to the ground did Robert look away. While he waited for his father, he scanned the inner bailey, absently noting the subtle changes since his last visit.

There were many.

Out of the corner of his eye, he saw a flash of brown. A young lad, no more than six or seven, raced across the courtyard to the chapel, his hair flying back from the sides of his head as he ran. Before he reached the small building, a woman emerged, her slow, heavy steps carrying her from the chapel toward the great door of the keep.

As the boy drew level with her, she leaned down to him, her head snapping up when the boy pointed in Robert's direction.

She started forward, her stride accelerating as she approached.

"Robert?" she called out, her voice firm, sharp, familiar.

Robert leaned forward, squinting to make out her face more clearly. It wasn't possible. The voice he knew, but not the form.

"Mother?" He barely breathed the words, so unsure the appellation belonged to the woman whose steps toward him had turned to a slow jog.

He slid from the back of his horse, taking no more than a footstep in her direction before he was met with a spear point laid at his chest.

"Halt!"

She'd drawn close now and he could doubt it no longer. It was his mother, her eyes, her expression so well-known to him, all encased in a face that had aged so much more than he expected. What could have happened to her in the months since he'd seen her last?

She ran now, lifting her hands to cradle his cheeks when she reached his side. "Robbie?" She whispered his name, tears filming her eyes. "Praise the saints, it is you. I kenned in my heart you'd return home to us one day."

The spear held to his chest wavered.

"You'll move that this instant, you worthless oaf," she ordered, slapping away the spear pointed at his heart before throwing her arms around him.

The guard took a faltering step back as if unsure of exactly what he should do next.

Margery MacQuarrie, though barely tall enough to reach Robert's breast, had always been a force to be reckoned with. He was glad to see that hadn't changed.

He enfolded his mother in his embrace, holding her tightly to him for only a moment before she pushed away, again lifting her hands to his face.

"I can hardly believe my own eyes. They told us you were killed in the king's service. But I'd no given up hope, Robbie. When they couldna bring yer body home to be buried, I told yer father they had to be wrong. I said my prayers and lit my candles daily. And now you've returned to us as I prayed you would." She let go of him and wiped a hand over her damp cheeks.

Robert stood silently watching while this amazing woman morphed from Mother to Lady Margery in less than a heartbeat. Her back straightened and the emotion swept from her face in the transformation of composing herself, as if only now she realized that everyone closely watched her actions.

"It's yer son, Hugh," she called, her eyes focused over his shoulder. "Come home to us at last."

Robert turned his head, words abandoning him for perhaps the first time in his life as he watched the large man headed in their direction, his progress slowed by a decided limp. Hugh MacQuarrie? The man was far too old to be his father. How was this possible?

Could their time travel have missed its mark by a few years?

The guards scattered backward as Hugh approached. He moved in closely to stare into Robert's face. After a moment or two, apparently satisfied, he threw his arms around his younger son.

"Welcome home, my lad, welcome home. We'd all but given up hope." Margery cleared her throat and he added, "Well, yer mother never did."

When his father stepped back, Robert was shocked to see a glassy sheen of tears in the old man's eyes.

"Mind yer manners, Hugh. Robbie's brought someone with him. A wife perhaps?" Margery rested a hand on Robert's forearm as she spoke. "Though much too young for you," she added quietly, her disapproval clear in her tone.

"Wife?" Leah squeaked from her perch on top of her mount. "No!"

Robert's own hurried "No!" all but drowned out Leah's protest.

He stepped to the side of her horse, holding up his arms to lift her down. Though he knew she would prefer to avoid his touch, after only the slightest hesitation she leaned into him, her hands grasping his forearms to allow him to lift her down.

A sharp pain twinged through his chest when he took her weight, and as soon as her feet hit the ground he dropped his hold. That was odd. She was such a tiny thing, less than he bench-pressed on a regular basis at the gym. Whatever it was, it wasn't something he had time to worry about right now.

"No my wife," he repeated, catching Leah's gaze as he continued. "My daughter."

Her eyes widened and her lips tightened but, to her credit, she made no comment refuting his claim.

He'd considered using this story from the start but had worried he'd have problems convincing them he had a daughter her age they had never known about. Still, it seemed his best ploy and was the only story he'd managed to invent. The result of an indiscretion he'd learned of only recently, a deceased mother, all good reasons to bring her here for their care.

In the seconds after his claim, his mother swept forward, a joyous smile breaking over her face. "A daughter! Och, Robbie, you've made me a happy woman indeed." She threw her arms around Leah, hugging the girl closely to her. "With nothing but sons of my own, you've no idea how I've longed for a lass over the years to join our family."

Robert tightened his hold on his emotions. Absurd to feel this pressure in his throat. Still, it did his heart good to see his mother so happy. Bringing Leah here had been a good thing all around. Though he'd never know the comfort of having his own children, his parents would feel the pleasure of thinking their bloodline continued in the form of a granddaughter.

As for Leah herself, though she was obviously surprised at the welcome, she handled it all quite well. This was going to work out even better than he could have hoped.

Now, before he had to face his brother, seemed an opportune time to come straight to the point.

"I've come to ask yer indulgence in allowing my Leah to remain here with you."

"And why would she no?" his father boomed. "As yer daughter, this is her home as much as yers."

His mother, arm around Leah's shoulders, herded the lass toward the keep, her expression shuttered as she cast one last look in his direction. "Bring her things, Robbie. I'll be about getting our bonnie lassie settled and then we'll have a grand visit, just the two of us."

His father's large hand clapped down on his back, accompanied by the booming laughter he remembered so fondly from his childhood.

"Aye, it's good to have you home, son. And with a

daughter as well! Perhaps 'tis a profitable score of years you've spent away from us, after all."

Robert's step faltered and he stopped in his tracks. *Score of years?* Could he have heard his father correctly? No wonder everything was so changed. From everything he'd seen, he'd suspected they'd arrived later than planned, but not by this much. This was supposed to be the same year he'd left, not twenty years later!

How could their plans have gone so wrong?

Mairi's parting advice about the Magic taking over danced through his mind as he tried to accept this unplanned change.

Twenty years. Twenty years had passed since he'd last laid eyes on this world.

What his eyes had shown him all made sense now. Little wonder his home looked so changed, his parents so much older.

Twenty years. What else might have happened in twenty years' time? A creeping fear spiraled through his gut at the thought. Had he completely failed his oath to Thomas? What might have become of his friend's poor little daughter?

Jogging forward, Robert caught up with his father, slowing his pace across the bailey to match his father's halting limp.

"I'm no as young as I used to be, Robbie. It's good you've returned to take yer rightful place at the keep. With you and the lass here, I can put away any worries about what will happen when I'm gone."

"Da! You've no call to say such as that. You dinna look ready to pass on to me. No yet." Robert smiled over at his father. "Besides, you've Richard here to look after things."

This time it was his father's step that faltered and stopped.

"Yer brother's at Edward's court, thanks to Elizabeth and her father. He calls himself an Englishman these days. He's even taken the Hawthorne name." Hugh straightened and started forward again. "He'll no have any part in the future of MacQuarrie Keep."

Robert shouldn't be surprised but he was. That, at least, explained the guard's comment. It wasn't bad enough that Elizabeth had broken his heart years ago. Now the red-haired bitch who'd used him as a stepping stone to get to his brother had managed to bring even more trouble to the MacQuarrie Keep.

"Come along, lad. Yer mother's no a patient woman these days." Hugh chuckled as if he found his own words quite amusing.

Considering twenty years had passed since he'd been here last, Robert had to admit he saw the humor himself, sad though it was.

Inside the door of the keep a young boy took the saddlebags from Robert, racing away up the stairs, presumably to Leah's new room.

His mother waited at the bottom of those stairs.

"You'll have time to meet with his lairdship after the midday meal. For now I'd ask you to join me in my solar."

He glanced at his father, who shrugged indulgently. "Best no to keep yer lady mother waiting. Any longer than you already have, that is. We'll have plenty of time to talk later."

Robert nodded and followed his mother up the winding stone stairs to the second level of the keep.

Just as he remembered, her solar smelled of flowers. Though he'd never stopped to consider it before, he realized she must keep dried bits and pieces tucked away in here. There certainly were no fresh bouquets available at the corner grocery in this time.

"Where's Leah?"

His mother motioned for him to have a seat next to her in one of the large chairs drawn up in front of the fireplace before she answered. "With Maisey. She'll bring the lass to join us here once she's settled in."

"My Maisey?" Now there was a name that brought back memories. The woman had been nursemaid to both him and Richard for the first eight years of his life. "She must be ancient by now."

Margery smiled, pouring a cup of spiced wine and handing it to him. "Aye. At least as ancient as I am."

He felt his neck redden as he realized his words had slipped out before he'd had a chance to consider them properly. "No, my lady, I dinna mean to say . . . that is . . ."

His mother lifted her hand to halt his ineffective apology, her smile even broader than before. "It's no matter, lad. I've many a day where I do feel ancient. But enough of that. Today is no one of them."

She took a sip from her cup and fixed him with a look he remembered well from his childhood. A look that put him on notice of what was to come. His mother, perhaps the most gentle, most loving female to ever step foot in the world, had always possessed the ability to pin her sons to the spot with that look. As they'd grown older, he and Richard had compared her gaze to that of a falcon as it eyed its prey.

"Perhaps you'd care to tell me where you've been this past score of years."

Stalling for time, he lifted his own cup to his lips and felt some of his apprehension slip away as he contemplated the story he would give her. The twenty years, though not at all in his plans, would actually make it easier to explain Leah's presence: a marriage, a deceased wife, a daughter in need of a woman's care. It would actually fit much more logically now.

"And while yer at it, Robbie, you can tell me who the lass really is, no this made-up story of her being yer daughter."

The wine caught in his throat and he choked, coughing as he gasped it into his windpipe.

His mother jumped from her chair, pounding him on the back while she lifted one of his arms above his head, just as if he were still a small child.

When he'd recovered, she returned to her seat, once again fixing him with "the look." "Well? I'm waiting. The truth, Robert."

He huffed out his breath, shaking his head. It was no use. He'd never once in the entirety of his life been able to sneak even the smallest deceit past this woman. How he'd ever allowed himself to consider the possibility he could carry this off was beyond him.

"You'll no believe me if I give you the truth," he muttered. "And I'd rather no have you think yer son has gone daft."

"That's my decision to make, is it no?"

Clearly she would settle for nothing less than the full truth, but where would he even begin?

"If I were to tell you a tale of magic and Faeries, what would you make of that, my lady?"

His mother looked down at her cup, her fingers clenching tightly around the vessel. "She's one of theirs, is she no? One of the Fae. She certainly has their delicate beauty about her."

It took a moment for him to realize his mouth had fallen open. His mother believed in Faeries? "How in the name of the saints . . ."

He stopped himself from speaking, watching his mother's grip gradually loosen on the cup she held while her expression calmed, as if she worked through some problem, at last reaching her decision.

"You ken the existence of the Fae, do you?" he asked when he thought her ready.

With a sigh, she slowly nodded, bringing her gaze back up to meet his. "Aye, son. I encountered one of them as a wee lass. I'd been allowed to accompany my father and brothers into Inverness for market day. The streets were crowded and we'd stopped at so many booths that morning, I'd grown tired, and gradually I fell behind the others." Her eyes glazed over with the memory of her experience.

"Go on," he prodded, not wanting her to stop now.

"I was terrified, unable to cease my tears. As I searched for my father, I found myself in a small alley, where a beautiful woman sat on the ground with her wares spread out on a cloth before her. She beckoned me closer and spoke kindly to me, assuring me I would find my family shortly. And though I dinna want to allow her to touch me, when she reached out to stroke my cheek it was as if I had no the power to move away from her. To this day, I remember her words, her voice, as if it were yestereve when I met her.

"'*Have no fear,*' she said to me. '*What you will do in life, the lives of those you raise, all are too important to the Fae for us to allow anything to happen to you this day. Hurry along, child. Even now your father searches for you.*'"

"I no ever heard you tell that story of yer childhood before." Though certainly his mother had delighted them with stories of her youth their whole lives.

"No. I've told that one only once, to my father, and no all of it at that." She shook her head, the faraway look still in her eyes. "I felt as though my feet were bound to the alley and I couldna move, no even when the woman dropped a necklace of ribbon and stone over my head. She tucked the bauble down under my shift where it would be hidden, and told me I'd find need of it one day. When she finally removed her touch from my skin, I ran as fast as I could. Blindly, out into the thick of marketplace, weaving through the masses, straight into my father's legs as if I were directed to him by a power not my own."

She paused to sip her wine once more, her expression returning to her normal composure.

"And?" Robert encouraged. There had to be more to this fantastic tale.

She smiled, again shaking her head. "I told my father of the beautiful woman and her words, but he dismissed it as nothing more than an encounter with a Tinkler, assuring me I was lucky to have escaped those who steal children as well as possessions. It was only after I was older I heard the other rumors about Tinklers."

"Other rumors?" Robert had read of them in history books. He knew that later they'd be persecuted as a people, driven from many places, and called by a variety of names, including gypsy.

"Aye. Many of the Tinklers are thought to have connections with the Fae."

"Mother . . ." What could he say to her? He couldn't very well tell her the Fae didn't exist. Coming from him, that would be a lie she'd see through all too easily.

After a moment of silence, she picked up the thread of her story as if it had never been interrupted. "To appease me, my father looked for the woman. Though we searched down many alleys that day, we never found any sign of her. And even at that age, even without having heard the rumors, I kenned the truth of what she was."

"What she was?" he echoed quietly, knowing before she spoke what his mother would say next.

"She was Fae, Robbie. Telling me of my future. Sending me safely back to my family that day that I might fulfill some purpose for the Fae later in my life. She protected me." His mother straightened in her chair with another smile. "As, of course, we'll help you protect yer Leah."

"Divine luck was with you that day, my lady, that the Fae you met was kindly. No all of them are. Some who walk this world are fair evil and dangerous to their core."

"As with Mortals, no? You find yer good and yer bad in everything." Margery tilted her head to the side, appearing to study her son. "I always believed you to be the reason the Faerie saved me that day."

"What?" His mother's words caught him off guard.

"From the moment I first felt you move within my belly, I believed you to be the one the Fae awaited. It's why I was so sure you had to be alive, no matter what they told me. No matter how long you'd been gone. I kenned the Fae had a purpose for you, Robbie."

His mother was wrong, of course. The Fae hadn't enough care for him to allow him to return to the proper time to keep his oath to a dying friend. Not enough care to allow him to rescue a small lass waiting for a father who would never return. It was obvious they had no more use for him than as a delivery boy.

"It's no me, mother. It's Leah. The Fae she encountered were no the kindly ones. They ill-used the poor lass in many a horrendous way. I felt she'd be safe here. Safe to grow and recover with yer gentle help, if you'll give it now that you ken the truth."

"If?" His mother's eyes widened with her indignant disbelief. "Robert. You should no have the least bit of doubt in this matter. Especially now that I do ken the truth. For all the world to see, she's yer daughter, and we'll raise her as such. She'll be cared for all her days, Fae or no."

"I'm not Fae!" Leah stood in the doorway, her face red in her anger. "I won't be. I renounce that part of me. I refuse to be something so horrible."

As tears trickled down the girl's cheeks, his mother hurried to her side, wrapping her arms around Leah.

"There, there, lass," she soothed. "Dinna you fash yerself over it. It matters no in the least. Yer home with us now. Yer a daughter of the House MacQuarrie and you've nothing to fear ever again."

Robert rose from his chair and headed toward the

door, intending to leave the two women to bond in the way of women. His mother's voice caught him just before he made his escape.

"You'll want to speak to yer father, Robbie. He's much to tell you. You'll want to know about Richard as well."

He looked back to see his mother leading Leah toward a chair by the fire, her low voice a reassuring murmur.

Though he felt as if half the weight of the world had been slipped from his shoulders, unease still rode him as he made his way down to find his father.

Now he faced the uncomfortable task of sharing with his parents that he was about to leave again on his quest to find his friend's child. No, he caught himself in that thought. Isabella wouldn't be a child any longer. He was twenty years too late to help the child Isabella. He could only pray he wasn't too late to help the adult she'd become.

From the conversation he'd just had with his mother, he sincerely doubted he'd be able to do that without telling them everything. Though *everything* would be a large bite for them to swallow.

Still, he could hardly expect their assistance if he didn't plan to offer them his honesty.

At least he wouldn't have to worry about Leah anymore. His mother, amazing woman that she is, would handle that from now on. The girl couldn't ask for better from her own mother.

One female settled in safely, one more to find. Only when he could assure himself of Isabella MacGahan's well-being would he feel truly at peace.

Chapter 5

⁓

*B*lood and slime spattered her dress, her face, her hair. It covered her arms from elbow to fingertips.

Isabella MacGahan couldn't remember the last time she'd been so happy.

When she'd first stumbled upon the young ewe trapped in the drop-off between the rocky outcroppings, she hadn't known the animal was so near giving birth. That realization had come only after she'd freed the sheep and it had followed her home.

Obviously her grandfather's shepherds hadn't cared enough for one missing ewe to bother after this poor creature. They'd abandoned her to make her own way, much as Isa's grandfather had absolved himself of any responsibility for her.

Their loss, her gain. Though whether her thought was to the sheep's situation or her own, Isa refused to explore.

"No matter. You've a home here now, dearling, and you'll have a name, too, as soon as I think on it a bit. You and yer wee bairn both." Isa smiled down at the tired ewe, busily cleaning her wobbly-legged babe.

Come to think of it, she could do with some cleaning up herself.

With a satisfied smile, she left the animal shed and headed around the building to her own tiny home. A good soak in a hot tub would be lovely for her tired muscles, too. She could feel the strain of the last few hours' hard work in her shoulders even now.

The ewe was lucky to be alive. She might be small but her babe certainly wasn't. Everything about the birth had appeared normal at the start of her labor. The nose and two black hooves had emerged first, but then one leg had gone crooked and Isa had been forced to pull the lamb's shoulders free. With what Isa had convinced herself was a grateful look from the exhausted ewe, the mother had managed the rest of the delivery on her own.

Still, Isa felt a marvelous exultation at the role she'd played in the event. She'd helped bring a new life into the world this day.

How could she not be happy? Spring was in the air with the smell of warming earth rising around her. As she followed the muddy dirt path around to the entrance of her little cabin, the sun burst from behind the clouds that had blanketed the sky for the past several days.

Isa turned her face up, halting her steps for a moment to bathe in the heated glow. A tiny shard of guilt flickered through her mind but she determinedly batted it away as she might a pesky midge.

If it was supposed to rain, the clouds would return soon. Besides, it had already rained for days. Her barrels were full. There was no lack of water. Whatever the cause of the sun's hasty appearance, she welcomed it.

With a sigh, she made her way to her front door, stopping to scoop up the wooden bucket she'd need for carrying water in to heat for the bath she planned. She eyed the little bench in front of her home longingly, considering a small rest might be in order in spite of the dried mess on her body and clothing.

Until she heard the slow, steady step of an approaching horse.

"Bollocks," she muttered under her breath as she dived through her front door, slamming it shut behind her.

Quickly she searched her memory. Could she have lost track of the days this badly? No, she wasn't wrong. It had barely been a fortnight since her grandfather's lad had been here last, delivering such goods as her grandfather decided to send.

She nudged a small wooden stool closer to the door and climbed up on it, lifting back the cloth that covered the tiny square hole cut high into her door. Through this opening she watched as the big horse carrying a small boy slowly made its way up her path.

"Mistress Isa?" the child called out, clearly searching for her. "Are you about?"

Isa leaned her forehead against the heavy door, an irritated sigh on her lips. Though she had no complaints about the lad himself, she thoroughly resented the interruption to her life he represented.

Why couldn't the old laird leave her in peace? He'd never once hidden the fact that he had no use for her. He'd been overjoyed when she'd broached the subject of moving from the castle to live out here in this little cottage on her own. It had taken him no time at all to have his men build an animal shed and provide her with her own chickens and goats. Granted, he sent someone to check on her each month, but it was obvious to her he did so only to collect the goods she had to sell. Or perhaps out of a sense of guilt.

"Mistress Isa?" the lad yelled, his voice rising on what sounded like desperation as the first fat raindrops started to fall.

The weather had turned again. Isa climbed off her stool and kicked it to one side before opening the door a tiny crack, struggling to calm her irritation. Whatever the child's purpose in being here, he'd certainly done nothing to justify her ire.

"Quite yer noise, Jamie," she called, her eye fixed to the small opening. "You'll frighten my animals and I'll have no eggs or milk from them for days. What brings you out here?"

The boy rolled to his belly on the big horse's back, sliding off to hit the ground feetfirst at a loping run, stopping only when he reached her door.

"His lairdship bids me bring you to the castle." The child spoke almost in a whisper. As always, he tried so hard to please.

She would say no to any other who carried her grandfather's bidding. Likely the laird understood this and sent the lad to ensure her compliance.

Before someone had decided Jamie was old enough

to make the trek from the castle on his own, he'd accompanied his grandmother, Auld Annie. This in itself was something Isa had planned to bring to his grandmother's attention the next time she spoke to her. The lad still seemed awfully small to be sent out alone on such a long trip.

"Please come, Isa." His voice quivered and he turned wide eyes to her before jerking his head away, keeping his face turned from her in a manner that broke her heart. "Master Roland says I'll have a beating if I dinna bring you in front of the laird today."

"Master Roland says that, does he?"

Isa felt her temper spike anew. Roland Lardiner, her grandfather's right hand and a distant cousin to her own father, overstepped his bounds with a threat such as that. It wouldn't surprise her one little bit to learn that weasel of man was behind the decision to start sending this wee child off on his own. She didn't trust Roland and, worse, didn't doubt for one moment he'd do exactly as he threatened if she didn't return with Jamie.

"Very well," she sighed, opening the door to allow the boy inside as thunder rumbled threateningly through the valley. "Sit yerself down by the fire while I prepare meself. Are you hungry?"

As if she needed to ask. The child was always starved. If she were ever blessed with such a son, he'd never go hungry. She'd see to that.

She pushed away the silly thought. A child of her own was naught but a dream, destined never to come to pass.

She poured a glass of milk fresh from this morning and set it in front of him, along with a large hunk of bread and piece of cheese. He smiled up at her, forgetting for a moment to shield his face from her.

The ugly burn scar marring the entire right side of Jamie's rosy face all but closed off the vision in his eye.

How could anyone treat a child so ill, especially a child who had suffered as much as this one had in his short life?

As if she needed to ask that question. They were men of the MacGahan, after all. Men so unlike her own father had been it was hard to accept her birthright to the clan.

She turned from the boy, yanking the ties from her hair and pulling it from its neat braid. A crazed woman would never take such care with her appearance. Free of their binding, her curls sprang wild, covering her face and spreading about her shoulders like a bright cape.

The mess dried on her hands and arms itched and pulled at her skin, but it would be best to leave it rather than clean it off. It suited her purpose all too well.

Still not quite enough, though.

She marched over to the fireplace, lifting a double handful of cooled ashes from the metal bucket she kept there. After sprinkling them into her hair, she wiped her hands over her face and turned to Jamie.

"Well? How do I look?"

"As you always do when you go to them," he responded around a mouthful. "Mayhap even worse than most times."

"Good. Slow yerself down there, lad," she cautioned as the boy stuffed another large bite into his already stuffed mouth. "We've no a need for you to rush through yer food. I'm no of a mind to leave until yer completely finished."

"Is there time for me to visit the goats?"

His little face was so bright with expectation, how could she possibly deny him the boon he sought? "Aye. But only for a little while. And dinna forget to close the gate as you did the last time." It had taken an hour to herd the animals back into their pen after his last visit.

"I'll remember. Thanks be to you, Mistress Isa, for the food and for coming back with me." Jamie nodded his pleasure, a smile curving the side of his mouth that could still move.

As if she'd send him back alone. No, she'd respond to her grandfather's summons. It was rare indeed for him to request her presence at the castle, and she was, after all, as curious as the next person.

Besides, it was well past time she had a chat with Cousin Roland. A chat she intended him to remember for a good long while.

Chapter 6

⟨ornament⟩

Robert kept to the shadows, leaning against a pillar at the back of the smoky hall. The great fires on either side of the enormous room barely seemed to cut through the damp chill brought on by the constant spring rains he'd encountered in this area.

Though he'd ridden hard for the last two days in his rush to reach Castle MacGahan, Robert saw this delay as providence. It suited his needs to wait for an audience with the MacGahan laird. It gave him an opportunity to study the people around him. An opportunity to assess the MacGahan strengths and weaknesses. An opportunity to listen for any mention of Isabella.

It also provided time to learn about the troubles of the clan before he broached his business with the laird. And troubles aplenty there seemed to be, if the grumbling of the servants was any measure to judge by.

The bawdy noise coming from the table of armed men at the front of the hall didn't bode well, either. The servants obviously felt the same way, darting in to refill the men's mugs before dashing away a prudent distance.

Robert had seen their ilk often enough to recognize them for what they were. Hardened warriors, dirty from the trail, here with an obvious purpose. They milled around their leader like bees buzzing around their queen. Violence held at bay emanated from the men in waves he could feel even from this distance.

Trouble definitely brewed in this hall.

Trouble, but no sign of Isabella.

He could only pray he wasn't too late. Twenty years too late, to be exact.

He turned his eyes from the front of the hall to scan the whole of the enormous room. His eyes but not his awareness. In his experience, it never paid to drop his guard, not even if the noisy warriors were of no concern to him. They held no interest for him and he certainly had no quarrel with them. His purpose here was simple.

Find Isabella and assure himself as to her safety or remove her to his family's home.

The old man who'd escorted him into the hall passed by, casting a suspicious glare in his direction and Robert drew farther back into himself. The smell of unwashed bodies wafted up his nostrils in the old man's wake.

Odd how he'd managed to live the first twenty years of his life in this world never noticing such things. Was it age or the influence of his new home that had sharpened his senses now?

Or had he simply grown soft over the past nine years?

A flurry of activity at the entrance told him this was no time to allow himself the distraction of such matters.

The laird had arrived, at last.

Though he'd never met the man, Robert would have recognized him anywhere. Randulf MacGahan reminded him of an older version of his long-lost friend, Thomas. He had the same massive build, the same penetrating blue-eyed stare. The old laird, though his hair was white, still walked tall and erect, his head held high as his gaze swept possessively over his hall.

Watchful guards surrounded him, each with an eye to the warriors at the front of the hall. At the MacGahan's side, head bowed, walked a demure blond-haired beauty. Isabella? The age would be about right. Thanks to the twenty years the Magic had robbed him of, Isabella should be only four or five years younger than him now.

If this were indeed the woman he sought, it would appear his worries had been for naught. Though he couldn't say whether or not she looked particularly happy, she was dressed well enough and didn't appear to be neglected in any fashion.

The laird's party made their way along the far wall, opposite the warriors' table, to the dais at the front of the great hall, where they took their seats. Keeping her eyes down, the woman seated herself next to the MacGahan laird's left as a granddaughter might. A good sign.

Perhaps Thomas had been entirely wrong in his estimation of his father's ability to raise the lass.

The chairs of the laird's party were still scraping against the floor when the obvious leader of the warriors rose from his seat, wasting no time.

"I'm no a man to keep waiting, MacGahan. I've been patient for too long now. Yer time is up. My armies will be at yer gates within a fortnight if yer no of a mind to meet my conditions to settle yer obligations."

"Calm yerself, MacDowylt. Early this morn I sent for the lass. As we agreed, she'll be here. Though it's little good it'll do you, as you'll see for yerself."

Robert sharpened his scrutiny of the man called MacDowylt. The old laird had sent for a woman at the warrior's demand? He didn't like the sound of that. Somewhere deep inside something stirred. Some sixth sense of impending trouble.

He'd learned long ago never to ignore that feeling.

Reminding himself he had no quarrel with the MacDowylt, he made his way to the side of the hall, edging along, slowly, casually, closer to the front to improve his view.

"Her visage is of no import, MacGahan. Nor the state of her mind. She's naught to me but a means to settle our debt without the cost of war."

At the man's words, the MacGahan leapt to his feet, knocking his chair over backward with his movement, his face a mottled red.

Robert's hand flew to his sword hilt, as did the hands of many in the hall. He waited, all but holding his breath, as the main players in this drama glared at one another over the distance separating them.

Seconds later, the tense silence was broken by a small boy loping awkwardly down the main aisle toward the dais. He darted around MacDowylt's legs, dropping to one knee as he reached the table.

The woman at MacGahan's side glanced at the child, then turned her head, her face a mask of revulsion.

"She's come," the boy announced breathlessly before rising and turning around toward the entrance.

Shock bolted through Robert's mind as the child's full countenance came into view. The right side of his face distorted, puckered and scarred, the bubbled skin an ugly shade of pink that reminded Robert of the bubble gum little Rosie MacKiernan loved to chew.

Robert looked to the woman on the dais again, her face determinedly turned away from the boy, her apparent disgust evident for all to see. If this were in fact Isabella, her father would be most disappointed in the woman his daughter had become. At the moment, he almost hoped it wasn't her.

A murmur rose from the back of the hall and Robert turned his gaze toward the entryway, anxious to see the woman MacDowylt awaited.

When she entered, Robert felt almost as much of a shock as he had at seeing the boy's face. Though he'd had no idea of exactly what he had thought this mystery woman would look like, the creature that made her way up the aisle now was certainly not anywhere in the realm of his expectations.

Wild red hair, looking as if it had never been tamed or even washed, surrounded her, curling wetly down her shoulders like a filthy cape. It hung in clumps in front of her face, hiding her features from all but those who might venture close. Her clothing hung from her, and— *Good lord!* Was that blood smeared down the front of her dress?

Even the brazen MacDowylt took a backward step as she passed by, ignoring him completely as if he didn't exist. She strode determinedly up to the dais, stopping only when she reached the boy's side. She placed her hands on the table and leaned in toward the old MacGahan laird.

"State the reason for yer summons and let me be on my way." Though she spoke quietly, her voice sounded wholly at odds with her appearance.

To Robert's ear, the sound was soft and melodious, as compelling as a cool breeze wafting down on a warm day. As if unable to help himself, he took another step closer to the dais.

The MacGahan's coloring had returned to normal and he again seated himself in the chair a servant had quickly righted for him. He lifted his tankard toward the warriors' table, a grim smile lifting the corners of his mouth.

"This is the woman you've awaited. The woman you say you'd have for yer bride, MacDowylt. Allow me to present my granddaughter, Isabella MacGahan."

Robert felt as if his stomach had plunged to his feet. This bedraggled creature was Isabella? This was the result of his failure to keep his oath to Thomas? Worse yet, it appeared that the MacDowylt was here determined to force a marriage to her.

Oh, he'd been wrong. Very wrong. It suddenly appeared he had a quarrel with the MacDowylt after all.

Bride?

Isa glared first at her grandfather and then at the stranger standing six paces behind her. Did they mean this as some sort of mocking gesture? Surely her grandfather knew better than to think she'd allow him to simply give her in marriage to some complete stranger.

"Ha!" she yelled, working to stifle the smile she felt threatening when the stranger jumped. "My answer is no. Discussion's over and done. Is that it? Am I free to go now?" She turned to face the table again, waiting to see her laird's reaction.

"So be it." The old laird spoke quietly, holding her eyes with his own before shifting his gaze to his visitor. "I warned you she'd no be agreeable to yer offer, did I no?"

Isa barely had time to register the surprise she felt in reaction to her grandfather's response before the air around her shifted and she felt movement behind her. The stranger—MacDowylt, her grandfather had called him—apparently didn't care for her answer. Or her grandfather's.

"You'd allow this . . ."—MacDowylt cast a look of contempt in her direction—"this crazed offspring of yers to determine the fate of yer people?"

"Isa," the laird cautioned, his hand visibly tightening on the tankard in front of him.

The warning floated to her on barely more than breath, obviously meant only for her ears. As she fought to rein in her temper, she looked back to his face and recognized the fear in his eyes. This felt more familiar, more along the lines of what she knew as normal. Fear was, after all, the expression she had grown to expect from her grandfather. Fear and loathing. Those were the emotions that had driven her out of this place that had never felt like a home.

Her thoughts sickened her, squeezing at her heart as much as her innards. At this moment, she wanted nothing more than to be in her own little house, far away from this castle and these people.

Away from the fear in her grandfather's eyes.

She turned from him, surveying the hall from behind the soggy curtain of her hair. Were there any here who still remembered her childhood? Any who, like her grandfather, had been there that awful day she'd learned of her father's death? Unlikely. Long ago, her grandfather had sent away all witnesses to that frightening display. All save one.

Only Auld Annie had approached her that day. Only Annie had pressed on through the howling winds and destruction to scoop up the devastated child Isa had been and hold her close. Only Annie had tried to ease the unimaginable pain of her loss.

But Auld Annie was nowhere in this hall. The eyes fixed on her now were those of people she barely knew. Eyes filled with disgust, contempt, perhaps even pity.

None of these people mattered to her in the least. Neither they nor their opinions. She didn't care one whit what any single one of them thought of her. And she certainly didn't want their pity.

Jamie waited silently at her side, his face blanketed in the innocence of childhood. One look at the lad and she remembered her vow to speak with Roland, her grandfather's second in command.

He sat to the right of the MacGahan laird, his lips drawn back in that arrogantly impassive sneer he always wore. How her grandfather tolerated the beastly man was beyond her. That she could be related to such as him by even the most distant drop of blood annoyed her greatly.

To her grandfather's left sat Roland's daughter, Agneys. That was a change from her last visit. Agneys was moving up in the world. Or at least she was moving up at the table. Agneys had always been perfect. Hadn't her grandfather held the girl's name up often enough over the years? Why must you be so difficult, Isabella? Why can't behave as a lady, like Agneys?

Well, the perfect Agneys could have her place at the table, right at the MacGahan's elbow. Be the perfect lady. Isa didn't care. Not one little bit. Though her curiosity was piqued as to what had brought about the new seating arrangement.

MacDowylt cleared his throat, jolting her back to the problem at hand. She took in a deep breath before facing him. The delay had done its work. She was in full control of her emotions once again. For the moment, both her curiosity about Agneys and her talk with Roland would have to wait. She had more important issues to deal with now.

The warrior remained several paces away, his fists braced on his hips. When she turned her gaze to him, he flexed the fingers of one hand and openly caressed the dagger at his belt.

The fool thought to intimidate her? Obviously he knew nothing of her beyond her blood relationship to the laird of the MacGahan.

She lifted her chin and placed her hands behind her back. Tilting her head, she studied this MacDowylt long enough to see the corner of his eye twitch.

Not so confident as he tried to portray. Perhaps he had heard stories after all.

Isa stepped down from the dais and circled the man, making a show of examining him. He was tall and big, obviously a man used to hard work, though she doubted he was more than a score and two, if that. She was sure that with his dark hair and startling blue eyes, he would find many a woman who would be pleased with his offer. But she wasn't many a woman.

At the conclusion of her circuit Isa stopped and shook her head slowly before looking back toward her grandfather.

"No. I'll no be changing my mind. He willna do at all. I've no desire to take such a pitiful example of manhood to husband."

The air around her thickened, the taste of violence so intense it almost masked the warnings of movement.

Isa pushed Jamie behind her as she whirled to face whatever came her way. She found the MacDowylt had closed the distance between them. He moved quickly, his fingers banding around her upper arm.

"Dinna mistake my offer for flattery. I've no interest in you as a woman. I'd only take such as you to wife to seal the MacGahan lands." He jerked her arm as he spoke, pulling her face close to his. "And I will have them for the debt I'm owed. Since yer laird refuses to sign them over, if you dinna agree to marry, our clans will go to war. Are you ready to sacrifice yer people? Because make no mistake, woman, if you dinna wed me, that's exactly what will happen."

It had all occurred very quickly. Her senses, normally so sharp, were dulled by the smell and feel of so many people crowded around her.

Her eyes fixed on those of the man who held her, his face so close to hers she could feel his breath hit her cheeks in short, sharp slaps. Her own breath came quickly now as she felt her control slipping.

A crash of thunder so close it shook the building drowned out any words the MacDowylt was saying to her.

Concentrate. She had to maintain her tenuous grasp on her emotions.

She retreated into her own mind, shutting out the noises coming from the table behind her. She focused on the pressure of his fingers digging into her flesh, on the red flush rising on his skin under the dark stubble of beard, on anything but how she felt about what he was saying. Anything that could keep the anger, the fear at bay.

Anger, fear—both were strong emotions, but combined they would be too powerful for her to control effectively.

She couldn't break down here. Not in front of her grandfather. Not again. She wouldn't allow that to happen.

Withdrawn into herself as she was, she missed the warnings of another's approach.

The shimmer of steel jolted her back to her surroundings as it flashed into the narrow space between her and the man who held her.

A sword tip poised over MacDowylt's hand where it clutched her arm.

"You asked the lady a question about her willingness to sacrifice." The voice was low, deep, almost mesmerizing in its tenor.

Isa's gaze slid along the wickedly sharp weapon hovering so close to her body to the man who wielded it. He was magnificent, a perfect example of a warrior, his deep brown eyes hard and withdrawn. As he stared at the MacDowylt she had no doubt this man could dispatch them both in one swift move of his muscled arm without giving the action a second thought. How could she have missed one such as this when she'd entered the hall? Could he possibly be her grandfather's man?

The emotionless smile he aimed at the MacDowylt sent a shiver down her spine.

"Now I have a similar question for you, MacDowylt. Are you ready to sacrifice yer hand? Because make no mistake, sir, if you dinna release the lady's arm, that's exactly what will happen."

The threat, a replay of the MacDowylt's own words, seemed to take the man by surprise. His fingers flexed and loosened on her arm, but he didn't let go.

"I dinna ken who you are, stranger, but you'd be best served to leave this place. This is a matter between the MacGahan and meself, and no business of yers." The reply sounded almost animal, more growl than words.

"That's where yer wrong, MacDowylt. Anything that concerns Isabella MacGahan is very much my business."

Around Isa, the air stilled as if the collective room held its breath, waiting to see which of the big men would blink first.

"Who are you to make such a claim? By what right?"

MacDowylt had asked the exact questions ringing in Isa's mind.

"I am Sir Robert MacQuarrie, oath-bound to see to the lady's welfare and protection." The stranger flicked his gaze to her for a moment and then back to MacDowylt.

In that moment, Isa was struck again by this MacQuarrie's eyes. Shielded. Eyes so hard they masked even the possibility of any emotion hiding behind them. What she wouldn't give for that ability.

"Oath-bound," MacDowylt repeated skeptically. "And just who would have had the audacity to accept such an oath from you?"

"Her father."

His words tingled down Isa's spine like tiny fingers brushing against her skin. What he claimed was impossible.

"What could you possibly know of my son?" the MacGahan laird demanded, once again on his feet, Roland rising to stand at his side.

"I know that his last words to me were of his concern for his daughter's safety. I swore to him I'd see to her protection."

Though MacQuarrie responded to her grandfather's question, he did so without taking his eyes from MacDowylt's face.

Roland snorted his disbelief, his normal sneer altered to one of contempt. "You'd have us believe you were there at his death? A score ago? You could have been no older than that filthy cur." He gestured toward the spot where Jamie crouched.

"Nevertheless." MacQuarrie shrugged as if their belief of his story was of no consequence to him. "I gave my oath to Thomas and I'm here to keep that promise."

His body shifted toward MacDowylt, an almost imperceptible action, but the threat it held was unmistakable. As if charged with his intent, the air around Isa began to shift and flow with his movement.

"I'll tell you one last time to release the lady's arm."

In the long moment that passed, Isa focused on the MacDowylt's face, watching for any sign of understanding. How could he not feel the tension building as the air stilled to stifling around them? Much more of this and she'd be forced to gasp simply for her next breath.

When the corner of the warrior's eye twitched again, she felt the tension blanketing her drain away.

He released his grip and lifted his hands in front of him as he slowly backed away.

Though MacQuarrie lowered his sword, he held it loosely in front of him, at the ready. Only then did he fully shift his gaze to her.

When she met his stare, she found herself captured. The eyes she'd found so hard and devoid of emotion only moments before were anything but empty now.

There, swimming in the brown pools, she could almost swear she saw something else. Something reaching out to her as if she were being invited into the very depths of the man's soul.

Ridiculous. Every bit as impossible as his having been old enough to have been at her father's deathbed to give the oath he claimed.

And yet . . .

In those depths she saw no deception. No dishonesty in the dark waters of his gaze. Nothing there but determination, solid and forceful.

"I can trust you?" To her own surprise, the involuntary words issued from her on a breath.

"You may believe me, my lady. Trust this to my care."

Believe him? No, she couldn't do that. His story was simply too unreasonable for the facts.

Trust him? Hardly. She trusted no one.

But allow him to deal with this situation? Leave her future in his hands as he'd asked? That, amazingly, she realized she could do. Especially since she was at a loss as to her next step in this delicate political dance.

She nodded her agreement and he smiled before turning his gaze back to MacDowylt.

That smile, a barely noticeable quirking of the corner of his mouth, obviously meant only for her, slammed into her, weakening her knees and her resolve.

This man, this Robert MacQuarrie, was something she'd never experienced before. Something that both frightened and fascinated her.

It was as if he were the human embodiment of a force of nature.

"Under the authority vested in me by the late Thomas MacGahan, I, Robert MacQuarrie, hereby proclaim my rights as Guardian to Isabella MacGahan. From this moment forward, she is officially under my protection and no other's. If you want something of her, you must go through me."

Robert noted with satisfaction that his speech was met by total silence. He'd take that as a good sign. He'd spent the better part of his ride to the MacGahan castle working out just the proper words to use if he found he needed to remove the young woman from her home. Granted, the words themselves were drawn from his memories of the hundreds of movies he'd watched over the last decade, but they seemed to have worked well enough.

One look at the mess that was Isabella and he had no doubts as to whether or not she needed to leave here. This was certainly no place for her to continue to live. No, she'd be much better off at MacQuarrie Keep.

What his mother would say when he brought *this* one home was more than he could imagine. For a fact, Margery would have her hands full turning this female into a lady, but if it could be done, his mother was indeed the one to do it.

"You?" the MacDowylt sputtered. "Dinna you think her grandsire will have something to say about that? She is the laird's only living heir."

Robert didn't wait to see if the man in question spoke up. What the old laird might have to say on the subject was of no interest to him.

"The MacGahan has had the past twenty years to prove his ability to watch over Isabella's welfare. As you can plainly see"—Robert cast an impersonal look her direction before facing MacDowylt again—"he's failed in that task as Thomas feared he would. It's in my hands now, and I reject yer offer of marriage on my ward's behalf."

"Thomas said that, did he?" The laird spoke up at last. "When he charged you with her care? What else did he say?"

Robert held his words for a moment, considering what would be in the old man's mind. Perhaps the truth would convince him and prevent any outbursts of violence.

"Yer son feared what you might do when you learned of his death. He told me you were not an evil man but that his daughter was 'different,' as her mother had been."

The MacGahan flinched as if he'd been struck. "Thomas told you of Elesyria?" He shook his head as if he could hardly believe what he heard. "That being the case, I canna doubt yer word, MacQuarrie. I relinquish authority over Isabella to you as my son requested."

"You've no a right to do this! You canna break yer word again." MacDowylt yelled toward the dais, his eyes flashing with his anger as he turned back to Robert. "You want the lands for yerself, I'd say, but it'll do you no good. They're owed my people in good faith. I'll have them if I have to lay waste to every living soul for miles."

Robert shrugged, keeping a tight hold on his response. What he'd like to do was show this blethering young idiot what happens to bullies who go through life spewing threats, but this was neither the time nor the place for such actions. Swords were being drawn around the hall even now and he had Isabella's safety to consider.

"And a fine lot of good that will do you, aye? With no one left to work the lands or tend the animals, you'll be no better off than you are now."

MacDowylt's face and neck had discolored to a dark splotchy red by the time he spoke again. "You'll no get away with this, MacQuarrie. Nor you, MacGahan. I'll be back, and then we'll see who has the upper hand."

With one last angry look around the hall, the young man turned and stormed from the room, his warriors following closely behind.

"If you'd but name me tanist, this would no be a problem any longer."

Robert looked back at the man who spoke. Seated at the right hand of the MacGahan, he leaned toward his laird, urging the old man to retake his seat. His hair hung in lank strings around his face, framing dark eyes filled with traits Robert recognized all too well. Cunning, greed, hatred—each emotion transcended his travels through time. There were men such as he in both the centuries Robert had inhabited.

"Isabella is the issue of my son and my heir in his place." The old laird's hand shook as he reached for his tankard. "I owe Thomas this much."

"A woman canna be laird of the MacGahan," said MacGahan's right hand. "You ken the truth in this. Look at her! You've need to see to the future of yer clan, no the memory of yer lost son. You should have given her over to MacDowylt. There's no a need for the fate of Clan MacGahan to be tied to her any longer."

Beside him, Isabella snorted her derision at the man's words.

"You speak as if you think I'd want anything to do with this castle or the clan. I want nothing more than to be left alone by all of you."

"And left alone is what you'll get." Once again the laird rose to his feet. "Begone with you and take yer new . . . *guardian* along as well."

"None too soon for my liking," she muttered, turning and starting toward the door.

"Hold on there!" Robert reached out and grabbed Isabella's arm as she attempted to push past him.

This was not at all what he'd had in mind. It was too late in the day for them to chance being caught on the road overnight, especially if MacDowylt and his men had camped somewhere nearby.

"We'll stay here this night and leave for yer new home at first light."

"New home?" Isabella drew back from him, appearing to study him through the matted red curtain of her hair. "Dinna be witless, man. I've no intention of going anywhere but my own home, and I'll be about doing that right now. I've animals waiting on my return."

"You canna stay here," the laird interrupted. "I'll no have her spend even one night under my roof against her will. As she says, you must leave now."

Robert looked around him in disbelief. He was surrounded by sheer insanity. What Isabella proposed, what her grandfather insisted upon, was nowhere in the realm of logical behavior.

Still, the MacGahan guards who'd stepped forward, swords drawn, gave emphasis to the fact, logical or not, he and Isabella would be leaving this keep as soon as possible. There could be no argument about it.

She'd taken barely two steps when she stopped and turned back toward the large table with a muttered, "I almost forgot."

Robert edged closer as Isabella leaned over the table toward the man who'd spoken earlier.

The finger she pointed at the man before she spoke was long, delicate and caked with ash. "One last thing for you, Roland. I'll no take kindly to hearing of any further ill-treatment of the lad, Jamie. Do you ken my meaning, Cousin? Dinna make me come back here angry."

The man's lips drew back in distaste, but any retort was halted by the laird's hand to his shoulder.

"Dinna fash yerself over the lad, Isa. No harm will come to him as long as I live. You have my word. Now be off with you."

Apparently satisfied with her grandfather's promise, Isabella turned, sweeping past Robert and down the aisle between the tables.

With one last look at the men on the dais, their heads drawn together in hushed discussion, Robert hurried after her, catching up as they exited the great hall.

The late-afternoon rain had slowed to a steady drizzle by the time they walked out the main doorway. There was no point in his new charge getting drenched again.

"If you'd like to wait inside, I'll go see to our horses and bring them around."

Isabella drew the edges of her cloak together, attempting to shut out the misting rain. "I have no horse for you to see to."

No horse? "How did you get here?"

"On the rare occasion the laird summons me, he sends a lad along on horseback. I ride with him. Now I suppose I'll ride with you." She lifted one shoulder carelessly. "Or I'll walk. It's of no consequence to me how I go, as long as I do."

"Wonderful," Robert muttered, stomping down the steps toward the stable.

First they were headed off to Lord only knew where with precious little time before dark would overtake them. On top of that, there was the possibility of MacDowylt's men waiting out there for them. Now, for the perfect finishing touch, they'd be doubled on his mount, slowing any escape they might need to make.

This whole nightmare just kept getting better and better. But what could he expect? He should have known it would be like this the minute he'd learned Isabella MacGahan was a redhead.

Chapter 7

The rains ceased once they lost sight of Castle MacGahan. Robert's worries about being caught in the open on the road lessened about the same time, as Isabella directed him to turn their mount into the heavy forest.

If only he could eliminate his worries about Isabella herself as easily.

His failure to see to a small child's welfare had obviously forced her to live a ragged, dirty existence on the fringes of society. He had always known about hermits. They inhabited both centuries he'd lived in. He'd just somehow convinced himself they were mostly able-bodied men who had made their own choices in life, not unprotected women who eked out a solitary existence because their families had rejected them.

"Only a bit farther now and we'll be home." Isabella's

cheerful announcement broke the silence between them.

Her words were welcome news to Robert. Their uneventful ride had lasted perhaps two hours, by his estimation, and it was growing late. The sun had dipped low on the horizon, and dusk already colored the deep recesses of the forest they rode through. Though it was unlikely they faced any danger so far away from the main trail, he would feel much more comfortable when he had her safely behind solid doors.

He just hoped wherever she lived actually *had* solid doors. Though the MacDowylt had gone away, he'd be back. Robert had not a single doubt of that fact. It was only a matter of when.

With a seeming lack of concern for her own safety, Isabella sat astride his horse in front of him. The top of her head was level with his nose, while her hands draped over the saddle horn. Her fingers, though dirty, were long and unexpectedly delicate.

Her hair, drying at last, tickled at his nose, filling his senses with the not unpleasant smell of woodsmoke.

How odd. From her appearance, the odors he would expect to find wafting up from the woman would be far from pleasant. And yet that wasn't at all the case.

Inclining his head, he breathed in deeply, drawing the scent of her into his nostrils. Again he smelled woodsmoke lightly overlaying something fresh, something that made him think of sunshine on a warm spring day.

He must be mistaken.

When he sniffed in a second time, she stiffened, tilting her head to the side as if listening.

"What's wrong? Is there something out there? Are we being followed?"

"No, my lady. I apologize if I startled you. I suspected something amiss, but there is no one out there."

Without a doubt, however, something was amiss. All was not as it seemed with the wild redhead in his arms.

"Here we are," she almost sang as they broke through into a picturesque clearing in the woods.

A small, tidy cottage with a neatly thatched roof lay straight ahead of them. Off to one side was an open area of freshly cleared land, obviously intended to serve as a garden. On the other side, a running stream wound its way down the hill and into the woods. While small and far from elaborate, it hardly looked like the home of the mad hermit the woman seated in front of him portrayed herself to be.

The longer he was around Isabella, the more of a puzzle she became. A most enticing puzzle he had every intention of solving.

What in the name of all that was holy was she going to do with this man now that they'd reached her home?

Isabella fidgeted in the saddle, impatient as Robert dismounted. Normally she would have simply slipped feetfirst to the ground, but this horse of his was a monster, easily larger than any she'd ever been on before. The ground was uncomfortably far away from her present perch.

When he lifted his arms to assist her, she leaned into him and his hands fastened around her waist. His grip tightened as he took her full weight, pulling her closer, his face all but buried in her breasts. Her breath caught in her lungs and she placed her hands on his shoulders to steady her descent, feeling for a moment as if time stood still.

Lord, but she'd thought sitting so close to him on the journey home, his arms stretched out on both sides of her, had been difficult, but this!—*This* was a *thousand* times worse, face to face, sliding down the length of his hard body. Her heart pounded in her chest and a strange sensation shivered through her, warming her cheeks and shooting that heat throughout her, to the pit of her stomach and lower still. Closing her eyes, she fought against the need to catch her breath in quick little gasps as her toes touched solid ground at last.

He released her as soon as her wobbly legs took her weight, and she looked up to find his handsome features distorted in a grimace. The sight of what had to be his disgust at being so close to her felt like the shock of falling into a frozen winter pond.

She stepped quickly back from him, dropping her eyes to the ground. This warrior, who had only moments before set her heart skipping in her chest, found her completely repulsive. So much so, in fact, that his face had distorted as if in pain when he'd held her.

As it should be. That had been her goal, had it not? To keep the world away from the old crone's door? To convince everyone that she wasn't worth their time or bother. She should be happy she'd been so successful in her deception.

She should be, but she wasn't. His reaction hurt, cutting as deeply as any weapon ever could, and the heat that suffused her cheeks now was stoked by the fire of humiliation. She simply wanted to be rid of the man and his hateful grimaces.

"Thank you for seeing me home. I've no more need of yer assistance now, so yer free to go as soon as you like."

Free to go and let her get back to her life as usual. That should come as a welcome relief to the man.

"Go?" Neither his look nor his tone conveyed relief. If anything, he sounded incredulous. "I'll no be leaving unless you've decided yer ready to make the move to my own home."

Now it was her turn at incredulity. "Yer home? Oh, I dinna think so, sir. I've no intention of going to yer home." Or any other place with a man such as him. No, the farther away she was from him, the better.

"You canna remain here, Isabella. The MacDowylt will come back."

It could be as he said. He did seem to be a man who would know of the world. But MacDowylt would be returning to the castle, not to her woods.

"I'm no leaving my own home," she repeated stubbornly.

He bowed his head as if he were a man accepting his laird's judgment. "Then I stay here with you. I made a promise to yer father to look after you and, late or no, now that I'm here, I've every intention of keeping that promise."

Oh no, having him here would never do.

"In that case, Robert MacQuarrie, as my father's only living descendant, I release you from yer onerous vow."

She envisioned him, at her words, gratefully mounting his enormous horse and riding quickly away into the distance. He did neither.

Instead he laughed.

"I'm sure yer pleased to have yer freedom back, sir, but I dinna see a need for you to be quite so rude about it." You'd think the man would have some small regard for her feelings. He had vowed to see to her well-being even if she had released him from that promise.

"My apologies, my lady." Though his laughter ceased and he dipped his head respectfully, the corners of his mouth continued to quirk upward. "I can see you value yer independence, but getting rid of me will no be so easy as that. As the subject of said vow, yer no in any position to release me from it. Simply put, if you stay, I stay."

"Stay?" Isabella's stomach tightened in a knot of nerves. What would she do if he seriously meant to stay? How long could she keep up her pretense? She'd never needed to carry on for more than a couple of hours at a time. Even now the ashes matted in her hair were itching at her scalp. "For how long?"

He crossed his arms over his large chest, following along behind her to the cottage door. "A month, a year, five years. I canna say. I'll stay until I'm either satisfied this is the best place for you to be or I've convinced you to allow me to take you somewhere better."

What had felt like a good idea in her grandfather's hall, allowing this man to be her guardian, no longer seemed quite so appealing. In fact, she was beginning to feel as if some giant trap were closing in on her.

She opened her door and stepped inside, turning at

the last moment to peer up at the handsome warrior. If she couldn't send him away, perhaps she could drive him away.

"Do as you want. But hear this: I've no a use for you or any other intruders in my life. I like my own company and no other's. If yer to stay here, you'll keep yerself out of my way." With one step back, she slammed the door shut and leaned up against it, drawing in a deep breath.

There. That should convince him he wasn't welcome. As soon as her body stopped trembling, she'd drag her stool over and climb up to watch him riding away.

The nerve of the woman! She'd slammed the door right in his face. Another inch or two and he'd be straightening out his nose even now.

Thick, dark clouds had begun to build, so he pounded on her door, pleased to see it seemed heavy enough to provide her some protection. After a long pause, followed by a scraping noise, she finally answered.

"Have you no left yet? What do you want?"

Robert shook his head, fighting back a smile at Isabella's transparent actions. She thought he'd leave simply because she warned him off and slammed the door in his face? She had a lot to learn about him.

"Have you a place where I can shelter for the night?" he called.

"No," came the muffled reply. "If yer to remain here, you'll have to make do for yerself. I canna be expected to feed and shelter you."

Remembering her apparent compassion for the boy back at her grandfather's castle, he decided on a different tack.

"I've no such expectations for myself, my lady. But is there a place where I can feed and water my horse? A storm looks to be gathering and he's tired after carrying the two of us all the way here." Not exactly a complete truth—that animal had been bred and trained for much harder exertion. But Isabella didn't know that.

A few moments passed this time before she responded.

"There's a stable around back. And feed. Mind you dinna frighten my animals, though."

Robert walked the short distance back to his horse, taking up his reins and leading the animal around to the back of the little house just as the first snowflakes began to drift to earth.

Bizarre spring weather for the highlands indeed.

As Isabella had said, he found an enclosed stable butt up against the back wall of the cottage.

He ducked his head as he entered the building, waiting for his eyes to adjust to the dim surroundings. For a stable, particularly a stable in this time, it was remarkably clean. There were rushes strewn about the hard dirt-packed floor as if it were someone's home rather than a pen for animals.

Strange indeed, but it would do just fine, for both his horse and for him.

He leaned down to loosen the straps holding the saddle, frowning to himself. He'd told Isabella he was prepared to stay here as long as necessary, but he had absolutely no intention of doing so. MacDowylt had claimed his armies could reach the gates of Castle MacGahan within a fortnight and Robert planned to be long gone before that happened.

Isabella might not want either his help or his protection, but she was damn well going to get it.

Though she was a growing mystery to him, at least he'd been right in his earlier assessment. Isabella had a soft spot for creatures in need. A soft spot he wouldn't hesitate to use to his advantage whenever necessary now that he'd found it.

Perhaps a very fortunate discovery, considering he had less than two weeks to convince the woman of the necessity of making her escape.

Chapter 8

Though the broth was weak, it soothed its way down Isa's throat and settled warmly in her stomach. She'd leave the pot to simmer through the night over a low fire, and once she added her oats tomorrow, she'd have a savory porridge for the day's meals.

If only she'd thought to set it onto simmer before she'd left this morning, it would be done by now, but food hadn't been her priority then any more than when she'd arrived home.

Once she'd assured herself that MacQuarrie wasn't going to make any attempt at forcing his way inside, she'd heated water and bathed the filth of the day from her body and her hair. Only then had she thought of putting her kettle on to cook.

Now she was comfortable and warm, snug in her heavy nightdress, sitting in front of her cozy fire. She plucked at the folds of the soft woolen draped across her lap, telling herself what a lovely evening this had turned out to be, even if her dinner did leave a little something to be desired.

She, at least, had a warm dinner.

No! She attempted to swat away the guilt nattering around her head like a pesky summer fly. It mattered not to her that the light fluffy flakes of early evening had quickly turned into a cold heavy rain.

So what if MacQuarrie was out there somewhere in the dark, huddled into his plaid against the weather. It was his own fault and none of hers. That he remained, braving the wet, supping on what cold food he carried with him was the result of his own poor choices. She had told him he was free to leave—had, in fact, all but demanded he go. But he'd refused. So how could any of this be her blame? It couldn't.

Anyway, likely as not, he'd taken shelter in the stable with his great horse. He'd be fine there.

Steam from the mug in her hand wafted up across her face, bringing with it a fresh wave of guilt. Though her stomach growled at the enticing smell, she found herself unable to take that next sip.

What if it *were* her fault? No, she'd not made the choice for MacQuarrie to stay, but she had been unsettled by the whole of the day, and most especially by his decision to remain with her.

As unsettled as the weather.

"Nonsense," she muttered, ripping a small chunk of bread from the loaf on the table next to her and dipping it into her broth.

Spring weather was frequently unsettled. It had

nothing to do with her reaction to the warrior, and she certainly didn't intend to waste another minute thinking about the man. She'd told him she wouldn't take on the responsibility for his feeding and care, and she'd meant it!

She shoved the bite into her mouth, chewing with much more enthusiasm than she actually felt.

She refused to think about how he'd stood before her grandfather and claimed his right as her guardian to protect her, or how he'd stood up to the MacDowylt for her, championing her cause against the greedy man. Most especially she would not think on how she had felt as he'd lifted her up onto his horse in front of him, encasing her within the warm, protective circle of his arms.

And what had she done to thank him for his efforts? She'd left him without benefit of hearth or fire, to suffer through the long dark night. Alone. Hungry. Perhaps in danger of freezing in a storm that could very well be of her own making.

"Fie on it," she said aloud, tossing the woolen from her legs onto the floor.

She'd get no peace this way. She could spare a cup of broth. It would be no hardship for her. It wasn't as if she were actually taking on the responsibility of caring for him. It was no more than a simple cup of warmth handed out to one in need.

Besides, in weather such as this she truly should check on the ewe and her new lamb.

Dropping to her knees on the floor beside the box where she stored all her treasures, she pulled out the tall metal and bone lantern that had once belonged to her father. Beside it, wrapped in soft wool, lay her dwindling supply of fine beeswax candles. She fit one into the lantern before filling a mug from the bubbling pot that hung over the fire. Isa strapped on her pattens, tossed a cloak over her shoulders, and lifted the cover to her head before lighting her candle. She didn't really need the light to find her way around back to the stable, but it would be too dark inside to adequately check on the condition of the new lamb.

Cold rain spattered her face when she stepped outside. Clutching the mug in one hand, she braced the lantern against her body while she closed the door.

Stepping carefully along the muddy path, she shuddered as the smell of wet dung stung her nostrils. Must be time to clean the stables again.

From her childhood, Isa had hated the odor of filth and its vile feel on her body. Her grandfather had claimed that her constant bathing would send her to an early grave and declared it was her mother's fault, insisting that her unnatural heritage made her an aberration in nature.

Even after all these years, the memory of his words set Isa's teeth to grinding. The great laird of the MacGahan was wrong. Wrong on so many counts.

The differences Isa had inherited from her mother enhanced her life. Anyone with eyes could see that nature loved cleanliness. She washed the earth with her rains on a regular basis. Isa could do no less.

She paused outside the door to the stable, looking up toward the blanket of clouds that hid the stars from her. Fat drops of clean, cold rain pattered her face, caressing her skin as they rolled down her cheeks.

In truth, not all of the differences she'd inherited

from her mother enhanced her life, but this rain tonight felt too comfortingly natural to have been her fault.

Holding on to that reassurance, she pushed open the big wooden doors and slipped quietly inside.

Light from her lantern barely pierced the curtain of black, as if she moved about inside a small, dimly lit cocoon. The flickering candle sent strange shadows wavering around her and the silence of the stable beat at her ears. The calm she'd felt only moments before began to slip away.

The giant black warhorse loomed as a massive dark mound at one end of the room. *He* lay next to the animal, huddled into his plaid for warmth, just as she'd imagined he would.

Her hands full, she tried to ignore the need to pull her cloak tightly around herself, to retreat into the warm safety of the wool's heavy folds. Instead she tiptoed nearer, stealing a closer look at MacQuarrie.

The eyes that had so mesmerized and intrigued her when open were shut now, allowing her to study the warrior's face without embarrassment.

Only to ascertain his well-being, she assured herself, and for no other reason. She would not enjoy the task of dealing with his great body should he take sick and die on her out here.

Tendrils of dark brown hair escaped the plaid pulled snugly around his head, curving softly over his strong, whisker-shadowed jawline. His lips, slightly parted in his sleep, were full and strong, and for an instant she allowed herself to wonder how they might feel against her own.

His nose, which she'd earlier thought straight and perfectly aligned on his face, on closer inspection appeared to be slightly crooked, as if it might have been broken at some point in his life.

Not that it made a difference in his beauty. She allowed herself to honestly admit he was the most starkly handsome man she had ever laid eyes upon.

She bit down on the exclamation that bubbled to her lips so as not to wake him. What had happened to her practicality? What a ridiculous thought for her to harbor—as if she were in any position to compare the qualities of men's beauty. Her of all people! It wasn't as if she saw men every day. Didn't months at a time go by where wee Jamie was the closest thing to a man she encountered?

Shaking her head at her foolish flight of fancy, she sighed and turned to spot her small wooden milking stool. Moving as silently as possible, she placed the mug of broth on the stool. It would cool quickly out here but there was no point in her carrying it back with her. Besides, he might awaken during the night in time to appreciate its warmth.

She stopped at the sheep's stall, where the new mother opened a wary eye.

"Be at peace, Maisey," she murmured, realizing only as the words left her lips she'd decided on the ewe's name. It had come to her mind as she'd spoken as if from the sheep herself.

Maisey closed the discriminating eye, acknowledging Isa was no threat to the lamb sleeping peacefully beside her.

Isa watched the mother and babe for a moment more until she was satisfied that all was well and she could leave. Her coming out here had been silly to begin with, but perhaps now she could go inside and relax. There was nothing out here to give her worry.

Comforted by that knowledge, she'd barely touched the latch when a large hand closed around her throat, choking the scream that burst from her lungs.

Robert awoke with the first footfall outside the stable, his hand instinctively closing around the dagger at his waist.

Too light to be a full-grown man. Would MacDowylt have sent a boy? A scout, perhaps, sent to seek Isabella's location?

The steps paused, far enough away they'd be standing in the open. Careless, whoever it was. He'd expected better than an untrained boy from what he'd seen of MacDowylt and his men.

The moment the door opened, Robert realized his error.

Not a scout, and certainly not a boy.

Isabella.

Her unique scent preceeded her into the stable, wafting ahead of her, fresh and distinct.

After a pat to ensure his steed ignored their visitor, he forced himself to remain motionless as she drew near.

What the hell was she thinking, wandering about after dark? Anyone could be outside her doors, waiting to attack her. Was the woman that naively trusting or simply the brainsick hermit she had appeared in her grandfather's great hall? Whichever the case, the more he learned of her, the more difficult he realized his task would be.

Her footsteps hesitated and then stopped very close to him.

With his eyes closed, his sense of smell sharpened. The earlier woodsmoke was gone. Now her scent brought him visions of newly mown lawns, sparkling after a fresh rain.

With a sigh and a rattle of pottery and wood, she moved away.

Whatever the reason, Isabella seriously lacked the care for her own safety. Though they likely had a fortnight before MacDowylt could return with his armies, anything was possible. And while Robert grudgingly admired the man's attempt to avoid war in his campaign to add to his lands, this was one time he couldn't agree with his methods.

In spite of Isabella's rationale that MacDowylt would return to the castle, the man knew she didn't live within the security of the castle walls. At this very moment he could have men scouring every inch of the surrounding countryside, hunting for her location.

It's what Robert would do in his position.

No, there was no haven to let down his guard here. He could either watch her twenty-four hours a day or he could teach her that the sense of security she obviously felt in her surroundings was false.

Better yet, he could do both.

The melodious tones of her voice floated to his ear as he stealthily rose to his feet and tucked the end of his plaid into his belt before approaching her. She'd just reached the door when he struck. Slipping directly behind her, he slid his hand inside the hood of her cloak to curl his fingers around her slender throat and pull her back against his chest.

As her strangled scream shattered the night, he loosened his grip immediately but didn't let go. Instead he pulled her closer as all hell seemed to break loose around them.

The sheep's plaintive wail combined with the cries of frightened goats. Even his own horse bellowed, the whole of their cries all but lost in a crash of thunder, as if Mother Nature herself were venting her outrage along with the animals.

"Have you no understanding of yer place in the world, lass? Do you no see how easy it would be for someone to capture you, or worse," he demanded roughly, practically shouting to be heard over the din.

Her answer was a blow to his chest, delivered with a great deal more force than he might have expected. For an instant, he wondered if he'd missed some weapon she'd carried as the strike sent a knife-sharp pain slashing through his ribs. He staggered back from Isabella, holding his side as disbelief flooded his mind and he gasped for air.

She stumbled away from him into the dark of the stable, screaming again as she did so, heralding another round of ear-splitting cacophony, the braying of animals lost in the frenzy of the storm raging outside.

His pain disappeared as quickly as it had begun and he breathed in deeply, straightening in time to see flames from the lantern Isa had been carrying spread through the dry floor covering.

Falling to one knee, Robert pounded at the spreading fire with his bare hands, quickly losing the battle as the sparks fed on the dry rushes.

With a *whoosh*, Isa's cloak floated past his head and down onto the fire, suffocating the flames and leaving them both in total darkness.

"Are you hurt?"

Robert ignored her question as he staggered to the door, flinging it open to the howling wind and rain. Fresh air washed over him and into the enclosure and he gulped it in, steadying himself before he spoke.

"What the hell did you hit me with?" he demanded, the memory of the unexpected pain still fresh.

"I . . . nothing," she stammered. "I jabbed you with my elbow and nothing more. Did I hurt you?"

He snorted his disbelief and reached out to where he knew she stood from the sound of her voice. Grasping her arm, he pulled her along with him, toward the door.

"You belong inside yer cottage, behind a bolted door, where you'll be safe." Inside, where in spite of her claims he could see for himself whether or not she carried any weapons.

"Wait. I've a need to . . ." She pulled her arm from his loose grasp and leaned down before finishing. "I canna move with any speed wearing these pattens."

She darted out into the driving rain ahead of him, leading the way to her front door. This time when they reached it she held it open, allowing him to follow her inside. Not that he would have settled for any attempt on her part to keep him out as he had earlier.

In three steps he reached the hearth, and pulled his shirt up and over his head as he did so. He took only the barest notice of his blistered hands as he ran them over his chest, searching, amazed to find nothing there. Nothing but the familiar thin silver trail, a reminder of the wound that would have taken his life almost a decade past.

As he turned, Isabella gasped, her hands flying up to cover her mouth. When he met her gaze, he realized it was the scar that had captured her attention, but it was Isabella herself that captured his.

The woman standing before him now bore no resemblance at all to the one he'd seen earlier today.

Her hair hung over her shoulder, captured in a neat braid that easily reached below her waist. Wet tendrils curled around her face, framing eyes so intensely green he'd swear she wore colored contacts if he were home.

Though the nightdress she wore would be relegated to the oldest of grannies in the time he considered his own, it occurred to him the clothing was seriously underrated. The heavy wet cloth clung to her body, outlining her curves in a manner more enticing than anything he'd ever seen.

She seemed to come to her senses first. Her hands flew to her hair and her eyes rounded, as if she'd just realized she stood in front of him without her disguise. It was obvious when she also realized she wore only her nightdress, dropping her arms to cross them protectively in front of her.

To Robert's way of thinking, the gesture did more to highlight than to conceal.

When she looked to her feet self-consciously, he forced himself back to business, to deal with the situation at hand.

"You should get yerself into some dry things."

"And you as well," she responded, glancing up first at him and then to the door. "I'd ask you to turn yer back so that I might change in privacy."

"I can wait outside," he offered, strangely relieved when she shook her head no.

He turned his back and moved closer to the fire, locking his gaze into the dancing flames. Behind him, the slap of wet cloth hitting the stone floor jolted him hard enough he had to close his eyes to keep from looking around.

What was wrong with him? She was a woman under his protection, not someone he'd picked up in a bar. Everything about him felt off-center tonight, from the pain he'd experienced when Isabella had jabbed him with her elbow right up to the unusually strong attraction he experienced when he was near her.

Perhaps it was the leftover effects of the Faerie Magic that had sent him hurtling through time. That must be it. He could think of no other logical reason for his bizarre responses.

"MacQuarrie?"

Her voice was barely more than a whisper, but he jumped and whirled around as if she'd yelled at him.

Not a foot away, her eyes rounded again, and she took a step backward before lifting her chin and offering him the bundle she held.

"I've no shirt that will fit you, but yer welcome to this plaid. Though it's old, it's clean and dry."

"Old?" he heard himself echo lamely. His tongue felt glued to the roof of his mouth as he stared at her.

"Aye. It belonged to my father," she answered almost apologetically before she retraced her steps to the other end of the room, bowing her head and facing the wall.

His fingers fumbled clumsily with his belt as he turned his back to her. Behind him, she coughed when he began to unwrap his soggy plaid, and he couldn't stop himself from wondering whether or not she fought the need as he had to steal a quick look.

"Damn fool," he muttered as he twined Thomas's plaid about his body and refastened his belt.

He turned to find Isabella's rigid back still to him, her hands knotted in the soft material of the shift she'd donned earlier.

"I'm finished," he called, ashamed of his thoughts when she turned, her face red with her embarrassment.

Some fine Guardian he was turning out to be, lusting after the innocent woman he was sworn to protect.

Isabella fought the need to fan herself as she brushed past her visitor. The Fates themselves would surely strike her down for her audacity, but she didn't care. Whatever happened would be a small price to pay for the quick peek she'd had of MacQuarrie's fine, strong arse.

Lo, but the man was a beauty, with legs as sturdy as tree trunks. Though she'd stolen only the briefest of glimpses, his magnificent body had fair taken her breath away, and she'd been forced to cover her inadvertent gasp with a false cough.

Did he have any idea what she'd done?

She pushed past him, busying her shaking hands by filling two mugs with hot broth.

What if he'd caught her looking? The possibility sent a fresh wave of humiliation cascading over her, and she offered the broth to him without being able to make eye contact.

"Thank you."

His voice brushed against her mind like the finest cloth against sensitive skin, and she shivered as she sat on one of the little stools near the hearth.

She chose a spot close to where he leaned his back against the stone wall. Close to him. But not too close. Not so close that their arms might accidentally touch.

At the moment, she wished for nothing so much as to hear him speak again. She had only to say a word or two of her own and she'd be rewarded with the sound of his deep voice, lulling her as a cool breeze on a warm day might.

But her tongue was as heavy and her senses as dulled as if she'd overindulged in spirits, and she could think of nothing to say to start a conversation with the man.

"Why the disguise at yer grandfather's castle? Why pretend to be what you are not?"

Isa jumped when he broke the silence, her free hand flying up to her hair. The Fates certainly hadn't waited long to take their vengeance. She'd been careless and now she was caught.

"I ask only to be left alone. No one bothers a witless scold living deep in the woods lest she curse them." She allowed her eyes to travel up from her mug only to feel the breath catch in her throat when she saw the blisters on his big hands. "Yer burned! You should have spoken of it. I have a salve for that."

"You've no a need to disguise yerself any longer, Isabella. I'm here to see to it that yer left alone until I can convince you there's a safer place to be."

She didn't respond and he said nothing else as she fetched her herbals and gently fussed over his palm, finishing by wrapping strips of clean, soft cloth around his hand. He might think of himself as here to see to her privacy, but who would give her privacy from him? She shook off her concerns as she finished with his hand.

"It's no so bad, MacQuarrie. If you'll but use some caution . . ."

"Robert," he interrupted, flinching as she rubbed her hand over the back of his. "My given name is Robert."

She looked up into his eyes and froze. "No." The name didn't feel right. Besides, it was already hard enough to keep from thinking inappropriate thoughts about this man without allowing herself to become too familiar.

"Robbie, then," he countered, his gaze holding hers. "That's what yer father called me."

"Robbie," she heard herself murmur, as if she spoke against her own will. "Tell me of my father. Tell me how you came to give him yer oath."

"Thomas saved my life," he began.

She sank to the hearth and leaned closer, staring into the warm depths of his eyes as he continued to speak. This time she gave no thought as to whether or not their arms might touch or even to the words he spoke. She was lost in the music of his voice.

Robbie.

Now that felt right.

Chapter 9

⁓

"*I* am sorry, Father. His lairdship still refuses to repeat what he deems to have been a mistake." Agneys nervously twisted a strand of hair between her fingers as she spoke. "I've told him he must not deny me because I . . . I love him. Just as you instructed me to."

Roland glared at his daughter as he paced the length of her bedchamber. It was such a simple task he'd set her. Sleep with the laird, conceive a male child. An heir.

The laird's heir and Roland's as well, leaving Roland himself in control should anything . . . untimely happen to the laird.

A simple plan. A lovely young woman and a lonely old man. But there she sat, his useless daughter, unable to accomplish even that which any filthy tavern wench could have done.

Worthless. Just like her mother had been. All beauty and no brains.

"Do you carry his bairn?" He turned to her, pleased to see her flinch when he approached.

"I . . . I canna say just yet." The useless mare continued to fidget with her hair, scooting farther back into her chair as if she thought she could escape him. "I'm no even sure his lairdship succeeded in . . . in doing what he needed to do in order to get me with child."

"You'll keep those thoughts to yerself," he snapped, stomping back to stare into the dying fire.

Roland curled his lip in disgust at the frustrating turn his well-laid plans had taken. When he had first sent Agneys to the old laird, MacGahan had refused to bed her, calling it *unseemly behavior*. The great laird saw himself as such a fine, honorable gentleman, they'd been forced to ply him with an inordinate amount of whisky to lure him into Agneys's bed the first time. Now he refused to touch the spirit.

He also refused to touch Agneys.

Events of the past few days had spiraled completely out of control, much too fast for his original plan to succeed. That bastard MacDowylt had shown up out of nowhere, insisting on the payment Roland had promised, demanding marriage to MacGahan's idiot granddaughter, determined now to have these holdings in return for his debt.

"We'll see about that," Roland hissed through clenched teeth. He'd spent too many years kissing the old laird's arse, waiting to be named heir, to let everything slip through his fingers now that he was so close to his goal.

He'd figure out a way to deal with MacDowylt. It

would simply take a little time to come up with a proper course of action, but planning was, after all, his great strength.

As for Randulf, laird of the MacGahan?

There was no more time. If the old man wouldn't cooperate of his own free will, Roland would simply have to force him into action. He'd realized the necessity of speed as soon as he'd heard of the MacDowylt's approach. He was too smart to be outmaneuvered by the MacDowylt upstart or by the doddering old laird. Two days ago, he'd set the wheels of his plan in motion and now was the time for his next move.

Decision made, he whirled around and crossed to where Agneys cowered. Winding his hand into her hair, he used the heavy golden locks to jerk her to her feet. Her annoying whimpers ceased the moment he drew her face close to his.

"You will follow my lead, agreeing with whatever I say. Do I make myself clear?"

She nodded, her eyes watery with the tears she held back.

Her current visage would only add strength to support his claim.

"Come with me." Releasing her hair, he grasped her upper arm, dragging her out the door, to the stairs and down, not slowing his stride until they reached the closed door of the laird's solar.

"What . . . what are you going to—"

"Be still!" he hissed, stopping her question with a squeeze to her arm that brought yet another round of whimpers. "And dinna disappoint me by forgetting what I've told you."

After a short pause to ready himself to play the outraged father, he threw open the door.

"Fifteen years of faithful service to my laird and this is my reward?"

He shoved Agneys to the floor, where she fell in a silently weeping heap. Very nicely done, he had to admit.

Randulf's head had snapped up at their entrance, his eyes red rimmed with age and worry.

"What outrage is this?" the old man demanded.

"Outrage indeed," Roland snarled. "The lass has all but taken to her bed, unable to hold down the food she eats. She is with child. Your child."

To his credit, MacGahan wasted no time in denials, though his mouth tightened to a hard, straight line and a flush of color stained his face.

"You've no a call to fash yerself over this. Agneys will be well cared for."

"Well cared for," Roland scoffed. Her care was of little interest to him. Only her ability to produce a son for their laird mattered. "She carries the MacGahan heir in her belly."

Randulf crossed his arms, lifting his chin as he did so. "How am I to be sure the child she carries is mine?"

The question Roland had expected from the beginning. The one he had prepared to answer the moment he had stepped into the hallway on his way here.

"You took her maidenhood!" he shouted. "She's been with no one but her laird. She even thinks herself in love with you. You've taken my only daughter to bed. Now you must take her to wife."

Randulf's shoulders sagged and for a moment Roland almost felt pity for the old man, his only defense stripped away by a night spent so drunk he could barely remember it.

"Agreed. We will handfast on the . . ."

"No!" Handfasting would not suit Roland's purposes at all. He wanted the joining held in front of as many people as possible. A joining that could never be questioned or doubted. "My daughter deserves a formal marriage. In the presence of clergy."

Randulf crossed to where Agneys still huddled on the floor and held out a hand, assisting her to her feet. "Is this your wish, Agneys?"

"It is as my father says, my laird."

"Very well, Roland." The old man continued to gaze at the girl as he spoke. "I leave the arrangements to yer hand."

Roland bowed his head, hoping to leave the impression that he was mollified by his laird's decision.

In truth, he was quite satisfied. MacGahan's predictability, in some things at least, rivaled that of the sun and the moon. Counting on the old man's pride, Roland had sent a rider to summon the clergyman from Urquhart two days ago. The arrangements the old laird had left to him were already made.

Now he had only to deal with MacDowylt. And, of course, Isabella.

Chapter 10

⁓

The *thwack* of the great hammer resonated up through Robert's arms, jolting his muscles to life. Once again he raised the heavy tool over his head and smashed it down onto the wood, driving the stake farther into the damp ground.

Physical labor was exactly what he had needed this day. He had to find some way to keep better hold over himself than he'd managed to demonstrate so far.

As the rains outside had gentled to a fine mist, he and Isa had talked long into the early morning hours. At first she had wanted to know about her father, but soon she was asking questions about his own life. The battles he'd fought, his family, his home—she'd wanted to hear it all.

He had wanted to know everything about her life, hoping by some small miracle he could ease his sense of guilt at having abandoned her for so long.

The longer they'd talked, the more they'd shared, the more comfortable he'd felt, as if they had known one another forever.

It seemed insanity now, in the bright light of a new day, but last night he'd come close to telling her all his secrets as they'd sat together by the fire. In truth, perhaps the only thing preventing his having done exactly that was her dozing off to sleep, her head pillowed against his arm.

He could easily have carried her to her bed and gone back to the stable as he'd planned, but he hadn't. Instead he'd selfishly settled her against his body, enjoying the feel of her in his arms as he tried to catch an hour or two of sleep leaning against the hard stone wall.

The men he worked with always did say he could fall asleep anywhere. It seems he'd at last found the situation that proved them wrong.

As soon as the sun had risen, he'd slipped out, with every intention of keeping himself too busy to think of anything but how to convince Isa to leave this place before it was too late.

She'd spoken last night of readying her garden and of her ongoing battle with the small animals that raided her vegetables each season. Stepping out into the sunny morning, he'd decided that building a fence would be a logical use of his time.

Not that he intended for her to be here long enough to make use of that garden. All the same, it would keep him occupied and away from Isa, and considering he'd already discovered that being near her was taking more self-control than he'd imagined, his plan seemed wise.

It had required almost superhuman effort to drag his eyes from her as she'd gone about her morning chores.

Enough of this!

With another great swing of the hammer, he finished placing the final post. He stepped back to inspect what he'd accomplished and his upper arm began to tingle as if something brushed across his skin.

"I'm sure yer hungry after all yer hard work."

Robert whirled around to find Isa carrying two hollowed-out bread bowls filled with a thick, steaming porridge.

"I dinna expect you to stop yer work to feed me."

"It's no a bother, Robbie." She smiled shyly and shrugged before holding one out to him. "I was stopping for my own midday meal anyway. I thought perhaps we could take our meal together."

He dropped to one knee, not realizing how hungry he was until he took the first bite. "This is very good."

Her cheeks bloomed a bright pink as she sat down beside him. After her first bite she looked up at him and wrinkled her nose before scooting several paces away.

Good. Having her so close had made even thought difficult.

"It's a fair warm day, is it no?" she asked, as if searching for something to say. "And you've been working hard."

He nodded, concentrating on the food in his hands. Small talk was an art at which he had never excelled. Filling his mouth with another bite, he allowed himself to steal a quick glance in her direction.

She stared off into the woods. The silence that fell between them felt all the more uncomfortable because of their shared memory of last night's easy conversation.

In that silence Robert found himself entranced by her hair, staring at the way the sun glinted off individual strands. It looked like threads of deep burnished gold had been carelessly scattered among the bright, shiny copper. Sitting here next to Isa, it was all but impossible for him to remember his dislike of red hair.

Loose curls tossed in the breeze, framing her face. He fought the desire to reach out and capture one, to discover its fine texture between his fingers.

Instead he shoved another bite into his mouth.

Obviously whatever fool malady had plagued him last night haunted him still. For the life of him, he couldn't begin to imagine why he was so obsessed with a woman he'd met only a day ago.

Another gentle puff of wind washed past, and her scent tickled at his nose like fresh mowed lawns on a lazy summer day. For an instant, his mind was filled with an image of her ankle-deep in one of those lawns. Her hair was loosened, floating around her shoulders in the breeze, as that fine, soft shift she'd worn last night slid the length of her curves to pool at her feet. When the mirage lifted her arms to beckon him closer, he actually leaned forward, jerking himself out of the erotic daydream.

"I have to go." He jumped to stand, dropping what was left of his meal. He could only pray he didn't sound as desperate to her as he did to his own ears.

"Yer leaving?" She sat still, looking up at him with those huge, innocent eyes of hers, blinking as if he'd confused her.

"It's the fence." He scrambled over his thick, useless tongue to come up with an excuse. "I need saplings for the wattle. I need to be about finding them before it's too late in the day."

"Oh." She rose to her feet, dusting her hands off on her apron. "I can help, if you like."

"No!" Good lord, he was so desperate to put some distance between them, he'd all but yelled it at her. He tried again, more quietly. "No, you've yer own chores to do. I'll be back before dark. I can stay to the stream and find my way."

He started off at a jog, stopping only long enough to grab the axe and rope he'd laid out earlier for the task.

The fence might need saplings but he'd reached a point where he needed the hard work of something much larger than cutting down a few twigs. He was thinking more along the lines of a big tree. He needed something that would exhaust his body and clear his thoughts.

With one last look back at the beauty watching him go, he cut into the woods, picking up speed. By all the Faerie Magic in the world, he sincerely doubted any place on the planet held a tree massive enough to allow him to drive that sight from his mind.

"Well, this is getting nothing done." Isa spoke aloud as she was accustomed to doing, forcing herself to move at last. She had no idea how long she'd remained where she was, staring into the spot where Robbie had disappeared.

How stupid of her to feel disappointed that he hadn't wanted her company. Wasn't she the one who disdained the company of others? And wasn't it beyond idiocy to feel lonely because he'd gone?

"Brainsick, that's me," she said to the world in general. Perhaps these past eight years of pretending to be a simple-minded dullard had taken their toll at last.

She did have work that needed doing. Too many tasks to waste her day dreaming after a man who was little more than a stranger. A kind stranger. A hard-working stranger.

"But a stranger nonetheless," she said firmly, stopping at the woodpile to load up her arms.

The fire for her oven wouldn't build itself. Without the fire there would be no bread for tomorrow's meals. And hadn't she promised herself this was the year she would try to build the drains depicted in her father's old manuscript?

Perhaps she'd show the papers to Robbie tonight.

He might be a stranger, but he was a stranger whose company made her oddly happy.

With new purpose, Isa threw herself into her chores over the next few hours, losing track of time. Her bread was baking and a new pot of porridge was on to simmer, this one with bits of dried meat.

She'd just rounded the cottage, heading toward the stable to check on the ewe, when her goats began to nervously toss their heads and paw the ground.

Instantly alert, she knew that meant only one thing. They heard something she didn't yet hear.

Gathering her skirts up in one hand, she raced around the building to her front door, stopping only long enough to pick up the faint sound of approaching hooves.

With haste, she barred the door and dragged her stool close, climbing up to peer out the little hole. Her stomach tightened in apprehension. Was it possible Robbie's prediction that MacDowylt would find her was coming to pass?

Within minutes her question was answered.

"What in the name of all that's holy," she grumbled, hopping off her stool and throwing open the door. "What are you doing here?"

From his perch atop an old horse, Jamie grinned down at her.

"I come bearing official news."

"Well, then, lad, climb down off there and deliver it."

She tried to hold her stern expression, but it was nigh on impossible when the child was so obviously excited. He stood as straight and tall as his battered body would allow, closing his eyes as if he prepared to recite a speech he'd memorized.

"Yer presence is required two days hence at his lairdship's nup . . . nup . . ." His bright blue eyes flew open and his lips tightened in irritation before he leaned forward, all pretense of official messenger forgotten. "I canna remember the word, Mistress Isa, but yer grandfather is to wed Mistress Agneys and he especially asked me to see to it that you come to the castle for the ceremony. They're having a clergyman all the way from Urquhart."

Isa felt the shock of Jamie's news like a slap to her face, but whether it was her grandfather's marrying someone her own age or his wanting her there for the wedding that surprised her most, she could not say.

"Yer guardman is to come as well."

"Guardian," she corrected absently. Yes, strangely, she did want Robbie there with her. She should go find him and tell him they'd need to go back to Castle MacGahan day after tomorrow.

"You've been baking this day?"

Jamie's innocent expression didn't fool Isa in the least.

"Aye. Are you hungry?" She waited for his eager nod before reaching out to clasp his hand. "When did you last eat?"

"Yesterday," he answered apologetically. "I was working in the stable and too late for a meal last night. Then the laird sent me with the message for you before I'd finished my chores this morning."

And, as Isa had learned from the boy on an earlier trip, with the new cook in charge there was no morning meal until chores were completed.

"What does yer grandmother say about yer missing yer meals, lad?"

They were inside now, with Jamie eagerly seating himself at her small table while Isa brought out bread and cheese.

"I dinna see her much. The kitchen lasses tell me she's ill and has no time to be bothered with the likes of me."

He ended all conversation by stuffing his mouth full, though he nodded vigorously, his eyes lighting in anticipation when Isa offered a mug of fresh milk.

His own grandmother, too busy for the likes of him? She couldn't believe that. Not of Auld Annie. Annie had been the head cook at Castle MacGahan in the days Isa had been as young as Jamie, and even then the woman had always made time for her. Nothing had gone past Annie's notice—no flower picked, no hurt feelings, nothing.

Surely she'd do no less for her own sweet grandson. This didn't sound right at all.

"How about you stay here for the night? I've a nice thick porridge for our evening meal. If you'd be willing to help me by watching over it, that is. Keep it stirred for me while I go find Rob . . . um, my guardian, to tell him yer news?"

"Aye, Mistress Isa. I'm always ready to help you. Can I visit the goats after I finish my food?"

He always asked to visit the goats. "Of course, dearling. And there's the new lamb for you to see as well. But dinna forget—"

"To shut the gate," he finished for her with his little half grin. "I will. I promise."

With a nod of satisfaction, Isa set off, pleased that at the very least she'd know for a fact the child would have one more good meal. Since she'd be at the castle herself in a couple of days, she would check on his grandmother for herself to see exactly what was going on.

She stopped at the edge of the woods, the exact spot Robbie had disappeared into hours earlier, noting the broken twigs. Lucky for her he'd been in such a hurry when he'd left. Not that she should actually need to track him. He'd said he would keep to the stream. It shouldn't be difficult at all to find him.

Chapter 11

⁓

"*T*hat should do quite nicely."

Robert straightened after tying up the last bundle of saplings, an annoying little pain zinging through his chest as he did so. He must have pulled a muscle somehow last night.

Looking over his handiwork for the day and, thinking of those bundles he'd left waiting all along his path down the mountain, he felt sure he had more than enough to finish the entire wattle fence.

If he could only be equally sure he'd worked his way through the little problem plaguing him. The little problem of his unaccountable infatuation with the woman he was supposed to be protecting.

Hours ago, he'd given up on trying to figure out the whys of his situation, concentrating instead on how to deal with all these unexpected and inconvenient feelings. The cause wasn't important. Only controlling his reaction to Isabella mattered.

From the time Robert had passed outside the protective walls of MacQuarrie Keep bound for his first battle, he'd determined to present an impassionate face to those around him. As his father had often counseled both him and his brother, the best way to avoid having the world poke fingers in your hurts was to prevent their seeing your soft spots.

Robert's soft spot had always been his emotions. After Elizabeth's betrayal, he'd spent a lifetime pretending to be the aloof observer, building walls between himself and the world. In spite of his efforts, he knew better than anyone how easily those walls could be breached over time.

The odd thing with Isabella was that it had taken no time at all. Whether it stemmed from his guilt over abandoning her or his surprise at her not being what he expected, one evening spent sharing stories in her company and he found himself completely infatuated.

And infatuation it had to be.

The sort of fleeting, false emotion a schoolboy might have for his first teacher, or a patient for his nurse.

Or perhaps a Guardian for his charge?

That was the case and nothing more. It had to be. He only hoped it would pass quickly.

Not even this latest rationalization could erase his concern. He rubbed his hand over the back of his neck, wincing when an errant breeze brushed past him.

No wonder Isa had taken her distance of him. He smelled like a ditch digger in the desert who'd never heard of soap and water.

The sun was moving lower in the sky and he still had work to do. There were too many bundles for him to carry back. He should have brought his horse along, but that would have required his having used logic and sense when he set out from Isa's cottage, and logic and sense were nowhere to be found in his emotional arsenal at that moment. Base lust had pushed everything else aside.

He was none too sure his arsenal was back to normal even now.

Remembering the small waterfall and pool he'd spotted in the distance farther up the mountain, he decided on a short detour in that direction. If the setting sun did catch him, he'd only need to follow the stream that ran from the pool straight back to Isa's cottage to find his way even in the dark.

Without the weight of any saplings or his axe, he covered the distance quickly. In no time at all, he'd chucked his plaid and shirt and plunged into the deep, dark pool.

Once the shock of the cold had passed, the water enveloped his body, soothing his aches and pains. He ran his hands across his chest, looking down quickly as his fingers brushed over a sensitive spot.

His scar. Odd. It had been almost ten years since he'd taken a sword to his chest saving Connor MacKiernan's life, but the scar looked much newer. Pink and sensitive to his touch.

He didn't think Isa's elbow to his chest last night could have somehow caused new damage, but he had felt a sharp pain with her blow.

What foolishness! Surely it was a trick of the fading light and nothing more that caused the scar to look strange. No time to go blaming Isa.

Even if she *was* a redhead.

He glanced to another jagged silver line, this one on his forearm near his elbow. There had definitely been a redhead to blame for that one.

It was the summer he'd turned fifteen. He'd gone to Inverness with his father and Richard to sell the flock of sheep his father had given him the year before. The silver he made from the sale was the first money he had been able to call his own. He'd invested months into dreaming of how he would spend that silver.

And then he'd met Marie.

Robert and his brother had waited until their father was meeting with a group of merchants. They'd hastened off to one of the seamier local taverns, though they'd been strictly forbidden to go there.

Marie had struck his eye the moment they'd entered, and a short while later, emboldened by the heat of forbidden whisky burning in his chest and Richard's goading, he'd approached her table.

It had seemed like a dream when she'd invited him to her room in the back of the tavern, where she'd given him another tankard of drink, promising him a trip to heaven when he finished it down.

Whether the whisky was drugged or just too much for his young system, the next thing he remembered was waking in a haze, to find her sneaking out the door. He had tried to stop her but his legs refused to work properly. He managed to grab her skirts, but she attacked him with his own dirk and he fell backward, hitting his head. When he awoke the next time, Marie was gone.

And along with her his silver.

No, he had no doubt that redheads were dangerous. It had taken him only two encounters with them to learn that lesson and learn it well. He had the scar on his arm from Marie and another on his heart from the even more treacherous Elizabeth to prove that fact.

He closed his eyes, splashing water over his face as if he could wash the memories of those two women from his mind. While the first had been an embarrassing lesson, the second had driven him to leave his family, trekking across the world, throwing himself into battle, risking his life on foreign soil. The campaign where he had met Isabella's father.

Isabella. Another redhead.

To clear his tangled thoughts, he swam over to the waterfall, allowing it to crash down over him like an icy shower.

It wasn't as good as what had become part of his daily ritual back home, but it would do. Next time he came up here, he'd have to bring along some soap so he didn't end up stinking on a regular basis.

Like everyone else in this time.

The thought had barely formed before he realized with a start it was a falsehood. Not everyone smelled bad.

Isa smelled of a summer breeze and fresh-mown grass, not the common stench of unwashed body. Even now, if he let his mind wander, he could recall her enticing scent as if she were somewhere nearby, but, of course, that was no more than his overactive imagination.

The same overactive imagination that forced his body to harden with need at the thought of her.

He dove under the water and turned, pushing off from the bottom to propel himself to a shallower spot before he stood. Breaking through the surface, he rose, lifting his face to the setting sun, hoping the waters would wash away his impure thoughts of Isa.

To no avail.

The memory of her standing before him, her wet nightdress clinging to every enticing curve, filled his mind even as her scent filled his nostrils, stronger than before.

Surely she should be asking some higher power for forgiveness. She was wicked. Truly wicked. She should back away as quietly as she'd come upon this scene. Back away, run down the mountainside to her cottage and forget she'd ever seen any of this.

And yet, Isa could not bring herself to turn away.

Ahead of her, Robbie bathed in the waters of her pool. What she'd only glimpsed last night, she stared at openly today.

He dove, then burst up through the surface, water sheeting down his sculpted body as he stood. When he flung back his head, droplets from his hair glinted in the sun's last rays as they flew into the air, forming a shining arc around him. Not even the scars on his body could detract from his allure. He was more beautiful than any nature god could ever hope to be.

Isa sank to her knees and huddled next to a broad tree trunk. She was ashamed of her inability to turn away, ashamed of hiding in the foliage where she could continue to watch. Ashamed of the physical need building inside her.

She might be inexperienced in the ways of men and women, but that didn't mean she had no knowledge of such things. You couldn't function in the natural world or raise your own animals without knowing the ways of life.

Except that the difference between the knowledge of what happened and the feelings she actually had coursing through her body right now was vast beyond belief. It left her with a frustration beyond anything she'd ever encountered.

Once. To have a man like that take her in his arms and sweep her off her feet. To crush his mouth to hers and lower her body to the ground underneath him. To put an end to the heavy wanting filling her loins right now. What she wouldn't give to experience that for herself just one time.

Her freedom. That's what she wouldn't give.

She pressed the heels of her hands into her eyes, rubbing as if she intended to force the vision of his naked beauty from her memory.

Pointless, of course. And damned unfair.

She'd realized long ago that people simply served to bring grief and unhappiness into her world and she would be better off without them. All of them. As a result, she'd spent the last eight years building her own life of solitude, away from everyone. She'd learned to hold her emotions tightly in check and spend her days doing as she pleased.

Now *he'd* come along, determined to insert himself into her life whether she wanted him in it or not, bringing with him all these . . . *feelings.* All these wants. All these needs.

And if she gave into these feelings? If she followed the path her body urged her down?

She would never be rid of him. Any man who held on to an unfulfilled vow for twenty years took honor much too seriously to dally with a woman he saw as his responsibility and then leave simply because she told him to.

She wanted him gone. Didn't she?

She opened her eyes and focused on an early wildflower blooming just in front of her, crushed by her own footstep when she'd first arrived in this place. The delicate weed had struggled to make its way here, alone in the forest, constantly pushed aside by the larger plants, wanting nothing more than a bit of sun and rain. It had needed so little to live.

It had needed to be left alone.

There was only one choice open to her. Robbie had to go, even if it meant driving him away.

That should be an easy enough task for her. When she was younger, Auld Annie, the cook who'd looked after her, had always said her bad attitude could force the saints themselves to run away in terror.

That was it, then.

Her decision made, she looked up to find Robbie had moved to deeper water, his gaze fixed directly on the spot where she hid.

Bollocks.

She was caught.

She rubbed her damp hands down the front of her apron and stood up, defiantly jamming her hands onto her hips.

"And what do you think yer doing out here?" she demanded.

"I might ask you same, missy. I wondered how long you planned to spy on me before showing yerself."

Isa felt the red heat crawling up her neck and onto her face. That would never do! Better to attack and take him off his track.

"Plan? I have no plan. I'm no spying. It's only my disbelief of yer rude behavior that kept me here. Splashing about with yer dirty self, fouling up the water I use for cooking my food, the water I drink."

She paused for a breath, surprised to see him headed toward her, a smile growing on his face. A few more steps and he'd reach the shallows!

"What are you doing?" she screeched, oblivious to the fact that she repeated her earlier words.

"I thought you wanted me out of yer water. I'm getting out."

He took another step, his smile so broad now it danced in his eyes, and she wondered if he'd be bold enough to keep going.

Two could play the game of dares if he liked. She was every bit as stubborn as he could be, if that was what it came down to.

"That's exactly what I want." She crossed her arms over her chest, waiting.

When he took the next step, she felt her knees weaken.

The dark waters swirled below his waist and her eyes fastened on the enticing trail of hair that moved down his abdomen and disappeared into the lapping waves.

The water flowed up as he pushed forward yet again, and her hands dropped to knot in her apron at her sides. Anything to keep from reaching out to touch him as he drew near.

The waves that had flowed up as he moved now withdrew, caressing his skin like silver fingers as they fled away, exposing all of him. She turned her back as quickly as she could, but not so quickly she missed one last look at the whole of the man.

Her blood pounded in her ears and her face flamed, even as low in her belly she felt a matching burn.

Lo, but he was a beauty.

When, a moment later, his warm breath tickled her cheek, she lurched forward—and would have fallen had he not grabbed her arm.

"A word of advice, my lady. I excel at poker. I'm no a man to walk away from a bluff. Never point a weapon if you dinna intend to fire it."

"I've no need for any of yer so-called advice." As if she needed him to tell her what to do. As if what he told her made even the least bit of sense. "Everything I do I do with a reason."

"Is that so?" He leaned in closer. "Then perhaps yer real reason for standing so long in trees was that you wanted to join me in the pool?"

"Hardly!" She jerked her arm from his fingers and stepped a pace away, all too aware of the heat his body gave off, even as water dripped from his hair, forging a cold trail down the side of her neck. "Now get away from me, you great oaf. Yer getting me wet."

She didn't turn at his strangled reply nor did she give him the satisfaction of responding when the sound turned into laughter.

Infuriating man.

So, she'd been too weak for this particular game of

dares after all. No matter. It only confirmed she'd been right from the beginning.

Robbie MacQuarrie had to go.

She was a feisty one, all right.

Robert smiled to himself as he watched Isa now, her head bent low over Jamie's as she helped him make a soft pallet on the floor by the fire. Seeing her like this, it was hard to believe she was the same woman who'd argued with him all the way back to the cottage this evening.

Attempted to argue with him was more accurate. Considering the circumstances of their meeting at the pool, there was no way he was allowing her to drag him into her verbal sparring. Some men might be able to channel their emotions into words but he wasn't one of them. He felt what he felt and preferred to act upon those feelings, not talk them to death.

When he'd seen her there in the woods, the hunger sparking in her eyes as she'd watched him, he'd known it would take very little to push him over the edge.

He'd tried to warn her.

One more dare. One more challenge. One more anything and they'd likely have found themselves on the ground, going at it like wild animals in heat.

That wasn't an option he could allow. So he'd ignored her verbal jabs though her underlying meaning was clear. She thought to drive him away with her sharp tongue and hateful comments.

But all that had changed mere feet from the cottage.

"Jamie's inside," she'd warned, her demeanor instantly transforming from scolding nag to mother tiger. "You'll be kind to him or you'll deal with me for it, you ken?"

The memory brought another smile to his lips as he watched the two of them now, the boy's face shining with happiness when Isa sat down next to him on the pallet. There was something about the child, something so familiar, and yet he couldn't put his finger on it.

"Come on with you, lad. Lie down. I ken that it's hard to get to sleep in a strange place, but we've a great deal of work tomorrow if we're to be ready to leave for the castle." She patted the blanket beside her and Jamie climbed under the covers, snuggling his head into her lap.

For his part, Robert finished off the mug of weak ale Isa had offered earlier. Relaxing in his spot against the rock wall, he was amazed that he could feel so comfortable, so natural, so at peace. The moment was almost perfect. A man, a woman, a child. If he had his little dog, Charlie, here, the scene would be complete.

Isa stared down at the boy in her lap, one long finger delicately stroking the side of his poor, misshapen face as little snores wafted up from him.

"What accident befell the lad?"

She looked up, startled, at his question, as if she'd been so lost in her thoughts she'd completely forgotten he was even there.

Not exactly a major stroke for his ego.

"Fire," she answered at last, running her fingers lightly through the child's hair. "Though his grandmother swore to me it was no accident, their home burning to the ground. He was just a wee thing at the time. Must have been going on five years ago? Maybe six. I dinna believe he was even walking when it happened. Annie, his grandmother, was the one who pulled him from the flames. Burned her hands so badly she couldna ever fully return to her duties as cook."

"His parents?" From the ill-kempt look of the child, he had a pretty good idea what her answer would be.

"His mother died in the fire. He had no father. Well—" Here her eyebrows lifted in a knowing manner. "No father that ever stepped forward to claim the poor lad."

Robert nodded. It happened. People were people. The only thing worse was that he knew it would continue to happen. The passage of time wouldn't much change people for the better.

"Was the battle you fought near here?"

This time it was his turn to be surprised by a question.

"Battle?"

"I could no help but notice yer wound this afternoon. The one on yer chest." Her cheeks colored and she fastened her gaze back on the sleeping boy. "I've no great experience with battle wounds, but yers looked to be serious. Was it recent?"

"No. It was a long time ago." Another lifetime ago.

Her eyes cut to him, her brow wrinkled. "But I could have sworn . . . It looked to no to have been healed too long."

His gaze locked on hers until she looked back down.

The old scar had looked oddly pink this afternoon, but he'd reasoned that was likely a trick of the fading light. Or perhaps the result of her having elbowed him in that exact spot.

Surely it couldn't be anything more serious than that.

"Of course, I am no a healer," she muttered, cradling Jamie's head in her hands as she slipped out from under him. She lay the boy down gently as she stood, then stretched out her back before hurrying to the other end of the room. There she bent over her wooden chest before returning, her arms wrapped around a thick woolen.

"I suppose I'd best take my own advice and get some rest." Her eyes flitted nervously around the room, refusing to light anywhere.

Was she waiting for him to go?

"Well, then, I guess I'll be out to the stable." He rose to leave but she stopped him with a hand to his forearm, which she removed as quickly as she'd touched him.

"There's no a need for you to do that. Yer welcome to take yer rest here by the fire, with the boy."

She held out the bundle in her arms as if in offering. When he took it, his hands covered hers and her eyes widened, the spark he'd seen in the woods this afternoon returning. A tingling rushed through his body and the mark on his arm felt alive with movement.

Isa jerked away and stepped back. Averting her gaze to the floor, she clasped her hands tightly behind her.

"I . . . I've a boon to ask of you, Robbie."

As if the look he'd just seen in her eyes wasn't enough, her familiar use of his name sent a rush of heat chasing after the tingle that dove straight to his loins. He lowered the bundle in his arms, holding it in front of him like a shield to protect him. Or a screen, to hide the effect she had on him.

"Do you suppose you could find something for Jamie to do for you tomorrow? Odd jobs to keep him here for another day until we're ready to travel to the castle?"

The thrill he'd felt building fizzled away like cold water tossed on embers. Was she so desperate to keep the boy here because of him? How ridiculous! Why on earth would she feel that was necessary? She didn't need protection from him. He was sworn to *be* her protection.

"I suppose he could . . . he could maybe help me gather the saplings and bring them down for the fence." He stumbled through his response, stung by her lack of trust in him.

"I would be most grateful to you. It's only that he tells me of his grandmother's illness and I want to keep him here long enough to be able to check on the woman for my own self when we go to the castle. I dinna believe he's being cared for at all, and he's half starved every time I see him." She gripped the edge of her apron, twisting and tormenting the material in her grasp as she spoke, her words racing out as if she couldn't speak them fast enough to suit her needs.

As her words died out, her face a flaming red, it occurred to Robert there might be more to this situation than his injured pride was allowing him to see.

It might not be that she wanted the lad to protect her from him. It just might be instead that she wanted the lad to protect her from herself.

Chapter 12

Like proud roosters, they marched back and forth, Robbie and Jamie, admiring the fence they'd labored over the day before. They could well be father and son, those two.

Isa bit back a smile as she watched them through the opening in the door.

She couldn't have imagined when she'd impulsively asked the big warrior to find a way to keep Jamie busy here that he would turn out to be such a kind and caring teacher for the boy. Over the past day and a half the two of them had been inseparable, Robbie patiently taking the lead, with Jamie at his heels like a noonday shadow.

She'd never seen Jamie so happy, not even when he was eating.

If she weren't so determined to make the man leave, she might just find herself wanting him to stay.

"Which is exactly why he has to go," she muttered as she closed the door behind her. The Fates had never been kind to her, but this—this taste of what other people have in their lives dangling in front of her—was the unkindest cut of all. Their last few evenings together had been idyllic, as if they were the perfect family she'd always dreamed of.

"Dinna you go brainsick now, Isabella MacGahan," she said aloud, needing the encouragement.

Time to put away the fantasies and face what life had actually dished out to her.

Even if a man like him did take a fancy to her, she was too dangerous to live among people. One unguarded flare of her temper and lightning could take them all down or they could drown in the rains she thoughtlessly provoked.

No, fantasy would have to be packed away like the treasures in her little wooden box.

For now, it was time to head to the castle. She'd finished her preparations.

Nervously she smoothed her hand down the front of her filthy dress, the action sending waves of foul odors swirling around her as she stepped outside.

"There she is," Jamie called, running toward her. "Are we ready to go now?" He stopped a short distance away from her, the good side of his face wrinkling in distaste. "Lo, but that's foul, Isa."

Even she had to admit she might have overdone it a bit this time. Perhaps the goat droppings in her pockets were a little over the top. Still, it was a big event and a good chance to impress upon everyone the necessity of keeping their distance from her.

"What the hell have you done to yerself?" Robbie demanded, an angry frown creasing his handsome features. "You stink to high heaven!"

"This?" She tried to ask it innocently enough. "Only what I always do."

"No. Yer no going about like that. No anymore." Robbie crossed his arms over his chest, shaking his head as if he could tell her what to do. "Go in the house and clean yerself up. We'll wait right here for you."

"I'll do no such thing." Was he witless? She'd carefully cultivated her disguise over the past eight years. She wasn't about to ruin all that hard work. "I'm ready to go as I . . . *urmph*."

The wind was knocked from her lungs when Robbie lifted her from her feet, tossing her over his shoulder and walking away.

"What do you think yer . . ."

Before she could even finish her sentence, she was flying through the air and landing with a splash, on her bottom, waist deep in the stream that ran beside her home. The only sound her brain could form was a scream of rage.

Thunder rolled and lightning streaked across the sky as a distant storm raced in their direction, but Robert seemed not to notice anything as he glared at her.

"Now climb yer pretty arse out of the water, get inside the house, and get yerself ready to go. I told you once before, you've no need to pretend to be anything other than yerself. I'll no have you humiliating yerself, yer father's memory, and yer grandfather on his wedding day. He deserves better from you."

"My grandfather?" She yelled at him, indignation filling every inch of her soaking wet frame. "What do you ken of my grandfather? Nothing! You ken nothing of my life or of what my grandfather deserves."

One look at Jamie's white face, peering at her from behind Robbie's massive body, and she gasped for air, fighting to regain her control. Of all the things in the world she might want, frightening the lad was not one of them.

"I ken he was laird and father to my friend Thomas. And I ken that Thomas loved his father as he did his daughter. And though I may not understand the troubles between the two of you, I have enough care for Thomas's memory that I'll show his father respect. And you'll do the same as long as I'm here."

He reached out his hand to help her up and she stared at it a long moment before accepting his assistance. How dare he try to shame her into changing her behavior.

"Then perhaps you should get on yer big horse there and go, Robert MacQuarrie. I dinna want you to stay. I dinna need you to watch over me."

For a second, she thought he might let go of her hand, plunging her back into the water. But then his expression hardened and he pulled her to her feet, though a bit more forcefully than necessary, to her way of thinking.

When she was on the bank, he released her hand and stepped back, holding out his arm as if he were a great gentleman inviting her to enter her own home.

"Dinna keep us waiting long, woman." He crossed his arms in front of him, one eyebrow cocking imperiously. "And for the record, Isa, whether you want me to stay or go is of no matter to me. I pledged my word to yer da to watch over you, and watch over you is what I intend to do. As long as yer here, I'm here, so you might just as well get that through yer stubborn little head."

It would do no good to argue. That much was plain to see. Swallowing her anger, she stomped off toward the cottage.

He knew nothing of the man her grandfather was. Nothing. How dare he throw her father's feelings in her face.

Damn him. Damn the Fates for bringing him here.

Thunder rumbled again in the distance as she slammed the door closed behind her, still struggling to bring her roiling emotions back under her command.

She fought back the tears that clouded her vision and the tightening in her throat, refusing to even think about whether they came from rage or sorrow.

Had she thought the Fates were unkind earlier? She'd been absolutely wrong. They weren't unkind. They were downright vindictive as hell.

So there was indeed a temper to match all that red hair. Robert stared at the back of the retreating woman he'd just plucked from the waters. He wasn't sure he'd ever met a woman who bottled up her emotions as tightly as Isabella did. She was going to blow one of these days, and when she did, heaven help whoever set her off.

"It's because of her mother," a quiet little voice said from behind him.

"What?"

Robert turned to find Jamie all but cowering a few feet away. The sight almost broke his heart. He strode over to the boy, and reached out to place his hand on Jamie's shoulder. When the boy flinched, Robert felt a flush of guilt and dropped to his knees, facing the child.

"Isa would not like to have me tell you so, but it's because of her mother that his lairdship wanted nothing to do with her when she was little. Please dinna be angry with her. It's no her fault." Though his chin quivered, he met Robert's eyes with an oddly familiar piercing blue stare, his shoulders back like those of a little soldier.

"I'm no angry with Isa. Dinna you worry yerself about that, lad." Robert forced a smile for Jamie's sake, relieved to see the boy visibly relax. "How do you come to know about these things you say?"

Jamie shrugged. "My grandmother used to tell me stories about when Mistress Isa was a girl at the castle. She said his lairdship hated her mum because she'd up and left Master Thomas with a broken heart and that Isa was the very image of her mum."

Robert nodded as he stood, ruffling Jamie's hair with one hand. The backstairs grapevine always had been the best place to learn what went on in a keep.

"Come along with you, Jamie. Let's get mounted and ready to go." He lifted the boy up onto the back of the old horse he'd ridden from the castle before climbing into his own saddle. "Thank you for telling me about Isa and her grandfather. It helps me to know. I guess

I can see how a father might resent the woman he thought had hurt his son. And if, as yer grandmother says, Isa looks so much like her mother, I suppose it would stir old feelings."

The door to the cottage slammed again and Robert turned, watching as the Isa he'd come to know over the past few days made her way toward them.

"Aye," Jamie agreed. "Between the way she looks and the terrible magic she inherited from her mum, she and his lairdship have had a hard time of it."

"The what?" Robert swiveled his gaze back to the boy.

"Magic," he answered innocently, waving as Isa approached. "Isa's mum was a Faerie."

Chapter 13

⁓

"The laird's solar is just down this way." With an emphatic nod, Jamie loped off ahead of them down the gloomy hallway at Castle MacGahan.

"As if I dinna remember where my own grandfather's solar is located," Isa muttered irritably, pushing in front of Robert to follow the boy.

The whole of their trip from the cottage she'd been quietly irritable. On the rare occasion where she seemed to feel the necessity to add her comments, they'd been snippy, as now. That her temper was on display was a given.

Robert had quickly decided that if this was her convoluted female logic trying to teach him a lesson by not talking to him, she had sorely misjudged his need for conversation.

So she was angry with him, that much he understood and accepted. Fine. She could be as angry as she liked. It didn't change for one moment what was right and proper. He might have missed his opportunity to guide Thomas's child, but he wouldn't allow the adult she had become to dishonor her father.

He also wouldn't allow her to continue to dishonor herself. She was a beautiful, intelligent woman who deserved the respect of her clan, not their pity and derision.

She'd have it, too. He'd do whatever was necessary to see to that. And if her being angry and refusing to talk to him was the price he'd have to pay, so be it.

Besides, he and Jamie had passed the time pleasantly enough discussing their fence and making vague plans for future projects, so her lack of participation was of no concern to him.

Jamie's claim that Isa's mother had been Faerie was another matter altogether. It had to be a flight of imagination, a story told by an old woman to a small boy to bring on sleep.

Though he knew better than most the reality of the Fae, stories of the Faerie were rife in the legends of the Scots. And while he suspected that some of those legends might be based in fact, this particular story was difficult to accept without some proof. That his whole life could be so intertwined with the Fae seemed simply too much of a coincidence. And yet, this could certainly explain Thomas's contention that Isa, like her mother, was "different."

Whatever the truth, he planned to learn more about this story, though the opportunity to follow up hadn't appeared yet. He was especially interested in learning whether or not Isa knew anything of it.

"Here we are," the boy whispered loudly before pushing open the heavy door to announce their arrival. "They've come, yer lairdship. I've brought them directly to you, just as you commanded of me."

Jamie bowed his head and moved to the side of the old laird's chair while Robert followed Isa into the room, stopping two steps behind her.

Randulf MacGahan stared at his granddaughter, the thoughts behind his piercing blue gaze impenetrable. At length, he rose from his chair.

"Apologies for my delay in welcoming you, Isabella. When you first entered, it was as if Elesyria herself were standing in the room."

"I canna help the way I look," Isa muttered, her hands tightening into fists at her sides. She stepped back a pace, casting a dark scowl over her shoulder in Robert's direction before returning her attention to her grandfather. "I've come as you ordered, for yer wedding to . . . to that Agneys. Though I canna for the life of me ken yer decision to tie yerself to that woman."

The anger in her words surprised Robert, giving him pause to consider that Isa's behavior this day might actually have less to do with him than he'd originally suspected.

"It was no an order, Isabella. Only the request of an old man to have his granddaughter at his side on this day."

Though Robert could not see her expression, the rigid line of her back gave clue aplenty as to her mood.

"I should no be surprised. You made yer choices known long ago. And either way, you have what you wanted, do you no? You'll guarantee the perfect little Agneys will be at yer side now for all time."

"Isa." The laird extended his hand and started toward her, but she held up her hand as if to stop him.

"I canna do this now. I've a need to speak with Auld Annie. Is she still in the room off the kitchens?"

Randulf's hand dropped to his side and he nodded his answer.

Isa turned, bumping into Robert in her haste to leave the room, her eyes filled with unshed tears as she pushed past him.

"My son Thomas chose his daughter's guardian well."

"Thank you." Robert backed to the door, wanting only to follow the footsteps he could hear even now fading down the hallway.

"No. Thank you, MacQuarrie. For bringing my granddaughter back to me."

"I can take no credit for that." Robert dipped his head in Jamie's direction. "It was the lad there who brought us both to you."

"No." The old man shook his head sadly. "I'm no speaking of yer physical presence here, lad. It's yer bringing home the lass who left here eight years ago. The lass I thought was lost to the madness I'd driven her to."

Before Robert could respond, the laird seemed to recover himself, his emotions once again masked.

"Know this, guardian, yer work is far from done here. I've a concern for Isabella's safety. You've a need to stay close to her side while she's here."

"And I will, Laird MacGahan. Now, if you'll excuse me, I'd like to do just that."

At the doorway, Robert paused one last time, thinking to leave with some appropriate pleasantry, but any words he might have spoken fled from his mind. The vague familiarity he'd sensed earlier suddenly crystallized for him.

Jamie had risen to his feet to stand at the old laird's side. Both the boy and Randulf had fixed their attention squarely on Robert.

Two identical piercing blue stares of expectation followed him as he took off after Isa.

Outside the room, Isa picked up her pace. Though she stopped herself just short of running, she couldn't get far enough away fast enough to suit her.

This entire day had been sheer hell, from her inglorious dousing in the stream this morning to her meeting with the MacGahan laird just now. As if having to watch her grandfather wed a woman who had been the bane of her life growing up wasn't going to be bad enough, having to face him stripped of the protection of her disguise certainly had been.

Perhaps she should have been thankful he hadn't cringed in fear at seeing her. Though accusing her of looking exactly like her mother was hardly any better. It had taken every bit of her control to hang on to her emotions and avoid disaster.

She knew she should have kept to her disguise.

The tatters and the filth had encouraged people to keep their distance. They'd turned away, ignoring her as if she didn't exist, secretly hoping that when they looked back she'd be gone. Without the disguise, she felt as if she were the center of curiosity, every head turning as she passed.

Slipping around the corner into the hallway behind the kitchens, she pulled up short to avoid running down a maid headed in her direction.

"Stop right there," the young woman demanded, stepping in front of Isa. "Are you one of them tinklers? Master Roland warned us to be on our guard for the likes of you lest you steal everything not nailed down. Who let you into the castle anyway?"

Isa briefly considered claiming to be exactly that, but quickly decided such an assertion would likely get her tossed out on her ear faster than admitting to her own identity.

"I am no one of the tinklers." Isa lifted her chin and glared at the maid. "I'm on my way to see Auld Annie."

"Oh no." Shaking her head, the maid again stepped in front of Isa as she attempted to go forward. "That's no allowed for any but those who see to her care. Master Roland's orders."

"Master Roland's orders, is it?" Isa asked, allowing the contempt she felt to color her words. "No that it's any of yer business, but I've just left the company of the MacGahan himself, and I'm visiting Annie with his full knowledge and permission. Now, as I recall, the laird's word overrides that of Master Roland, does it no?"

The young woman's face wrinkled in her confusion. "I . . . I suppose. I can show you where—"

"I've no a need for yer help," Isa interrupted, pushing past the maid. "I ken the way on my own."

When Isa had lived at the castle, the room had been for little more than storage. But after the horrendous fire that had taken the life of Annie's only daughter and nearly killed both her and Jamie as well, the laird had granted the old woman lodging in the castle itself. She'd chosen this room over any other because it kept her close to her beloved kitchens even though the burns to her hands and arms kept her from returning to her position as head cook.

Isa pushed open the door, stepping down into the dimly lit room. At the far end, Annie sat in front of a low-burning fireplace, looking small and lonely, swathed in a mound of woolens.

"Annie? How are you feeling?"

The old woman turned her head slowly, her eyes lighting in recognition. "Isabella? Is that you, lass? Come closer and let Auld Annie have a look at you."

Isa hurried over, dropping to her knees at Annie's feet to clasp the old woman's hand. This was the one person she'd been able to turn to when she was growing up. The one person who'd been here from the time she was born and yet passed no judgment on her. The only person who'd ever seemed to care what happened to her.

"What ails you, Annie? Jamie said you were so ill they wouldn't allow him in to bother you."

Annie made an irritated clucking sound with her tongue that Isa remembered from her own childhood.

"I suppose that explains why I've no had a visit from him in so long. Him or anyone else, save the lasses who bring my meals."

"It's by Roland's orders no one's allowed in to see you." Orders that Isa was at a complete loss to understand. "Why would he want to keep you isolated?"

Annie ducked her head, refusing to meet Isa's eyes. "I canna imagine why."

"I can."

At the sound of Robbie's deep voice, Isa jumped to her feet, whirling around to place Annie at her back before confronting him.

"What are you doing here? Did you follow me?"

"Aye." He stood like a guard by the door, his hand resting casually on his sword. "It's no as though I'm likely to let you roam unprotected through these halls, is it?"

"Yer no my . . ." Isa stopped herself, the word *keeper* about to roll off her tongue. It would do no good to argue with the stubborn man since that's exactly what he saw himself as. "Well, then, if you know so much, just why would Roland think to keep a harmless old woman locked away from everyone else in the castle?"

Instead of flashing that disarming smile of his she'd expected, he focused his gaze beyond her shoulder to Auld Annie. "Yer friend there may indeed be harmless, but the secrets she keeps are no."

"Secrets," Isa scoffed. This was Annie, the woman who had been her only confidante as a girl. Annie wouldn't be keeping secrets from her. "Dinna be ridiculous, Robbie. What secrets could Auld Annie possibly have?" Even as the words left her lips she felt the air around her waver and thicken with the smell of fear.

He didn't answer right away, instead staring silently at Annie, as if he were stalling for time. Or giving the old woman a chance to speak up. When he did respond, his eyes took on that hard, unfeeling warrior look she'd first admired.

"Perhaps the identity of Jamie's father?"

"Yer as mad as she pretends to be," Annie muttered, dipping her head toward Isa. "There's naught about wee Jamie to interest anyone, so you've no need to be bringing his name into our conversation."

"Really?" Robbie's eyebrow lifted with his question. "I'd think being the laird's bastard would draw a great deal of interest."

"No!" Annie surged to her feet, woolens falling around her like dead leaves. "Dinna ever speak those words aloud. I'll no risk losing Jamie as I did my poor Jone. I'll go to my own grave first."

The old woman's emotions clouded the air, swirling and tangling with Isa's own confusion, forming a mix so heavy Isa fought to catch her breath.

"Roland fancies himself the next laird. He'll no allow any challengers to that goal." Robbie's tone carried no question, only a statement of fact, as if he were putting together a list. Then, his eyes lighting as if he'd found the missing piece of a broken pottery, he turned his gaze on Isa. "A fact that would explain the MacGahan's concerns for Isabella's safety."

"What are you saying?" Isa pushed the words from her mouth, fighting against the heavy air around her. "Yer making no sense."

No sense at all, but the fear continued to pour off Annie in waves, beating at Isa like storm-driven swells hitting the shore. Isa's vision narrowed as she struggled for air, stumbling forward.

Suddenly Robbie was there, his arm around her shoulders. The bubble of clean, clear air surrounding him filled her lungs as he urged her toward the exit.

At the doorway she looked back at Auld Annie. Though the woman's emotions blurred the air as they shimmered in the distance between them, the truth was also visible. There was age but no illness in Annie. She stood erect, her cheeks pink and healthy. The woman was prisoner, not patient, pure and simple.

"Dinna fash yerself over Jamie's welfare. I'll no let anything happen to him," she assured the older woman.

"That's beyond yer power, I fear. Only by hiding who he is can I hope for his safety."

"But, Annie . . ." she stopped as the old woman held up her hand.

"No, lass. Mark well my words, MacQuarrie. You must take her far away from here. Far away where she'll be safe from those who would do her harm."

"My plan exactly, madam," Robbie murmured, shoving Isa out the door and closing it behind them.

Robert's original intent in following Isa had been nothing more than to ensure her safety. Once he'd seen her with the old woman, though, he'd realized there was more to her relationship with Annie than met the eye.

Before he left Castle MacGahan, he intended to find a few minutes to chat with Auld Annie again, but without Isa around. He suspected if anyone could shed some light on Jamie's story about Isa's mother, this woman would be the one.

All that would have to wait for now.

Something he didn't quite understand had happened in that room back there. Something that had physically weakened Isa. Something that had set the mark on his arm to tingling like bugs crawling under his skin.

At this moment, he didn't really care what was the cause. He simply wanted to get her away from the room, away from that woman and away from this castle as quickly as possible.

That she had allowed him to hustle her out of there with no resistance spoke to him of the serious nature of what they'd encountered. In his experience, Isa did nothing against her will without a battle.

"Once yer grandfather has spoken his vows, we'll slip out to the stables and make our way beyond the castle. Until then, yer not to be out of my sight unless I say it's safe to do so. Yer especially not to be around this Lardiner fellow. Do you hear me?"

One thing was clear to Robert now. Castle MacGahan was rife with political intrigue. He'd seen it often enough before—he should have recognized it on his prior visit. But he'd been distracted, first by his need to find Isabella and then by the woman herself. He might not know who all the players were, but he did know there were battle formations being drawn in this hall, and clearly he and Isabella were caught behind enemy lines.

It grated on his nerves that he'd walked into the situation willingly. More than willingly. He'd actively encouraged Isa to come here today.

"If it's no the devil himself," Isa murmured next to him, her gaze fixed ahead of them.

Down the hallway, Roland approached, accompanied by two men who were obviously his personal guards. Not that they posed much of a threat. Robert had little doubt he could deal with all three of them easily enough, though he wasn't at all fond of trying to do so in this confined hallway with Isa at his side. Too great a risk that she might be hurt in the scuffle.

"Well, well, MacQuarrie. It would appear you've been a busy man. Isabella looks almost like a normal woman." Lardiner, a sneer lifting his lip, stopped several feet away, his guards on either side of him.

"I'm afraid you have the advantage of me, good sir." Robert felt the ice of impending battle settle over him. He smiled as he stepped a pace ahead of Isa, keeping his hand on her forearm just in case he needed to quickly shove her behind him. "You are?"

Roland's jaw tightened, but he managed a cursory tilt of his head.

"Roland Lardiner, second in command to the laird of this castle."

"Ah, yes." Robert wrinkled his brow as if searching his memory. His friend Jesse had long extolled the virtues of what he called pushing an enemy's buttons to test their mettle. "I remember now. My father has an underling such as you at our keep."

The man's face colored like a mottled beet.

"May I ask yer purpose in being in this particular hallway?"

"I came to see Auld Annie," Isa blurted out before Robert tightened his grip on her arm.

"I trust you had a pleasant visit with the old woman?" Lardiner's beady eyes narrowed with his question.

"I encouraged Isabella to come, though I would no go so far as to call the few moments spent in a dank sickroom pleasant." Robert eased a little farther in front of Isa. "Nonetheless, our visit here seemed a good opportunity for Isabella to say her final farewells since she'll be coming away with me once the laird is wed."

"Indeed?"

"Indeed." Robert locked eyes with Lardiner, holding his gaze until the other man looked away. "And now, if you'll excuse us, we'll be out to the courtyard for some fresh air to wipe away that nasty experience, won't we, Isabella?"

To her credit, she said nothing as he pulled her forward. As discreetly as possible, he maneuvered her ahead of him when they passed by Lardiner and his men, placing his own body behind her as a shield.

Just in case.

"What did you mean by . . ." she started, but he cut her words off.

"Not here. Outside, where we won't be overheard." The walls of this time period might not have the electronic bugs he'd encountered in his new time, but the people who inhabited these castles were often lingering in dark corners. Listening.

Listening and carrying tales. Which probably accounted for their meeting with Lardiner and his men in that hallway. Robert would bet money someone had scurried off to tell the second in command that Isabella had broken his no-visit rule.

He hurried her forward, relaxing only a little after they'd made their way out to the bailey. At least here he could see what might be coming at them.

He almost stumbled over her when, in the middle of the courtyard, she abruptly halted, whirling to face him.

"We have to do something about the way my grandfather is treating Auld Annie. She's being held prisoner in her own quarters."

"That's no yer grandfather's doing, lass. It's Lardiner who's given those orders."

She rolled her eyes and leaned in toward him, her hands on her hips. "Roland is naught but a toothless lapdog for my grandfather. He does the laird's bidding."

Isa had been too long away from the company of others if she believed that. Lardiner looked to him to be a dog with very sharp teeth. But this was neither the time nor the place to try to convince her of that fact.

Instead he shrugged and shook his head. "Say what you will."

"Explain yerself, MacQuarrie. And for that matter, what was that blether about Jamie? What was going on in Auld Annie's room?"

If the dangerous glint in her beautiful eyes hadn't warned of her anger, her use of his surname certainly did. But he had questions of his own that needed answers.

"I might well ask the same of you. What happened to you in there? You looked as if you were suffocating."

Isa's lips drew into a thin line, and her eyes quickly darted away from his and back again. "That's no what I meant. How could the laird have fathered Jamie?"

She obviously thought to ignore his query. He wouldn't be sidetracked as easily as that, but if she wanted to parry words, he was more than up to the task.

"In the usual way, I'd imagine. You do have a knowledge of that process, do you no?"

Her cheeks flushed an attractive pink and she turned

to look out across the courtyard, her arms crossed under her breasts.

Now there was a sight to make a man's mouth water if he'd ever seen one.

"Because if you dinna ken how it's done, lass, I'd be more than happy to demonstrate for you once we're away from this place."

The pink in her cheeks morphed into an overall dull red.

"What are those men doing?" she asked, walking away from him in the direction she faced even as she spoke the words.

"Wait!" he called, looking ahead as he hurried to catch up with her.

Did the woman just live to make his life difficult?

Ahead of them, a group of men and boys had gathered near the large gates that opened into the bailey. Their growing noise, angry jeers and laughter, must have been what first attracted Isa's attention.

They had formed a circle around a man and woman holding a small child, hurling insults at the couple. He could feel the crazed excitement of the crowd building momentum, each person stoking the anger and suspicion of the one next to him.

How careless of him! He'd been so distracted in his banter with Isa, he'd failed to notice what was going on right under his nose. As he drew up beside her, he reached out to grab her elbow.

Too late.

She dodged his arm and bulldozed her way forward. "What do you men think yer doing? Stop that! Stop that right now!" Isa, her head barely level with the men's shoulders, stepped into the center of their circle to where the couple stood, taking a stand in front of them.

Robert elbowed his way through the men, too, likely shoving a bit harder than was actually necessary in his irritation. The instant he'd realized what was going on, he should have remembered her affinity for the underdog. Seeing the quarrelsome mob surrounding her triggered his own anger.

"What's going on here?" he demanded, sizing up the situation even as he spoke.

The crowd that had gathered was little more than stable hands and castle servants. Dealing with the lot of them would be easy enough should it come to that, but Robert didn't like their position in the least. Having both Isa and the woman with her child inside this circle was unacceptable. His most immediate priority was to shift them to a more easily defended spot. A spot with no one at their backs.

He chose the most expedient means he could think of to get people moving away. He drew his sword, pulling it hard against the scabbard to ensure the ring of metal would carry through the air.

The circle evaporated, with men and boys scattering off to both sides, all keeping their distance as he backed the couple and Isa toward the open gate.

"Now," he demanded loudly. "Would someone like to tell me what the hell is going on here before I'm forced to lose my temper."

"It's them dirty tinklers," one of the men called out from a safe distance away. "We caught 'em sneaking in through the gates. They're here to steal something."

"We dinna sneak," the man at his shoulder asserted. "And we've no need to steal anything these people might have. My wife and I walked through the gates in broad daylight. We accompanied the cleric from Urquhart thinking to offer our goods and services for the wedding celebration to be held at this castle."

"Who are you to be protecting them dirty tinklers?" one of the braver voices called out.

Before Robert could respond, another in the crowd answered for him. "He's that warrior what claims to be guardian over the laird's granddaughter."

More rumbling ensued, but most backed away a little farther.

Robert spared the tinkler only a quick glance, keeping his attention focused on the men around them.

"This is no place to bring yer family, sir. There's no amount of silver to be made that's worth risking something so precious in a place as unsettled as this."

Behind them, the wife edged closer, lifting one hand to her husband's shoulder. "He speaks the truth, William. Can you no feel it on the wind? We should be away from here. Quickly."

"Agreed."

That was all Robert needed to hear. Once again he lifted his voice to call out to the crowd. "These people have meant you no harm and I mean for no harm to come to them. Do you ken my words? Now get away, all of you. Go back to what yer supposed to be doing."

Gradually, in groups of two and three, they began to drift away, grumbling, casting suspicious looks over their shoulders as they left.

"Where are the guards to let this happen?" Isa's cheeks were still pink, but Robert suspected the color resulted from her anger.

"Ha!" the man scoffed. "There's none likely to come to the rescue of a tinkler, miss. Making your aid, good sir, all the more impressive." He held out his hand to Robert. "William Faas, in yer debt. And this is my wife, Editha, and our son, Sean.

"He's adorable." Isa reached out a tentative finger, stroking the child's soft plump cheek as she spoke.

"Thank you." Editha's shy smile broke beautifully over her ruddy face. "As my husband says, we're in yer debt. If yer ever in need of us, you've only to call upon us for aid."

Editha hefted the small boy higher up on her hip and turned, following William out through the gates to their wagon beyond.

"Right," Robert muttered, watching the retreating couple. "I'll keep it in mind if I ever find myself in need of a new pot." He could only hope William Faas had learned a valuable lesson this day about using more care in where he led his family.

"I suppose it begins," Isa murmured, brushing past his shoulder to move in front of him.

The doors of the great hall had opened and groups of people drifted down the stairs, all heading toward the little chapel at the far side of the courtyard. Robert and Isa followed, keeping to the edges of the crowd.

The MacGahan laird took his place on the steps of the chapel, Roland Lardiner at his side.

Robert studied the two of them, searching for any signs of trouble. The MacGahan laird must suspect something was amiss at his castle, otherwise why would he have made a point of asking Robert to watch over Isabella? Did he see that the danger came from his own second in command, or was he so close to the man as to be blinded?

"What worry's filling yer thoughts now, Robbie?"

He looked down to find Isabella staring at him, her gaze penetrating.

"Nothing," he lied.

"You canna expect me to believe such as that when yer forehead is puckered up like a large dress tied about a small woman. Those wrinkles tell me yer worrying over something."

When had Isabella become the expert at reading him?

"I was only wondering if the laird's new wife might not be in danger from . . ." He stopped, looking around at the people close to them. "From the man we were discussing before," he finally finished.

"Hardly," Isa scoffed. "Agneys is Roland's daughter."

Roland's daughter? "But that should mean . . ."

"Isabella! There you are!" Laird MacGahan's voice rang out over the noise of the crowd and the people quieted, all heads turning to look in their direction.

Isa grabbed Robert's hand, as if for support, scooting closer to him before the old man called out again.

"Join me up here on the steps, lass. I'd have my granddaughter at my side on this day."

She looked to Robert, her eyes rounded, and he nodded his reassurance before leading her through the opening that formed in the crowd between the laird and where they'd stood. He gave her hand a squeeze before she let go to stand beside her grandfather.

He moved back, but only a couple of steps. Though he wanted to watch Isa, to be able to give her encouragement if she needed it, his attention was completely taken by Lardiner.

The man glared at Isa in a way that made Robert remember the saying, "If looks could kill." Which made no sense at all.

After all, Roland's daughter would shortly be the wife of the MacGahan, so what threat could he possibly see in Isa?

Chapter 14

*I*sa fidgeted uncomfortably in her chair. She'd never been seated on the dais next to her grandfather before, and his insistence that she stay for the wedding feast and occupy this place next to him now was most confusing.

She sat on his right with Agneys on his left. Roland sat next to his daughter, his expression as close to a smile as Isa could ever remember seeing on the slimy man.

The only positive in her grandfather's table arrangements had been that he'd seated Robbie next to her. More than once this evening she'd felt the need to let her foot linger close to his under the table. Each time, the look he'd sent her had settled her nervous stomach and given her strength to continue to sit here amid so many stares.

She slid her foot next to his now, waiting to catch his eye. The almost-smile he gave her warmed her heart and seemed to make the air in the room easier to breathe.

Not that anyone else would recognize his expression as a smile. Even with his sword hanging from his chair rather than strapped to his back, her guardian looked every bit the warrior tonight, his emotionless mask securely back in place.

She'd been fooled the first time she'd seen him, thinking the man was truly without emotion, but she knew better now. There was much more to her Robbie than mere warrior.

She'd seen with her own eyes the kindness in his face when he'd gently taken Jamie under his wing, slowing his progress on the task at hand to allow the lad to work with him on the fence. She'd watched this afternoon as justice had lit his expression when he'd come to the rescue of that family of tinklers in the courtyard.

And without a doubt, she'd seen the heat of desire in his expression a time or two.

If only her life had been different, she would have chosen a man such as Robbie to spend it with. A man of intense emotions but always in complete control of them. A man to fill her days and share her nights. A man to father her children.

She sighed at the hopeless daydream. Even if a man such as he were the least bit inclined to care for a woman like her, the knowledge of what she was, what she was capable of, would send him running in the opposite direction fast enough.

The clanging of metal tankards against the large

wooden tables jerked her attention back to the present. With a guilty start, she found Robbie staring at her, and she felt her face heat as if he could read her thoughts.

"Raise yer cups in celebration," Roland announced. "Of our laird and his lady, Agneys." He paused, waiting for the cheering to subside. "You've news yet to share with yer people, have you no, my laird?"

If Isa didn't know better, she'd think her grandfather uncomfortable with the question. Though the idea seemed impossible to her, she could have sworn he stiffened in his chair before responding to Roland.

"I'm no sure what yer speaking of, Roland." Randulf reached for the full tankard sitting on his left.

"Here, now, my laird. This is no time to be a modest man. Yer people deserve to hear from yerself the good news you and yer lady have to share with us."

Randulf looked out over the faces in his hall before turning his gaze to Isa.

Isa had always believed her grandfather had the most piercing stare of anyone she'd ever known. When he'd trained that gaze on her as a child, she'd imagined herself a rabbit in the falcon's sight. As she met his eyes now, she wondered how she could have ignored how much like her father's eyes his were. How like Jamie's. Frosty blue, like storm clouds on the horizon.

At this moment, with their gazes locked, she could almost allow herself to believe he was trying to share his thoughts with her through those eyes.

But, of course, that was ridiculous. Her grandfather had shared nothing with her since that awful day he'd come to tell her he'd received news of her father's death.

At five, she'd had no understanding of how to control her emotions. She'd felt swallowed up by an unimaginable sorrow to know her beloved da would not be coming back to her. When the tears started, she couldn't stop them any more than she could halt the thunder or the rain or the quaking of the earth that had followed.

Her fault, her grandfather had accused. The fault of her mother, the treacherous Fae whore who'd broken his only son's heart and left him with a dangerous halfbreed to raise.

Thunder boomed outside now and Isa closed her eyes to break the strange connection with her grandfather. To break the connection to her past. To stop the horrible memory that was all that she shared with the old man sitting next to her.

To her amazement, her grandfather patted her hand.

"Our laird is ever the modest man so I'll share his news, my kinsmen." Roland, still standing, seemed as if he could hardly contain himself. "Even now, our laird's new wife carries his heir. In a matter of months, we'll welcome the next MacGahan laird into the world!"

Cheers and applause and shouts of congratulations greeted Roland's announcement, with people banging their tankards against their tabletops and stomping their feet on the stone floors.

Isa studied her grandfather's pale face as he pushed back his chair and rose slowly to his feet. He looked so much older than she'd noticed before, the lines of his face etched more deeply than she remembered.

"Aye, what Roland tells you is true. My . . ." He paused, looking down at Agneys next to him before continuing. "My wife, Agneys, tells me she carries my, our, child. And today, before all of you as witnesses, I declare that should this bairn be a male child, he will be the next MacGahan laird." Here he paused again, allowing the hall to erupt into more cheers and clapping until, at last, he lifted a hand, motioning for silence.

"You also stand witness to this—should the bairn Agneys carries be a female child, I hereby name my granddaughter Isabella as my rightful heir, and declare that whoever Isabella chooses as husband will be the next MacGahan laird."

A hush fell over the room and Isa felt as if every pair of eyes in the room bore into her. Under the table, she laid her hand on Robbie's thigh, not caring whether or not it was appropriate behavior. When his big fingers closed around hers she felt for a moment as if she might weep with relief at having him there with her.

After what felt like an eternity, a scattering of applause broke out across the room until, at last, all joined in.

The MacGahan laird held up his hand once more, quieting the crowd. "Now, my kinsmen and friends, let us drink and eat and enjoy the celebration of my wedding feast. Let the music begin!"

From the corner of the hall, notes from a pipe and a harp floated into the air, all but drowned out as conversation in the hall resumed.

Robbie gave her hand another squeeze and then stood, leaning down to whisper into her ear.

"Yer no to leave this table until I return. Stay at yer grandfather's side. Give me yer word you'll do as I say."

She started to refuse, to demand he take her along with him or at the very least tell her where he was

going, but, in all honesty, she simply didn't have the
energy left for it. The day had been too long and she'd
dealt with too much. Her mind was awash in the com-
plexity of all she didn't understand. From Robbie's
claims about Jamie to her grandfather's inexplicable announcement, she needed time to process it all. The last
thing she wanted right now was to argue with Robbie.

"You have my word."

With one irritated look back at the table on the dais,
Robert hurried through the door and out toward the
kitchens.

Damn the laird for his thoughtless need to name an
heir tonight! Surely the old man must realize he'd all
but signed Isa's death warrant with that public decla-
ration. If he hadn't known before he spoke, the black
anger on Lardiner's face afterward should have clearly
shown him his error.

This would likely be Robert's only opportunity to
speak to Auld Annie—now, while Isa was surrounded
by her grandfather and his guards. He wanted to learn
as much as the old woman would tell him about Isa's
childhood. Perhaps somewhere in that knowledge he
could find the key to persuading her she must leave
this place and journey to his family's home, where she
would be safe.

Because if anything, this day had convinced him that
they would find safety neither inside this castle nor at
her cottage. Her grandfather's performance minutes
earlier had assured that Isa was a marked woman.

To make matters worse, they would be staying overnight here at the castle. He'd rather have faced traveling in darkness than risking the night within these walls, but the laird had insisted and Isa had given in to his pleas.

Robert was thankful to find the hallway to Annie's room empty. The fewer people who knew he spoke to her, the better for all of them. Though he was anxious for whatever she could tell him, he certainly didn't like the idea of endangering her life. Or worse, Jamie's life.

Damn, but he missed the simple things he'd become accustomed to using. He'd give a small fortune for ten minutes' use of a flashlight. At least he'd been here earlier this day, or he'd likely not find the entryway to Annie's room in the darkened hallway. Trailing his fingers along the wall, he kept count of the doors he passed, knowing hers would be the fourth.

He gave only small thought to the lack of guards posted, suspecting the possibility that the door would be locked when he reached it. But the handle gave way easily and he slipped noiselessly into the dark, stifling space.

The room was strangely silent and pitch-black. He held his position, back to the door, waiting to see if his eyes would adjust.

"Annie?" He kept his voice to a whisper, knowing only that something felt wrong in this room.

Across from him, tiny dots of orange floated in the inky black. Embers in the fireplace.

He searched his memory for the layout he'd seen during his visit earlier today. Once he crossed to the fireplace, he should find a chair angled to the right and a bed off to the left. There should also be a small candle on the shelf by the fireplace.

Holding his arms out in front of him, he made his way slowly across the room toward the miniature orange fireflies. There'd been a stack of wood by the fireplace this afternoon, so why the old woman would allow her fire to burn down so low was beyond him.

When he reached the fireplace, he ran his hand over the wall until his fingers bumped into the candleholder. The acrid smell of the tallow hit his nose the instant he bent down and stuck the candle into the embers.

The light wasn't strong, but at least it was light. Shadows jumped around him when he turned to survey the room.

Across from him, a lump in the covers of Annie's bed drew his attention. Even before he drew the covers back, he knew what he'd find. He should have recognized the odd feel to the room when he'd first entered.

He held the candle closer, using caution not to allow the tallow to drip on the bed. No sense in letting anyone know he'd been here.

He wouldn't be learning anything from Annie this night. Or any other, for that matter.

Her head jutted out askew on her body like a misshapen doll, her neck obviously broken. From the looks of it, she'd been strangled. With extreme prejudice, to borrow a term from the movies back home. And though he was no expert, he'd guess from the feel of her skin she'd met her demise shortly after he and Isa had spoken to her this afternoon.

Robert pulled the covers back over the old woman's head and made his way to the fireplace. He stared at the candle, fighting his own private battle. The internal debate raging in his head at the moment was not a pleasant one.

The idea of what someone had done to that old lady made his palms itch to crack skulls. But he had Isa's safety to consider. And Isa was not going to take this well. Not at all.

If he told her what he'd found, that is.

"Yer no supposed to be in here."

Robert whirled around to face the woman who'd spoken, deciding as he did, the less he admitted to knowing, the better off he'd be. A quick scan of the room assured him she was alone.

"I came to visit Annie," he responded, keeping his voice to a hoarse whisper. "But I think she's sleeping."

"Ha!" the woman scoffed. "There's no a need to mind yer voice for her benefit. The illness took her peacefully, in her sleep, this very night. I'm here to clean her body and ready her for burial."

Robert doubted Annie's death had been peaceful in the least. The old woman had struck him as a fighter.

"Well, then—" he edged closer to the woman, holding out the candle as he did so—"I suppose you'll have more need of this than I will."

He backed into the dark hallway and pulled the door shut just as the first fist landed in his gut.

Chapter 15

Catching him unaware, that first blow knocked the air from him, ramming his back into the door he'd just closed.

Prepared or not, he'd been a warrior too long, had trained too hard to be taken out of any fight so quickly, and this one would be no exception.

In the dark, he paused only a second, listening, before he struck out with his left forearm, driving up and into what felt like someone's chin. At the same time, his right hand flew up to his shoulder, finding only empty air.

Dammit! His sword still hung on the back of his chair, where he'd placed it when he sat down for the feast.

On his other side a blow glanced off his shoulder. When he concentrated, he could hear them breathing.

There were at least three, perhaps four, of them, and while he gave blows as good as he got when they moved in on him, he wasn't about to step away from the solid door and leave his back unprotected.

He was ready for the next hit, grabbing the hand that connected with his shoulder. He twisted, bending it back until he heard the bone snap. He ignored the scream and the footsteps of someone running away as he took another well-calculated swing. His fist connected, hard. He heard the crack of bone and felt the solid hit vibrate through his arm, satisfied with the scream of pain that followed.

Two down, though he thought he'd heard perhaps two more.

What he hadn't heard was the door behind him open. He realized it had only when something heavy struck him between the shoulders. His reflex to the blow, throwing his arms in the air, left him open to the next hit. Something, perhaps a foot, landed a solid blow to his ribs, sending a shot of unbearable pain lancing through his side. Unable to catch his breath, his legs buckled and his knees hit the floor while he gasped for air.

A moment later, something hit the back of his head, and he pitched forward into darkness.

"Master Robbie?"

He heard the words, as if they came from very far away. He even thought he recognized the voice and honestly did want to answer, but the pounding in his head drowned out any sounds he might try to make.

"Oh, do wake up, Robbie. I dinna ken what to do to help you."

It was a little voice. Young. Helpless. Frightened.

Robert fought the haze blanketing his head and blinked his eyes, pushing himself up from the floor to sit.

Small hands caressed his cheeks and Jamie's face swam before his eyes.

"Are you hurt? Should I go get Mistress Isa for you?"

"No," he groaned. "Wait. Let me just sit here for a moment." Isa. The memory of what had happened to him flooded back. How long had he been out? "Is she still at the feast? With yer laird?"

"Aye." The boy nodded his head. "They are all still there. But Mistress Isa grew worried when you dinna return and summoned me to go find you."

Robert ran a hand over the back of his head, fingering a walnut-sized knot that had formed. He sat against the wall, tucked back in a corner and, from the smell of it, not far from a garderobe.

This certainly wasn't where he'd been when he'd lost consciousness. Whoever had managed to get the best of him must have dragged him here. For what reason he couldn't guess, any more than he could say the identity of who he'd fought, which made it all the worse. There were too many unknowns for comfort.

One thing he was sure of. Although he might not have any idea *who* had attacked him, he had a damned good idea of *why*.

"Well, lad, what say we see if you can help me haul myself to my feet?"

Sliding his back up against the wall, Robert pushed to stand, pausing to let a wave of dizziness pass.

Slowly, with Jamie at his side, he made his way back to the hall, where music and the joyous noise of people filled with spirits poured from the doors.

His head was clear now. The danger to Isa was too great for him to take any more chances. Not until he had her in her room, behind a bolted door, could he allow himself to relax his guard.

"Yer not going in there like that, are you?"

Robert froze, considering Jamie's words. He was likely a sight, if he looked at all like he felt, and drawing attention to what had happened was the last thing he wanted.

"Yer absolutely correct, lad. Would you mind going to fetch my sword and Mistress Isa? Bring them both here to me?"

"Aye, Master Robbie."

The boy's serious expression prodded Robert to stop him.

"Hey, Jamie. I just want to say, you'd make someone a fine squire."

The boy turned to look at him. "Do you mean that? Honestly?"

When he nodded, Jamie's look of disbelief cracked into a smile that all but broke Robert's heart. One side of the boy's face lit with joy while the other didn't move at all, frozen as it was in a mask of scar tissue.

If only he could get Jamie back to his time. Maybe something could be done to save his sight or ease his suffering in some way. But those were considerations for another time. For now he had to focus on getting Isa upstairs and behind bolted doors.

In moments she was at his side, her shock at his appearance evident in her expression.

"What in the name of all that's holy has happened to you? Who did this?" She whirled around as if to return to the hall, but he grabbed her elbow to keep her there.

"No. We dinna want any attention to this now."

"Someone's done this and they need punishing for it." Her eyes flashed with her conviction.

"No now, Isa. Please listen to me." He needed something, anything, to convince her to do as he wanted. "Just help me upstairs."

"Oh!" Her mouth rounded in a little circle, her eyes opening wide. "What a fool I am. Of course. Yer injuries want tending. Come along." She draped his arm over her shoulders as she sidled up close to him.

He should have remembered sooner. All he needed to do was let her think he couldn't take care of himself. His ego wasn't so large it prevented him from playing along.

"Here's yer sword." Jamie's arms shook as he held the weapon out. "I have to go now. The stable master will be angry if I dinna finish my evening chores."

Robert slipped the strap of the sword's sheath over his arm and allowed Isa to assist him up the stairs. When they reached her bedchamber, he entered first, searching the room to make sure no one waited inside.

"The chamber is clear. When I leave, yer to bolt the door and allow no one entrance, no matter what they say." He intended to find a spot in the hallway from which he could watch her door. Losing one night's rest would be a small price to pay for knowing she was safe.

"Leave? Yer no leaving anywhere until I've had a look at what's been done to you. Now sit yerself down on that stool and remove yer shirt while I light some more of my grandfather's expensive candles."

"There's no a need for me be taking off any of my . . ."

"I'm no hearing that," she barked, giving him a little push in the direction of the stool. "You favored yer side the whole way coming up the stairs so dinna you even think to deny it. Take it off."

Robert stifled the urge to laugh at Isa's demanding orders. "Yer a right bossy bit for a woman in danger," he teased as he took a seat.

"It looks to me as if it's you danger's found. Now, hush yerself and do as yer told."

He pulled the long shirt from his plaid, biting back a groan as he lifted it over his head and off. His shoulder was sore from the blows he'd blocked, but hardly worth noting.

It was the old scar over his ribs that concerned him. Swollen and tender to the touch, it looked like a wound only weeks into the healing process.

He had no choice but to face the obvious—that this wasn't any normal injury but the beginning of the danger that Cate and Mairi had feared.

Cate's warning rang in his memory.

"You're going back to a time when you're not supposed to exist. If the Magic seeks to equalize what should be with what is, you could be in real trouble."

The steadily worsening wound on his chest was trouble, all right. It seemed clear to him that this was the Faerie Magic working to set history to rights.

Which meant his time here, his time to get Isa to safety, would be coming to an end.

His muscles twitched involuntarily in response to the cold, wet cloth she stroked over the scratches on his face.

"I'm sorry it's cold. I've nothing to heat the water in."

He shook his head, but didn't reply, fighting to ignore his physical response to her hands on his body. Though her touch was gentle, as if she feared she might hurt him, it was the fire she trailed across his skin that made him flinch. When her fingers stroked over the Mark of the Guardian on his upper arm, he felt as if the air had been sucked from his lungs.

By the time she reached his chest, he could stand no more and grabbed her hands, holding them within his own.

"I need you to listen to me and think hard on what I say. Tomorrow morning, when we leave this place, let me take you to MacQuarrie Keep."

The shake of her head foretold what her words would be. "I canna do that, Robbie. I've animals depending on me. I have to return to my home. I've no desire to leave there."

His frustration got the better of him.

"Goddammit, Isa! Yer animals are the least of yer worries. There's MacDowylt to consider, and after yer grandfather's big announcement tonight, there's Lardiner. My time here is limited, and I've no stomach for leaving you at the mercy of men such as these."

She stared into his eyes, her expression serious and thoughtful, until at last she smiled, a sad little uplifting of the corners of her mouth.

"Yer a good man, Robbie MacQuarrie. You've no tried to force me to do this against my will and that means a great deal to me. If it will make you rest better, I'll think on yer request this night."

Force her? He could never do that, though he knew many a good man who would. Somehow, in this situation, it seemed wrong. Whether it was the knowledge of the Faerie edict against changing history or something else, something about Isa herself, he couldn't bring himself to drag her away against her will.

That she even considered what he asked felt like a major step in the right direction.

"Then I'll leave you to yer rest." He started to rise, but found himself unable to stand, unwilling to do so, when she pressed down on his shoulders.

"I'd rather you stay here. There's plenty of covers for me to make you a bed by the fire. And if whoever did this comes looking for you, it's yer room they'll search, no mine."

The invitation was tempting. It was those men coming after her that worried him. In spite of how it looked, he could take care of himself. Here, in her room, he could see to her safety as well.

Still, it wasn't right. Someone would see. Someone always did. Word would spread. "I'll no compromise yer reputation by spending the night in yer room."

"As if you suppose I care what anyone thinks?" she scoffed. Then, as if she could read the indecision in him, she stood and hurried to her bed, pulling covers off and bundling them in her arms.

"It's settled, then. Yer staying here for the night."

Chapter 16

～

The wind had picked up, moaning as it forced itself through the gaps in the wooden shutters high on the wall of the bedchamber.

Isa squeezed her eyes tightly shut, willing herself to sleep. It felt as though she'd lain here for hours, waiting for slumber that just wouldn't come.

She didn't want to think anymore. Her thoughts were jumbled and confusing, and no matter where they started, they always ended in the same place.

Robbie was going to leave her. He'd told her so. Told her his time here with her was coming to an end.

She should be overjoyed. That had always been her goal, to be alone. From the moment she'd been old enough to consider the possibility, being alone had meant freedom and a peaceful existence to her. It was all she had ever wanted.

Until Robbie showed up.

Somewhere in the short time since she'd met him she'd started to want more. To dream new dreams. Dreams of a man to love her. Dreams of having children of her very own.

Impossible dreams.

Now the thought of being alone just felt . . . lonely.

She turned over to her side, jerking at the too-big night dress that tangled around her feet. How was she supposed to sleep in this enormous gown the maids had left on the bed for her use? The pillow felt as lumpy as if someone had stuffed parts of the bird in along with its feathers. And the bed. She didn't even want to consider how long it might have been since someone had washed the bed coverings.

She was miserable and uncomfortable and lying in filth. And on top of all that, she was despairingly lonely, knowing those things she wanted most in life, those things that others took for granted as their right, she would never have.

No wonder she couldn't force herself to sleep!

Outside, the moan of the wind turned to a whistling howl, ominously rattling the wooden shutters as if demons were trying to claw their way into the room.

There were demons out there beyond her walls, all right. Her emotional demons. The demons of her unfulfilled wants and desires.

Enough of this! She couldn't allow herself to wallow in this pool of pity. It wouldn't do her, or anyone else, the least bit of good.

So he'd said he was going to stay and now he wasn't. It was all the same to her. His change of heart simply meant she could continue to do whatever she pleased, whenever she wanted. That had been her plan, after all—to drive him away. Besides, what Robbie MacQuarrie did made not the least bit of difference in how she lived her life.

Or did it?

She sat up in bed and gazed over at the fireplace, at the bundle of covers where Robbie slept.

Had it been only days ago that she'd watched as he bathed in the mountain pool beyond her cottage?

Watched and wanted.

She'd denied herself any possibility of experiencing what went on between a man and a woman because she feared that once she'd been intimate with Robbie, she'd lose her freedom. He would never leave.

But that was when she'd thought he intended to stay. Now she knew that wasn't the case. He would be going. Soon. He'd told her so.

Once. Just once. If she missed this chance, she would likely never have another opportunity. And he was so beautiful, inside and out.

She loosed the tie on her hair and worked at freeing her braid while she stared at his unmoving form, considering her options.

What was there to stop her?

He could refuse her. She knew nothing at all about the art of attracting a man. He could reject her when she offered herself. Though from the heated gazes he'd sent her way she found that result unlikely.

What if he didn't reject her and she conceived a child?

Her breath did a little hitch, as if her heart had missed a beat.

She could imagine only one outcome more desirable than that. A man to love her and a child in her arms was her heart's secret desire. To find even half of that fantasy would be heaven.

Tossing her covers aside, she swung her feet around and slid off the high bed. A shiver raced through her body as her toes met the cold stone floor.

"Robbie?" she called, barely more than a whisper.

From under the covers, a muffled grunt.

"Are you awake?"

"It's no like a man can get any sleep between you thrashin' about in yer bed and the wind making all that racket."

She waited, chewing her bottom lip, working up her courage.

"Are you frightened by the storm, lass?"

As if she, of all people, would be frightened by the weather. And yet, if that was what he thought . . .

"Yes," she whispered.

The roll of thunder joined in with the wind's howl as she tiptoed closer to where he lay. When she reached him, she dropped to her knees and pulled the covers from his head, fighting the instant desire to run her fingers through his tousled hair.

"I am," she lied. "And I canna sleep at all." That much, at least, was the truth.

He stared at her, his eyes dark and unreadable with his back to the flicker of the fire.

"Would you feel safer here with me?"

She nodded her head vigorously, and he lifted his covers, inviting her to join him.

When she sat, he put his big arm around her, pulling

her in, tucking her back up against his chest. He wore no shirt, nothing but the plaid wrapped around his hips. The heat of his body enveloped her like a welcoming cocoon and she stretched out one leg, tentatively rubbing it against his shin.

"Holy Christ, woman! Yer feet are like chunks of ice." He shivered and pulled her closer, draping his arm over her hip.

"Mmm-hmm," she murmured, drowning in the feel of him so close he was practically wrapped around her. All the wants, all the desires she'd had that day at the pool slammed back into her. Hard. It felt as if all the heat trapped under those covers had gathered itself into one big ball and dropped right into the pit of her belly, burning, churning, demanding attention.

Robbie's attention.

And her in this damned blanket of a nightdress, so huge it felt as if there were a whole mattress separating their bodies.

Robbie cleared his throat and scooted back from her just a little. "You let yer hair down," he murmured, and his breath feathered over her ear.

"The braid was uncomfortable and I couldna sleep." Again, truth enough that she couldn't sleep. "Does it bother you?"

"Not at all," he murmured, doing that sniffing thing he'd done the first day they'd ridden together on horseback.

The hateful shapeless nightdress gathered at her neck and tied with a ribbon. She couldn't think of a way to casually drag the whole thing up and over her head, but if she loosed the neck tie, it would pull out wide enough to allow her the freedom to slip it down over her shoulders.

Slowly she pulled at the tie holding her gown closed. With a couple of small tugs to the gathers, the neckline opening gave way, hanging loose.

Again he cleared his throat and scooted back a little more. "We'll neither of us get any rest if you dinna stop wiggling about."

"Sorry. I was only trying to get comfortable." She slipped the opening over her shoulder and down, freeing one arm. "I'm no used to sleeping so close to someone."

"Believe me, I understand." He removed his arm from her hip and scooted farther away.

It was all the room she needed.

Turning from her left side to her back, she pulled her second arm from the nightdress, tugging the loosened neckline down to her breasts. She had no doubt the opening was large enough now to easily slide down over her hips.

Slowly, carefully, she tugged at the tail of her nightdress, pulling it up to her knees, freeing her legs as well as her arms.

The hateful gown dealt with for the moment, she rolled to her right side, facing Robbie. His eyes were clamped shut as if he fought to force sleep as vainly as she had earlier.

Sleep was not at all what Isa had in mind. Not for either of them.

With her big toe, she traced the back of his calf.

His eyes flew open, wild and dark in the shadowed light. "What do you think yer doing?"

"Warming my feet?"

"Warming yer feet," he repeated, his tone making no disguise of his doubt.

"Aye." She reached out, laying her hands on his chest, feeling the muscles jump under her fingers. "My hands are cold, too."

"They dinna feel cold to me," he rasped oddly, his body tensing as if all his muscles had frozen into place. "They're more like hot coals."

Her eyes locked with his and she scooted closer, allowing the nightdress to twist lower. Her hands edged up his chest to his shoulders as if it were beyond her control to stop them.

When she slid her leg in between his, nudging his plaid up as she lifted her knee, he grabbed her arms.

"You dinna ken what yer doing, lass. You need to stop this. Right now." His voice had gone gravelly and as dark as his eyes.

She pushed forward again, meeting no resistance, until her bared breasts met the heat of his chest.

He sucked in his breath and she pushed against him, rolling him to his back, straddling her leg over him as they turned.

She looked deep into his eyes, feeling as if she could see her future there, knowing everything in her life was about to change.

Whatever powers watched over them now, there would be no forgiveness for her this time. Unlike her spying on him at the pool, what she did now wasn't accidental or beyond her control. What she did now was her choice.

"Isabella . . ." He spoke her name on a breathless moan.

Entirely her choice and entirely what she wanted.

She leaned down and lightly touched her mouth to his, feeling the heat of his breath on her face when she broke the touch.

"This is a very bad idea, Isa," he whispered, though the grip he kept on her arms held her close.

She dipped her head, tracing his full lower lip with her tongue before she answered. "Then I must be a very bad woman, Robbie, for this is what I want and what I intend to have this night."

"Yer no worse than me, love." He lifted his head to gently kiss her mouth, a truly wicked smile curving his lips and lighting his eyes. "We're two of kind in this."

With one hand behind her head, he rolled, flipping her to her back before she even realized he was moving. He lay between her legs, his mouth moving across her cheek and slowly down her neck while his big hands massaged her aching breasts.

When he took her nipple into his mouth as if to suckle, the ball of heat that had pooled low in her belly felt as if it exploded, sending the fire of need lower, to the spot between her legs where he pressed his body against her.

His tongue, wet and warm, curved around her nipple as he sucked, then teased her with quick little flickers of motion that drove her wild. She arched her back, pushing up against him, and his hands slid down her sides, leaving a trail of fire and goose bumps in their path.

"This has got to go," he muttered, raising his head from her breast and leaning back far enough to pull the nightdress down and off her legs. "And this."

She had no idea a plaid could be unwrapped so quickly.

And then he was on her again. She spread her legs around him as he traced his hands along her body, blazing a path from her breasts across her stomach and down to the sensitive area between her legs.

He brushed his fingers over her mound of curls and she thought she heard him murmur something about her giving redheads a good name, but her ability to think at all disappeared as he gently thrust a finger inside her.

She bucked up against his hand and he found a whole new way to drive her insane, running his thumb over her most sensitive nub while inserting and withdrawing his fingers.

"Slow, love. We'll just take it slow," he whispered, his hands doing magic things to her body.

She lost track of time as he continued. Deep inside, a pressure built, growing and demanding more until at last it felt as if something shattered. Something so wonderful, so fantastic, it sparked out through her entire body, leaving her legs trembling and her body weak.

"Are you ready?" he asked, grasping her hips with his big hands and tilting them up.

There was more? Of course there was more. She knew what was supposed to happen. She'd just had no idea it could possibly make her feel like this.

She was the most beautiful thing Robert had ever held in his hands. And if the Faerie Magic took him tomorrow, he'd go to his hereafter a grateful man.

Grateful for the honor she bestowed on him, entrusting him with her body, and grateful she'd decided to allow him to take her to MacQuarrie Keep, where he'd know she would be safe even after he was . . .

He pushed those thoughts away. What happened to him after tonight didn't matter. He prayed only that the Fae allowed him to live long enough to get her safely into the arms of his family.

For now, he wanted nothing more than to enjoy these moments with Isa. To see to it that she enjoyed them as well.

He pulled her forward, entering her as gently, as slowly as he could manage. God, she was so tight! It took every bit of self-control he could dredge up not to surge into her and end this right now.

He covered her body with his, kissing her face, her neck, her beautiful lips. Her mouth opened to him with no effort and her tongue danced with his as if her body knew his, as if they'd done this a thousand times before.

It would be so easy to lose himself in her.

He forced himself to focus. Gradually, a little bit at a time, deeper and deeper, slowly, until at last she gasped and jerked in his arms and he was there, buried deep inside her.

His body throbbed with his need so he held himself very still, clutching her to him as he fought for control.

When he pulled out, she grabbed his hips, digging her fingers into his skin and lifting her hips, as if trying to keep him inside her.

"No," she moaned.

He thrust back into her, slowly again, and she locked her ankles behind his back.

"Yes," she said breathlessly.

Yes.

He repeated the action and she lifted her hips to meet him. Again and again. So good. She felt so damn good.

And then his control was gone. Hands clutched around her waist, he pulled her against him as he thrust into her, and his world shattered around him in what looked suspiciously like lightning arcing through the room.

When he could move again, he gathered her into his arms and rolled to his side. She kissed his chin and snuggled into his embrace, her breathing slowing within minutes to tell him she'd fallen asleep.

What they'd done might well have been very, very bad, but they'd sure as hell done it very, very well.

Chapter 17

Roland fingered the delicate earthenware cup before hurling it into the stone fireplace, sending sparks and pottery shards alike out onto the stone hearth.

He flung himself into the chair to wait, his fury seething with no outlet in sight.

That Agneys still valued her mother's worthless trinket after all these years angered him.

Angered him, but didn't surprise him in the least.

His daughter was so like the needy cow who had birthed her. Useless. And now, when at last she had some small part to play to finally, *finally*, be of some value to him, even now she couldn't properly do what he'd asked of her.

A scrape sounded at the door and he was on his feet instantly, ready and waiting when she entered.

Her back to the room, she closed the door quietly, gasping when she turned and saw him there.

"Father! You frightened me. What are you doing in my bedchamber?"

"Waiting." He purposely kept his words short and clipped. There was nothing to be gained in lulling the dull harlot into any sense of security. "Have you done yer duty this eve? Did you lie with him or has he rejected you again? Is that why yer here now?"

Her eyes darted around the room. He knew the instant they lit on what was left of the little cup he'd destroyed. Her lips tightened and thinned with her displeasure, and when she met his glare, her face took on that pathetic sniveling look he so detested in her. As he had in her mother.

"Well? I'm waiting. It's an easy task. You've but to lie on yer back and open yer legs."

He took a step toward her and she flinched away, as if she anticipated the back of his hand. Perhaps she wasn't as stupid as he thought. She was, at the very least, trainable.

"I've done what I needed to do this night, Father. My laird sleeps now. He's asked that my things be moved to his lady's chamber, adjoining his, on the morrow."

What was that he heard in her tone? A haughtiness? He was across the floor, towering over her in an instant, his fingers crushing into her chin as he drew her face to him.

"Dinna you think for a moment that wedding the laird raises yer station, lass. Yer nothing more than you were last night. You never will be anything but the vessel to carry the laird's heir. My heir. And once we ken for a fact you carry that babe, we'll rid ourselves of the old man and I'll be in charge."

The dream of power, so close to reality now, energized him, thrilled him. He loosed his hold on Agneys, allowing her to stumble away from him, back to her bed, where she grasped the bedpost as if to hold herself upright.

"But . . . but what if the child is a girl?"

He turned on her, feeling the pulse in his head pound with his irritation. "It makes no matter. She will be the laird's daughter and under my control."

"And what of the laird's proclamation this night? That if the babe is a girl all goes to Isabella?"

That had certainly come as an unpleasant surprise. The old fool seemed determined to thwart his plans to the very end, even going so far as to clean up his half-witted granddaughter and try to pass her off as acceptable to his people.

But it wouldn't make a difference.

"Isabella can't very well inherit anything from beyond the grave, Daughter."

Another of her annoying tremulous little gasps. "You couldn't possibly mean to harm . . . not with yer own hands, Father."

What a disappointment she was.

"I won't need to. I've already dispatched a rider to find the MacDowylt and then I'll go to him. We'll lead him to Isabella, and in the struggle her guardian will no doubt put up, the laird's precious granddaughter will be a casualty."

"Neither her guardian nor MacDowylt will allow that to happen."

Stupid cow. No ability to think ahead at all.

"Perhaps not. But a few of my own men, well placed, can see to it. If all goes as planned, they can see to the MacDowylt being a casualty as well."

He wasted his time sharing his plans with her. She hadn't the wit to appreciate his brilliance.

At the door he paused. "I await confirmation of what I announced as fact tonight."

"Yes, Father. As soon as I can be sure, I'll bring word."

It would have to do.

Agneys stared at the door for several minutes after her father exited her room before going over to drop the bolt into place.

Madman.

She hurried to the hearth, picking up the pieces that remained of the little cup she'd used earlier this evening and tossing them into the flames.

In one of his classic temper rages, her father had destroyed for her the very item she'd hurried here to dispose of herself.

"*Never leave evidence behind,*" her grandmother had told her, and she had always followed that advice.

Though it was unlikely any could ever detect the traces of the dwale that little cup had held before she'd emptied it into old MacGahan's whisky, it was one risk she was unwilling to take.

She slipped out of her gown and shift, letting them pool at her feet before slipping the heavy woolen nightdress down over her head.

The herbal potion her father's mother had taught her to make had done its job well. The old laird had fallen into a deep sleep before he'd been able to do more than fondle her breast with his bony, wrinkled hands. Exactly as he had the first time.

As if she'd allow that old man to stuff his flaccid tarse into her body.

Something would have to be done soon, though. Her ingredients for the dwale were running low and it wasn't likely the traders who sometimes visited the castle would carry opium and hemlock among their regular wares.

Perhaps she could convince her new husband to allow her a visit to Inverness. Once there, it should be simple enough to slip away to that little shop as she had before. The young merchant had been more than willing to barter for the items she'd wanted and he'd filled all her needs.

All her needs.

Too bad the old laird didn't look more like that merchant. It would have been exceedingly pleasant to have all those needs tended to this night.

Now the MacDowylt, he was another story altogether. There was a laird she'd welcome into her bed without hesitation. He had the look of a virile man, one who'd have no trouble planting his seed in her belly.

And not carrying a child would soon become an issue to be dealt with. The people expected it, and certainly the laird did.

Once again, her father's thoughts for the future centered on making his life better, not hers. For too long he'd taken advantage of her for his own benefit. Underestimated her.

His thinking her the malleable fool would only make it easier for her to surprise him one day. For now she'd played the part he expected of her, following along with all his schemes, knowing a time would come when his plans would open a door of opportunity for her to walk through.

His rush to set his plans in motion, however, came as more than an untimely inconvenience. He'd pushed ahead so quickly, she hadn't yet decided on a proper course of action.

She slipped into her small bed, pulling the covers up around her neck, her mind a whirl of possibilities.

There were so many challenges she'd need to consider, her not being with child and the lack of any prospects to become pregnant chief among them. Isabella and her handsome guardian would be a problem, and perhaps it would be best to let her father deal with them as he'd planned, though she didn't like the idea of his killing Isabella. Not that she'd ever been fond of her strange cousin. Still. The idea of murder didn't sit well with her.

And definitely not the old laird. Not yet. And not MacDowylt.

Agneys could see too much potential for MacDowylt to allow her father to succeed in eliminating him right away.

No, she'd need to think on this situation. There were too many loose ends to satisfy her.

Still, she had time. A few weeks, at least, before she'd need to implement any plans of her own. Until then she would relax and enjoy her new life as the laird's wife.

Chapter 18

*E*ven with his eyes shut, Robert sensed the morning light trickling through the gaps in the room's wooden shutters. It would be a wondrous day. Thanks to one beautiful redhead, he felt refreshed, alive, invigorated. And ready for seconds.

He opened his eyes to find her staring at him from her perch on a chair a few feet away. She sat with her hands primly folded in her lap. Fully dressed.

He could change that quick enough.

Propping himself up on one elbow, he extended his free hand and wiggled his fingers in an invitation to join him.

"It's growing late, Robbie. And though I wouldn't mind doing . . . ."—here she paused and a lovely pink flush colored her cheeks—"*that* again, we need to be on our way."

She was right, of course. It would take a good two days of riding hard to reach MacQuarrie Keep.

With an exaggerated sigh, he reached for his plaid and stood, wrapping the garment around him. He plucked his shirt off the stool where he'd tossed it last night and dropped it down over his head.

When he looked back in her direction, he saw she sat unmoving, her gaze fixed on him. The expression on her face told him she'd spoken the truth earlier. In fact, he suspected that not only would she not mind doing *that* again, but that she'd likely welcome the opportunity as much as he would.

A good thing to keep in mind. Though they'd a long ride ahead of them, there was no reason they couldn't have a pleasant overnight along the way.

"Yer all ready, then?"

At her nod, he opened the door and held it for her.

"We'll collect Jamie and take him along with us, aye?" she asked, rising from her seat. "I promised Annie I'd see he was taken care of."

Annie. He couldn't tell her about the old woman now or he'd never get her out of this place. Her sense of justice would demand that they confront Lardiner, and that was something he simply couldn't allow.

"On our way to locate the lad we can stop in the kitchens and see if we can charm the cook into packing enough provisions to do us."

She had gathered the covers from the floor and carried them over to the bed, but now she stopped, hands on her hips, staring at him.

"Provisions? Food, do you mean? Why would we need to carry food along with us?"

Obviously she didn't realize how far they had to go.

He crossed the room to where she stood and gathered her in his arms, kissing the top of her head as he pulled her close. "It's a two-day ride to MacQuarrie Keep, love. We'll want something more than each other to nibble on along the way."

She pushed back from his chest to look up at him, her brow wrinkled in confusion. "What are you saying, Robbie? I've told you before, I'm no going to yer family keep. I've no intent to leave my home, no for any reason."

He stared at her, his thoughts a jumbled mess. "But last night . . . I thought that meant you'd agreed to do as I asked. I told you my time to get you to safety was running short."

Isa took another step back from him, fixing her eyes on the floor in front of her. "Last night meant only last night. If you have to go, then go. It's no like I'm saying you have to stay, only that I am."

"Goddammit, Isa, why will you no listen to reason?" He grit his teeth until he thought his jaw would crack with frustration as he struggled to find some words, some way to convince her.

Maybe it was time to ignore her feelings. Though some sixth sense told him it would be a mistake, perhaps he should ignore that, too, toss her over his shoulder onto his mount and take her to MacQuarrie Keep by force if she wouldn't go of her own free will.

It went against every natural instinct, but he had no reasonable choice left other than to stay with her until the Magic took him, and then she'd be left on her own. To face more dangers than he wanted to consider. Lardiner. MacDowylt.

No, his decision was made.

Until his gaze lit on the spot in front of the fireplace.

Burned into the stone, a blackened outline circled the place where their bodies had lain together on the floor.

It would appear the lightning he'd imagined when they made love hadn't been in his imagination after all.

Which would mean that Jamie's story about Isa's mother being Fae must be true.

And if there was one thing Robert knew about the Fae, it was that you couldn't force them to do anything against their will without there being serious consequences.

No wonder that sixth sense had been setting off warning bells.

How Robbie could possibly have assumed she meant to leave her home and go with him was beyond Isa's wildest imagining. Or so she tried to convince herself.

If only her damnable conscience wouldn't keep flashing bits and pieces of last night through her mind as a vivid reminder of why he might think she'd do whatever he wanted.

Isa picked up her pace, as if she could leave her guilty thoughts behind. Through the castle and out to the bailey she hurried until she was all but running to the stable to find Jamie.

"Slow yerself down or you'll draw attention to our leaving." Robbie's deep voice flowed over her, as soft and gentle as the hand he wrapped around her arm.

She nodded her agreement, almost stumbling as she changed her pace.

"He's there."

Robbie pointed across the courtyard to where Jamie stood with a young woman, his head nodding in quick agreement to whatever she was saying. When he spotted them, he waved and hurried in their direction.

Isa dropped to her knees to speak directly to the boy. "I spoke to yer grandmother, lad. She's asked that you come home with me to stay since she canna look after you. I'm going now and I'd like for you to come along with me. Will you do that for me?"

Jamie's one-sided smile faltered and he looked from Isa back over his shoulder to where the young woman waited.

"Oh, Mistress Isa, that will be wonderful since I never see my gran anymore. But I canna today. It's my turn at last to help with the churns. There's fresh butter on warm sweet bread as a reward when the butter's done. I've waited so long for my turn to help them."

"But, Jamie," she began, stopping as Robbie laid a hand on her shoulder.

"You go to yer churning, lad. And when you've finished, you come to Isa's cottage, aye? But do so in secret, lad. Dinna speak of it to anyone, you ken?"

"Aye," Jamie agreed, running back to the waiting maid.

"Why did you do that? If what you spoke of with Annie is true, he's no safe here." And the thought of Jamie being in danger curdled her stomach.

"Because making an issue of it here, drawing attention to the lad, creates more of a danger for him than simply having him go about his business as usual."

It made sense when he explained it that way so she

let it drop, following him into the stable and waiting quietly while he readied his horse.

Her nerves were on edge from her worry over Jamie's safety, and now, not knowing what would happen in the next few minutes was almost more than she could bear. She had no idea whether Robbie would lift her onto his mount with him to return to her cottage or simply ride away and leave her standing here.

Outside, the wind whipped through the stable yard, blowing bits of rubbish and sticks in harsh little whirl-pools of air.

She had to get hold of her thoughts and emotions.

"No another storm coming on," Robbie grumbled. "I'd appreciate at bit of calm weather, thank you very much."

"I'm doing my best," she muttered in return, not re-alizing she'd spoken aloud until he laughed as if she'd made a joke.

"Come on, then, let's get you mounted."

She hesitated, wondering if he understood she would go nowhere but to her own home.

"Yer taking me to the cottage, aye?"

"Aye."

His response was tight and clipped, as closed as his expression, not telling her at all what she really wanted to know. Learning any more would require swallowing a bit of her pride and asking.

Ah, well, pride was highly overrated anyway.

"And once we're there? You'll be leaving, I suppose. To return to yer family?"

Not knowing exactly what answer she really wanted, she couldn't bring herself to meet his gaze.

He, however, seemed not to suffer from that problem. He grasped her chin gently between his fingers, turning her face to his. The eyes she looked into were dark and troubled, but bore not the smallest sign of doubt.

"I mean stay at the cottage with you."

No, he was supposed to go! That was what she had counted on, what she had wanted. Wasn't it? She was so confused, she wasn't sure she knew what she wanted anymore.

But what she didn't want was another matter. She didn't want him staying with her because he felt some ridiculous responsibility as a result of having made love to her. She had to know the truth. Her pride would simply have to take one more hit.

"Are you staying because we . . . because of what we did last night?"

"No. What passed between us has nothing to do with my staying." He brushed one thumb up over her cheek. "Know this, Isa: Where you go, I go, as long as I am able. I'd have you safe in my family keep if I were to have my way. But if you'll no agree to that, then I'll stay by yer side to my last breath. That's my pledge to you."

His words slammed into her with a force of their own so that she barely noticed when he let go of her chin and lifted her to his horse or when he climbed up behind her and pulled her close against him.

"I'll stay by yer side to my last breath."

His words should terrify her, threatening as they did her freedom and independence. Instead her heart felt as warm as her body did, ensconced in his arms.

Chapter 19

~⚬~

"*A*gneys Lardiner MacGahan." Agneys shook her head and made another try at it. "Agneys MacGahan. *Lady* MacGahan."

Oh, she liked the sound of that! Perhaps she'd speak to the laird tomorrow and request that he order his people to address her by that title. She twirled in a little circle, reveling in the feel of the fine linen nightdress the laird had gifted her, clasping a tiny cup to her breast.

With a great sigh, she spun around once more, slowly this time, admiring her new bedchamber. All hers. The bedchamber of the wife of the laird.

What a fantastically lovely room! So much larger than the chamber she'd occupied since she and her father had first come to this place all those years ago. At one time she'd hoped to move into Isabella's quarters after that pathetic creature had slithered off into the woods to live alone, but the laird had refused her that boon, leaving her where she'd been for so long.

But now! This was so much better, from the beautiful tapestries on the walls to the rich, heavy curtains enclosing the bed. She loved it. She loved being the laird's wife.

Too bad she couldn't love the laird who'd put her here.

With another sigh, she crept back to the opening between their rooms, peeking through at the old man snoring loudly in his bed.

The racket he made was horrible, but the worst was when he seemed to hold his breath for long seconds at a time, finally gasping loudly before resuming his infernal snoring. In those moments she feared the potion might have been too strong this time or that she'd put too much in his ale.

Crossing the room, she dropped down into the big, hand-carved chair with its wonderfully soft cushions, facing the most beautiful fireplace she'd ever seen. The older servants told stories of the laird's devotion for his wife and how he had brought masons all the way from France to carve intricate details into the stones above the fireplace simply to see her smile.

Agneys closed her eyes and tried to imagine a young Randulf MacGahan so smitten by a woman that he'd spend all that money. It would be her dream to find a man who felt that way about her.

Just not the one sleeping in the adjoining room. The very thought of allowing him into her bed made her physically ill.

And yet she truly didn't dislike the old man. He'd always been kind enough to her. Kinder than her own father, in truth.

She certainly didn't want him dead. Not yet. Only asleep so that he wouldn't be pawing at her body.

Dead, and her lovely new existence would be complicated beyond reason. Dead, and her father would be in charge. And *that* was not an acceptable outcome by any means. She'd been under her father's thumb for too long as it was.

Lost in her thoughts, she almost missed the knock at her door.

Who in the world would bother her at this hour of the night?

Agneys opened the door a crack, only to have it shoved full open, her father striding into her chamber without even the pretense of respect for his laird's new lady—as if it were his right to enter.

"Well? I've had no word as to yer . . . condition."

"No word?" She all but snarled her response, forgetting to temper her words. "Are you fool enough to think I'd have a answer when it's been only two days since the last—"

The shock of his knuckles slammed into her jaw, his backhand sending her to the floor. The pain radiating through her face kept her there as her mouth filled with the metallic taste of her own blood.

Roland's eyes shone with the unholy madness of his anger when he leaned down over her. "Dinna you ever take that tone with me, Daughter. You may think yer something special because yer laird moved you into his wife's quarters, but yer no. You'll never be more than a worthless whore, no even capable of carrying an old man's seed to fruit."

Agneys threw her hands up in front of her face and he grabbed a handful of her hair, dragging her to her feet. Her muscles tightened involuntarily, preparing for the blow from his upraised fist.

"Christ's blood, man, stop that! What do you think yer doing?"

Randulf leaned against the doorway in between his bedchamber and hers, his plaid hanging around his bony hips, partially unwrapped as it had been when he'd fallen asleep.

"Disciplining my daughter, my laird, as is my right as her father."

Roland released his hold and Agneys stumbled backward, seeking to put distance between the two of them.

"It's no yer right anymore, Lardiner." Randulf took a step forward, his body unsteady. "You lost that right when you forced me to take the lass to wife."

It was obvious to Agneys from the laird's slurred speech and hesitant movements that the dwale still affected him.

Randulf licked his lips and reached out a hand to steady himself as he drew even with the big chair Agneys had sat in earlier. "I'll no have you attacking yer laird's wife. No you or anyone else. Yer banished, Roland. I want you out of my castle and off my lands this very night."

For a moment, Agneys thought her father might have swallowed his tongue as fury turned his face a bright red.

"You canna mean that. Yer mind is clouded by the

whisky, old man. You dinna ken the words you speak," Roland at last managed to respond.

"My mind may be clouded, but my decision's made. I want you gone, now, you wicked bastard. You've tormented poor Agneys for the last—"

Agneys screamed as her father launched his body at the laird, knocking the old man over backward, smashing his head into the corner of the hearth.

"You canna do this to me," Roland yelled, repeatedly slamming the back of the laird's head against the stones. "No after all the years I've given you!"

"Father, you must stop!" Agneys pulled at her father's shoulder, backing away as soon as he dropped his hold on the laird.

Roland slowly got to his feet before he turned to her. His earlier fury spent, his eyes lit in instant panic before he regained control.

Agneys hurried forward, dropping to her knees by the laird's body. "No," she moaned, the denial ripped from deep inside. *Not now. Not yet. Not like this.*

"It will look like an accident. Yer husband, well in his cups, attacked you, and then he staggered out for more drink, ordering you to wait in his bed for his return."

She struggled through her shock, through the emotions threatening to overwhelm her, fear and anger chief among them.

How convenient her father had a story ready to feed to the people of the castle. A story that covered everything, right down to the painful swelling he himself had left on her face.

Roland hurried into the laird's chamber, returning with the tankard that had sat on Randulf's table.

"This little . . . incident will simply speed up our original plans. Now get out of that nightdress and into his bed. You'll remain there until someone comes to tell you they've found yer husband. I'll throw his body down the stairs. Once he's found, I'll ride out to meet the MacDowylt as if it was what the laird had instructed me to do. No one will question any of it."

"Randulf MacGahan would never have struck me. No one will ever believe—"

Roland flew at her, his eyes glittering with his anger. Before she could run, he grabbed the neck of her nightdress, ripping in down the front with a force that caused the material to bite into the back of her neck, surely marking her tender skin.

"Now take off that rag and get into the old man's bed." He hissed the command through his teeth, spittle forming at the corners of his mouth, reminding Agneys of a mad dog she'd once seen.

As was necessary, the dog had quickly been put out of his misery.

She backed away from her father, turning once she was out of his reach to hurry into the laird's chamber. She stepped out of the tatters that remained of her lovely, soft nightdress and climbed into the high bed, pulling the curtains shut around her.

Damn her father! He'd stolen from her the time she'd hoped to use to come up with a logical course of action. His temper had cost her the weeks she'd expected to have for planning. Just as his impatience had forced her to pretend a pregnancy he still hoped would be true. A pregnancy she knew was impossible since the old laird had never actually lain with her.

Agneys wiped at the tears streaming down her face and curled under the covers, trying to come to terms with what had just happened.

Poor Randulf. He'd been nothing but nice to her over the years, and though she could never have loved him as his wife, she had cared for him in her own way.

With a deep shuddering breath, she fought to clear her mind. Everything had changed with her father's actions this night. She had to decide, and quickly, what to do next.

Within hours, the whole of the castle would know their laird was dead. Shortly after, the MacDowylt would arrive. Her father might have managed to trick the poor old laird, but she suspected he'd find less success in using his wiles on the warrior. Unless she missed her guess, MacDowylt wouldn't be satisfied with waiting outside the castle walls as her father planned. She had no doubt he'd be riding through those gates within a day or two, more anxious than ever to get his hands on that half-wit, Isabella, in order to secure a hold on the MacGahan lands.

None of these things worked to her advantage.

Or did they?

She rolled onto her back, concentrating on the thin edge of an idea. Perhaps, with some clever planning and a little luck, she could use her father's blunders to her advantage.

Thanks to his ill-conceived announcement at the wedding feast, everyone assumed she carried the laird's child. Her father told her he'd already sent for the MacDowylt to return and would be riding out to meet him tomorrow. Surely the warrior would want to come to the castle.

If she arranged to find herself in the MacDowylt's bed soon enough, a pregnancy might still be possible. It could be his child she carried. And with the old laird out of the way, MacDowylt could claim her in marriage.

Now that sounded like a scheme that would surely appeal to the handsome warrior. After all, he wanted the MacGahan lands and she wanted to be taken care of. It was an arrangement that would suit them both.

Her father's plans to deal with Isabella still bothered her, but she could only deal with what was before her right now.

That still left her father as a major loose end. He'd reached a point where his temper made him more liability than asset. And after what he'd done to Randulf? He needed to be dealt with. Perhaps a grateful MacDowylt could be persuaded to dispatch of him. Especially once he learned of her father's plans to have him killed along with Isabella.

In the dark, Agneys smiled to herself as she considered her new course of action. Her father's impatient bumbling could well have provided her all the cards she needed to play out this hand to her own advantage.

Foolishly Roland had always underestimated her. Because she had her mother's beauty, he saw her only as her mother's daughter. Too bad for him, he didn't seem to understand that she was her father's daughter as well.

Only smarter.

Chapter 20

———❦———

Robert stretched his legs out in front of him, crossing them at the ankle as he stared into the flowing stream that ran past Isabella's cottage. The dark ripples seemed to take on a mesmerizing life of their own as they reflected the light of the full moon.

After what felt like the longest two days of his life, he was not at all anxious to begin another night in the cottage. He needed time alone to unravel his tangled thoughts.

Time alone to face his demons.

He and Isa had made the trek back from Castle MacGahan in silence, his guilt and worry building a wall he wasn't sure he'd ever be able to scale—guilt over the secrets he kept from Isa, worry about his inability to ensure the obstinate woman's safety.

From the moment he'd seen the burn mark on the bedchamber floor, he'd begun to suspect that his relationship with Isa was far more than either of them had bargained for. That suspicion made his not having any control over what would happen to Isa when the Faerie Magic overtook him all the more painful.

And the Magic would overtake him. Of that he had absolutely no doubt. The daily changes in his old wound assured him of that fact.

He felt powerless for perhaps the first time in his adult life, and he hated it.

When had he so completely lost control over the direction of his life? That was easy. The moment he'd come in contact with his first Faerie.

The mark on his arm prickled, and he squeezed his eyes shut in a useless attempt to quiet his equally prickly conscience. Apparently the Fae Magic that infused his body wouldn't allow him to wallow in self-deception.

Fine. He'd admit that the Fae weren't entirely to blame for his current dilemma. Though he did fully expect the Faerie Magic would be the death of him, in fairness, it had also saved him. It had swept him into the future and allowed him the most amazing decade of experiences any man could imagine.

No, the problems troubling him tonight were of his own making. *He* had kept information from Isa. *He* had failed to convince her to leave this place for her own safety. *He* had slept with her. Willingly. Eagerly.

Then he had gone and made everything worse for the past two days by shutting her out, denying them both what little time they might actually have together.

"Great dunderheaded fool," he muttered into the night.

"Pardon?"

Robert's eyes flew open at the sweet sound of her voice so close. Her hair was loose, the long curls flowing around her.

"I dinna mean to interrupt yer . . . yer thinking time, but I worried when you remained out in the dark for so long."

She held her fingers laced together at her waist, so tightly, from the looks of it, that Robert doubted she could have any circulation left in her hands.

He'd managed this night to confront some of his demons. Perhaps it was time to confront one more.

"It's no so dark, really." He stretched up his arm, pulling her down to sit next to him when she took his hand. "The moon lights the land like a lantern tonight."

"I suppose." She nodded before laying her head against his chest.

"Isa, did you ever . . ." He swallowed his nervousness and draped his arm around her, pulling her close before he tried again. "When you were a small lass, did anyone ever tell you stories? Faerie stories, perhaps?"

Her body tensed against him, but he held her tight, waiting for her response.

"Mayhap," she said stiffly. "One or two."

"Sitting here this night brings a story to my mind. Would you like to hear it?"

"Aye," she whispered, seeming to relax a little. "It would please me to listen to yer telling."

"Long, long ago, long before man ever began to record his history, Fae and Mortal lived together in a harmonious world. For every man there was a mate. Two perfect halves, their souls destined to be together through eternity. As one life ended, the displaced spirit would take up residence in the Fountain of Souls, waiting until its mate arrived, and then they would both return to bodies to live together again. All was as it should be.

"Then came the Great War. A battle between factions of the Fae for control of the Fountain and the power of immortality it bestowed. The foundations of life itself were shaken. Soul Pairings were ripped apart, many never to be reunited, and the world was divided between Mortal and Fae.

"Since that time, the souls that were separated—the ones that survived, that is—have sought one another, lifetime after lifetime, their misery creating disharmony in both worlds."

Here he paused, listening to Isa's breathing, wondering for a moment if she'd fallen asleep.

"I've never heard such a sad story, Robbie. Does it have a happy ending?"

She lifted her hand and laid it on his chest, and he felt his heartbeat speed up under her touch.

"For some it does. Every once in a great while, two struggling souls will find one another, repairing a tiny piece of the damage that was done, returning a sliver of harmony to both worlds."

"That's a lovely tale," she breathed, turning her face toward his. "What was it about this night that brought that story to yer memory?"

He'd swear the moonlight pooled in her eyes, flowing out to set her entire body aglow—she was that beautiful to him.

"You," he whispered. "Standing there with yer hair wisping about in the breeze. And now, with you in my arms, it's as though the story is fact. You feel that right to me when I hold you."

She lifted her hand again, this time to trace her fingers down his cheek, and he felt his body tremble under her touch.

He lowered his lips to hers, swearing to himself he would kiss her once and nothing more. Knowing, even as he thought it, the oath was a falsehood he had no intention of keeping.

Her hand glided to the back of his neck, her fingers tangling in his hair as she leaned into him, deepening the kiss as if she were as desperate for his touch as he was for hers.

When she pulled away from him, her rapid panting echoing his own as her fingers flew to the ties on her shift, clumsy in their haste.

The ties were of no importance to Robert.

He grasped her shoulders, guiding her to her back, shoving her skirts up as he covered her with his body. His plaid slid up as he pushed himself in between her legs and she moaned, threading her arms around his neck as she drew his head down for another kiss.

Skin to skin, her body called to him in a primal way. In the space of a heartbeat, the need he'd felt building turned to frenzy, and he drove into her heat, not stopping until he'd buried himself deep inside her welcoming folds.

He had to get hold of himself or this would be over before it had even begun.

"Sorry. Trying to . . . slow down." He forced the words through gritted teeth, dropping his head to her shoulder.

Another of her sexy little moans and he felt his tenuous grasp on control slipping.

"Again," she panted, tilting her pelvis and pushing against him.

The thread of reason snapped.

Grasping her hips within his hands, he withdrew and drove back into her, reveling in his power as she demanded more. Again and again, he plunged into her, until her hips bucked up and the contractions of her orgasm drew him into his own mind-numbing release.

He pushed his weight off to one side, unwilling to separate their bodies for several minutes.

When at last his breathing had returned to normal, he looked down at her smiling face, her eyes closed, and he brushed a tangled curl from her cheek, tucking it behind her ear.

"That was even better than the last time," she murmured.

The laughter he felt building in his chest would not be denied.

With one arm under Isa's shoulders and another under her knees, he rose to his feet and carried her back to the cottage and through the open door.

Inside, he set her on her feet, tugging his shirt off over his head as she scrambled out of her overdress and shift. His hand froze on his plaid, forgetting what his brain had ordered it to do as he took in the sight of her standing there, her curves bared for his pleasure.

"Yer the most beautiful woman I've ever seen."

The words were pulled from deep inside as Isa stepped forward, pushing his hand from the waist of his plaid and unwrapping it for him.

Once again, he lifted her into his arms, ignoring the tearing burn in his side. Stopping at the bed, he stared down into her radiant face.

Her hand covered the Mark of the Guardian on his arm, and his skin felt sensitized to her touch as if all the energy in his body gathered in that one spot.

"The story you told out there, Robbie, the Faerie story? When I'm with you, I can almost believe it. And if it were to be truth? I'd wish to have you as the missing piece of myself. You and normal life to complete my soul."

She lifted her lips to his and he lost himself in the taste of her. His ears filled with a strangely familiar humming, and for just an instant he felt as if the world around him exploded in a burst of light.

His knees weak, he lowered Isa to the bed, climbing in beside her.

Outside, on the grassy bank, he had taken her hard and fast. And though it had been a magnificent coupling, this time he intended to take it slow and easy, pleasuring her long into the night.

The Magic might well take him on the morrow, but tonight belonged to him and Isa.

Chapter 21

"Yer wasting valuable time sitting here." Roland Lardiner paced back and forth, his eyes darting around the large guest bedchamber at Castle MacGahan as if following the flight of birds. "As I tried to tell you before you even entered the gates, you should no be here. You'd be better served by going out to retrieve the lass this very night. I'll send my own men along to assist you in finding her."

"You'll do that for me, will you?" Malcolm MacDowylt leaned back in the big wooden chair, lifting his booted feet to the small table in front of him. He tired of toying with this deceitful dog. "And why would you want to help me secure the means to take over the MacGahan holdings?"

More bluster from the idiot as he continued his frantic pacing. Nothing of any worth spewing from his mouth. There was little of any value this deceitful dog had to offer. A few well-placed silvers on Malcolm's last visit here had guaranteed him loyal spies within the household. He knew all that he needed to for the moment and had no reason to pay attention until the fool uttered the words he'd expected from the beginning.

"As the MacGahan's tanist, I can assure you . . ."

"Yer no that." Malcolm interrupted. "So dinna try to waste my time with that blether. The MacGahan named no tanist, only a succession order."

That stopped the fool's prancing about. Left him with his eyes bulged and his mouth opening and closing like that of a trout lying on the bank.

"Yes, Lardiner, I ken the whole of it. All that went on here. Yer daughter's marriage and the babe she carries. The babe that inherits only should it be a male child."

"But, but . . ." Roland sputtered.

"Yer absolutely right about one thing. Until I've decided exactly what I plan to do here I've no intent to let this Isabella slip through my fingers, either. While I'm inclined to have her brought here to me, I'll think on yer offer, Lardiner. And we'll talk on it tomorrow."

"But the longer you wait . . ."

"Leave me!" Malcolm shouted, watching in satisfaction as the annoying man scurried from his bedchamber.

"I wouldna trust that slime of a man as far as I could toss him."

Malcolm nodded his agreement as his brother stepped from behind the massive draperies hanging around the bed.

"There's something no right about his urging you to go after the crazed lass."

"My thoughts exactly, Paddy. And exactly why yer here with me." He offered the tankard of ale, setting it back on the table when his brother shook his head in refusal. "Tomorrow I'll have the rat and his men bring the woman here to me."

"As you say," his brother acknowledged. "Do you think it might be wise for me and some of the boys to follow along? At a proper distance, of course."

"I do at that." Malcolm agreed.

Therein lay the beauty of naming his own brother as his tanist. They'd worked together so well and so long, it was as if Patrick anticipated his thoughts.

Malcolm pulled his dirk from the strap on his boot and cut a slice of cheese off the hunk on the table, tossing it to Patrick. His brother grinned and snatched up a piece of the bread as well, dropping down into the chair across from him.

Though they'd need to stay on their toes, Malcolm felt confident the MacGahan holdings would soon be his, made all the sweeter by the fact that he wouldn't have to raise his sword against anyone in the process.

"Agneys? Agneys! I order you to open this door at once!"

Agneys dropped into her chair, clutching the polished silver mirror to her breast. She had absolutely no intention of opening that door to her father. Not this night or any other.

She'd known the instant she'd seen the MacDowylt enter through the big gates this afternoon that her father would end up in a crazed frenzy of anger. MacDowylt at the castle was not what he had planned, and he detested having his plans go awry.

Nonetheless, Agneys had plans of her own and too much to accomplish this night to subject herself to Roland's madness.

With the MacDowylt only two doors away in the castle's best guest chamber, her father would be unwilling to raise too much of a fuss and risk drawing the man's attention. At least she hoped that would be the case.

Events had reached a point where her father had become a serious danger. If all went well, MacDowylt would eliminate that danger for her. And if not?

She knew of a potion or two that would do the trick. And wouldn't poison be an ironic death for her father? Perhaps she would use the very one he'd used to rid himself of her mother.

"You dinna think I ken what you did, do you, Father?" she whispered in the direction of the door.

But she did know. She'd learned the herbs from her grandmother when the woman had come on a visit from France after her mother's death. She knew the signs, and she remembered what her mother's face had looked like when she'd found her that morning.

Agneys had no intention of ending up as her mother had.

Long, tense moments passed before the sound of retreating footsteps reached her ears.

Finally.

She let out the breath she had held and strode to her

bed, propping the small mirror against the covers so that she might have one last look at herself.

The nightdress she wore had belonged to the laird's first wife, making it inappropriately snug across her ample breasts and around the curves of her hips.

Inappropriate, but perfect for her needs.

"Oh!"

She'd almost forgotten about her hair.

"Wearing yer hair loose is something only for unmarried lassies. Especially now, to show respect for the laird's memory, you must be seen as the lady." Her old witch of a maid had made the annoying claim this very morning as she'd pulled Agneys' hair into the uncomfortably tight and ugly braids.

Agneys removed the bindings and worked her fingers through her hair, fluffing the golden locks over her shoulders and around her face.

She smiled as she considered the humor of her situation. In light of how she had dressed for tonight, an inappropriate hairstyle hardly mattered.

With one last admiring look into the mirror—and one last adjustment of her breasts to ensure they were displayed to their best advantage—she tossed her cloak around her and peeked out her door before slipping into the darkened hallway.

Two doors down, she stopped. She could do this. She could do anything to save her own life. And if she didn't free herself from her father, it would eventually mean her life, she had no doubt.

One deep breath to settle her nerves and she rapped her knuckles lightly against the heavy wooden door, putting *her* plan into action.

* * *

When the knock sounded on Malcolm's door, he looked up from his tankard, his gaze locking with his brother's.

"You dinna think the fool is back to have another go at changing yer mind, do you?" Patrick shook his head, mirroring the disbelief Malcolm felt.

With a shrug of his shoulders, Malcolm stood. "Only one way to find out. Let's invite our guest in." He motioned toward the entryway, waiting as Patrick crossed the room and threw open the door.

"Looks as though we were wrong, Colm." Patrick's grin when he stepped aside to reveal their visitor said it all. "I'm guessing this might be a good time for me to go check on our men, aye?"

Malcolm nodded his agreement, his gaze fixed on his lovely visitor. "Dinna forget to close the door on yer way out."

He'd seen this one before, perched on the dais next to the MacGahan laird.

"Would it be the MacGahan's widow herself I have the honor of hosting in my bedchamber?"

"It is," the beauty murmured, seeming to float across the room to stand in front of him. "I've a proposition for you, MacDowylt."

With a flick of her wrist, the ties of her cloak came loose and the garment fell to the floor at her feet.

Little wonder the old laird would wed something as desirable as this. His body responded to her immediately, but even in his surprise he had the good sense to keep his weapon between his own legs until a time of his choosing.

"I'm sure you do." He gave her his best leer, attempting to put her on the defensive. "And I must say, yer a fine-looking piece for a woman who's rumored to be with child."

"Rumored," she repeated. "Aye, that's the key here, MacDowylt. And the proposition I have for you is no exactly what yer thinking. It's business. Though"—here she trailed a delicate finger carelessly around the low-cut neck of the nightdress she wore—"it has the potential to be more. Much more."

Malcolm took a step back, holding out the chair his brother had earlier vacated for his beautiful guest. "Have a seat, my lady, and we'll discuss this . . . *business* of yers."

He returned to his own chair, leaning forward as he sat to disguise his obvious response to this woman.

No point in letting her know of his physical interest in her. Not yet anyway. She was, after all, the daughter of Lardiner. And as much as he distrusted that man, he trusted this woman even less.

Roland, his world a red-hot haze of fury, kicked the tinder basket off the hearth in the laird's solar, scattering bits of wood and wool as it tumbled across the floor.

Where the hell was Shaw anyway? He'd sent that deformed idiot lad to fetch the man. How was he to function as laird if his second in command didn't come when he was called?

And Agneys! His ungrateful bitch of a daughter would pay for her disobedience tonight. The bruise she wore on her cheek was nothing compared to what he'd

leave her with next time. As soon as he had this annoying MacDowylt out of the way, he'd see to her punishment personally, laird's widow or no.

Conspiracy! He could see it clearly now. They all
conspired against him, just to make his life more difficult than necessary.

They'd pay. "They'll all pay," he vowed, looking for
something to throw to vent his anger.

"I've brought him for you." Jamie stood in the doorway ahead of Shaw, with that pathetic half smile of his.

"Get out of here, you misshapen whelp!" he yelled,
coming as close as he had all evening to happiness at
the fear in the lad's eyes.

The child's voice grated on his sensitive nerves. The
burn-scarred deformity of his face disgusted Roland.
Looking on the whoreson made him think of . . .

"It's no my conscience," he muttered aloud. That
bitch, Jone, had brought it on herself by sleeping with
the laird in the first place. Her brat should have died in
that fire with her.

"I beg yer pardon, Lardiner . . . er . . . my laird."
Shaw stumbled over his words, his eyes darting to the
door as if he thought of escape. "Were you speaking to
me?"

"No!" Roland yelled before catching himself. He
needed this man to follow his commands flawlessly.
Angering the fool would not serve his purpose at the
moment. "No," he repeated, quietly this time.

"You sent for me, aye?"

Roland felt much calmer now. In complete control
of his emotions. "I did. On the morrow, MacDowylt
will, I am sure, accede to my wishes and go after the

MacGahan half-wit. As we discussed, you've picked the men you can trust to go along with you when you accompany him?"

"I have indeed. The most generous payment you offered was incentive enough to recruit them."

"Good." Roland rubbed his hands together. At last his plans were coming together. "You'll make sure they understand, aye? Neither Isabella nor the MacDowylt are to make it back to the castle alive."

As Shaw nodded his agreement, a noise outside the door caught Roland's attention. An odd scraping sound.

"Go," Roland ordered his man as he flew to the door, throwing it open and lurching outside. Down the hallway, his pathetic limp having slowed his escape, Jamie cowered against the wall.

In a fury, Roland reached the child, grabbing a handful of his filthy hair and dragging him up off his feet.

"You dare to spy on me? Yer laird?"

"Yer no my laird," the boy cried. "You killed my laird. I saw you on the stairs after you'd pushed him down."

The red haze filled Roland again, and he flung the boy into the wall, fighting to catch his breath as the small body crumpled into the corner.

"You'll regret those words," Roland said, kicking his foot into the soft little mound hunkering in front of him.

Ignoring the child's screams, he had drawn back his foot to kick again when a weight landed on his shoulder, pulling him back and off balance.

"Here now, what's this?"

A large man, much larger than himself, moved in between him and the object of his fury.

"This is none of yer business, whoever you are. Be on yer way." He'd deal with the intruder later.

"Oh, I dinna think so. My business or no, I'm no going to let a full-grown man bully a wee bit of child."

Roland's whole body shook with his fury as he attempted to push past the man only to find himself flipped around, his face ground into the stone wall with his arm wrenched up behind him.

"You have no idea who yer dealing with. I'll have yer name," he sputtered. "And on the morrow, I'll have yer head mounted in the courtyard."

The interloper had the nerve to laugh—laugh!—as he let go of Roland's arm, allowing him at last to turn around.

"Patrick MacDowylt, at yer service, Lardiner. Yes, I ken who you are, and I'll tell you honestly, it's no *my* head I'd be concerned about if I were you."

A second MacDowylt? Roland watched as the man strolled away, realizing only after he was out of sight that the child had managed to sneak away as well.

Roland smoothed his shirt and plaid back into place as he returned to the laird's solar. His solar now.

It didn't matter. None of it mattered. They'd all be dead within days. The MacDowylts and that rotten child, too. Dead. He'd see to it if he had to slice them apart himself.

No one would take from him what he'd worked for years to achieve.

He was the MacGahan now.

Chapter 22

*I*sa stretched her back before squatting down to fill her bucket with water from the stream. The muscles in her legs trembled, deliciously tired, as if she'd played on the slope of a steep hill all night long.

No hills, perhaps, but she certainly had played.

She grinned like a crazy woman, not caring one bit what anyone might think of her this morning.

And what a beautiful morning! Everything around her seemed brilliantly sharp and new. The sweet-smelling spring air caressed her face with its warmth and she felt the promise of new birth carried in that gentle breeze.

Time to begin her planting today. Robbie should wake soon, and they could have their morning meal while the water heated for her bath. She needed to put on a new porridge to simmer for tonight.

Jamie should arrive this day. She'd expected him yesterday, but he must have been delayed with his chores.

So much to do, so many things to organize now that Jamie would be staying with her. With them. Just like a family.

Such a lovely day. Even the waters felt warmer than they had only days ago. Holding her hands down beside her bucket, she allowed the stream to ripple through her fingers. The waters caressed her skin as if they were alive.

Or perhaps she simply felt more alive.

Chuckling at her own silliness, she reached for her bucket and froze.

What in the name of all that's holy?

She dropped to sit on the grassy bank, staring at her hand. A mark covered her palm. A mark that hadn't been there yesterday. A mark identical to the one on Robbie's arm.

Plunging her hand back into the water, she scrubbed at her palm, but as if the mark were a part of her, nothing happened.

What could it mean?

"Robbie?" she called. "Robbie!" Louder, as she rose to her feet, running toward the cottage.

He met her halfway down the path, one hand clutched to his chest as he ran toward her.

"What?" His face was pinched with worry and he grabbed her shoulders. "What's wrong?"

In answer to his question, she held out her hand, palm up.

He stared at her hand, much as she must have, before meeting her eyes. "Where did that come from?"

"I was hoping you could answer that since it's identical to the one you wear on yer arm. Where did yers come from?"

He didn't answer right away, but instead trailed a finger over the mark on her palm, setting her skin to tingling as if feathers brushed against it.

"It's no exactly the same. It's much smaller." He looked away, reaching up to scratch at the mark on his arm.

What did *smaller* have to do with anything? And why did it suddenly feel so odd?

"Look!" Isa held up her trembling hand, staring at her palm, watching in fascination as the mark slowly disappeared. "It makes no sense. It's gone. I scrubbed it in the water, before, and there was no even a smudge. And now . . ." She let her words trail off.

The mark might be gone but she felt as if hundreds of tiny, invisible creatures covered her skin. Her hand continued to tremble, beyond her ability to control, until Robbie grabbed it, clasping it between his own.

As suddenly as the whole bizarre experience had begun, it now ended.

"It's no gone. See for yerself." He turned her palm over and there it was, now on the back of her hand.

"I dinna understand any of this, Robbie." Certainly she'd seen more than her share of strange occurrences, but this one frightened her.

Robbie half turned from her, rubbing his hand over the back of his neck. "We need to talk, Isa. Though I canna explain *why* this has happened, I may have an idea as to the source."

"And?" she asked even as a hard lump settled in the pit of her stomach. This had the feel of the Fae to it.

It must be her mother's people behind this, but why? Why would they plague her now, just as she'd finally found some measure of happiness?

"It's long past time I told you how I came to be here."

"But why would that have any bearing on . . ."

He held up his hand to stop her words, his head tilted to the side as if listening. "Do you hear that?"

In the distance, a horse approached, its gait slow and unsteady. "That would be Jamie come at last. You should probably finish with yer clothing before he gets here."

In all the turmoil over her hand, she hadn't even noticed that Robbie had barely taken the time to wrap his plaid around him, throwing all the excess over his shoulder to trail on the ground before coming to her aid.

"Go on with you. I'll wait here for him," she said

He nodded his agreement, his eyes dark and serious. "But after. We still need to have that talk."

"Aye," she agreed. "And we will. Now go."

She watched him walk away, gathering the excess of his plaid into a ball and holding it against his bare chest.

Even in a loosely wrapped plaid that man had the finest backside she'd ever had the pleasure to admire.

With a sigh, she turned her face toward the sound of the approaching horse and headed down the path in that direction. She could see them in the distance now, through the trees. As she'd surmised from the sound, it was the old horse Jamie always rode.

She called out his name and lifted her arm to wave in greeting, but he didn't respond, though his mount stopped and lifted her head.

Odd, that. As odd as the boy riding all hunched over the horse's neck that way.

"Jamie?" she called out again. Lifting her skirts and walking more quickly, she accelerated her pace, running until she reached his side.

"No." Her agonized groan was ripped from deep inside as she pulled the little body down from the old horse's back. "Jamie? Jamie!" she cried, falling to her knees with the child in her arms.

Blood crusted down the side of his face, the skin that had been smooth and clear now scraped and raw. When his good eye fluttered open, she felt as if her heart might burst.

"Thank God," she sobbed, rocking him in her lap, pushing his tangled hair away from his face.

No matter what had happened to him, he would recover from it. He had to. In that brief moment she'd thought him already gone she couldn't breathe, couldn't think.

His whimper snapped her back to reality and she struggled to her feet, stumbling back up the trail toward the cottage, her long skirts catching between her legs as she tried to run.

"Robbie," she yelled, gasping for air, hardly aware of the tears streaming down her cheeks as she ran. She needed Robbie. He'd know what to do.

And then he was there, lifting the boy's weight from her arms, guiding them back to the safety of her cottage as the terror gripping her heart quickly turned to fury.

"Isabella! You must calm yerself or you'll wake the lad."

They'd tended to Jamie's scrapes and bruises as best they could. It was the wounds they couldn't see that worried Robert now.

Both Jamie's and Isa's.

"I am calm," she hissed, stabbing her poker into the fire with a force that sent sparks flying. "I'm sure his little rib is broken and I just canna see how Roland could be such an animal as to do that to a wee lad like Jamie."

Robert had wondered that himself.

"Do you believe me now that it's no safe for you to stay here? No you or the boy, either one. When he wakes, we can be on our way to MacQuarrie Keep." Where his family could see to their safety when he was no longer able to.

Isa whirled, throwing the poker to the hearth. "Do you think I can simply turn my back on this? You heard what he said of Roland. If it's true—if that whoreson has murdered my grandfather—I canna let him get away with that any more than I can allow him to go unchallenged for what he's done to the lad."

Robert didn't question the truth of what the boy had said in the least. It was, in fact, because of what Jamie had told them that Robert felt so much urgency. He had to make her see reason.

"There's more. Things I dinna tell you. The night of yer grandfather's wedding, when those men waylaid me, the reason I dinna want to spread any alarm was that I suspected Lardiner was behind it. I kenned the truth of it then that he'd do anything, even murder. It's why I tried to convince you then of the need to come away with me."

If only she would agree. He didn't want to hurt her by telling her what he'd found before meeting those men in that dark hallway.

But it seemed her stubbornness knew no bounds.

"Suspicion is one thing. What we see with our own eyes, what that beast had done to poor Jamie, that is something else altogether. Roland might batter a wee child, or push an old man already in his cups down the stairs, but he's a lowly coward. He'd no lay his hands on me."

She left him no choice.

"Yer wrong about the man. I've good reason to believe he laid his hands on yer friend, Auld Annie. I'd gone to her room that night, hoping to speak to her again. But when I arrived, I found her dead. Strangled, by the looks of it, though the maid who walked in on me assured me she'd died of her sickness in her sleep."

"That canna be. She was no sick when I saw her. Only frightened."

"Exactly. They murdered her. I saw her body with my own two eyes. It was coming out of her room I was attacked, but when Jamie found and wakened me, I'd been moved to another part of the castle."

It broke his heart to watch the pain wash over her face, but she had to know, had to understand how important it was for her to get away from here. Surely she'd see reason now.

"You saw this? At the castle, before we left? And you dinna tell me? Surely you had to realize I would want to hear of this travesty against Auld Annie." Her face had lost its color, as if shock were setting in.

"That's exactly why I dinna tell you. Yer safety was more important to me than any revenge you might seek." And with her temper, he didn't doubt for an instant she'd want justice for her old friend.

"It's no a matter of revenge. Roland must be made

to pay for his crimes." The color that had drained from her face when he'd first told her about Annie flooded back, washing her cheeks a deep dull red.

"Isa. Think about what you say. With Lardiner in charge, you and I alone canna take on the whole of the MacGahan clan. You canna ask that of me. Think of the boy. Let me get you both to safety. You and Jamie. Once we reach MacQuarrie Keep, I'll lead men back here if it's what you want, but listen to reason for now, lass."

She glared at him, eyes glassy with unshed tears, her lips pressed into a thin, tight line. Then, as if a door had opened, her expression blanked before turning into a small, sad smile.

"As you say, Robbie, I canna ask that of you." She wiped her hands down the front of her shift and crossed to him, leaning in to kiss his cheek. "We'll need to make sure enough feed and water is left for the animals to carry them over until yer people can come back for them."

Finally! He gathered her into his arms, covering her mouth with his for a kiss she met boldly. He knew she hated to leave her home, knew it saddened her. But this was the only viable option, and he thanked the saints she'd seen the truth of that at last.

"I'll see to the animals. You gather rations for us to carry on our journey. Though it will add an extra day, I'm thinking we'd best go the long way around to avoid Castle MacGahan."

He stopped at the door, glancing back to reassure himself it was real. She had already spread out a cloth and even now placed two loaves of bread in the middle of it.

"Go on with you, Robbie. We've much to do this day. Both of us."

With a sigh of relief, he strode out the door toward the stable. For the first time since he'd arrived in this century, he felt as though the weight of the world had been lifted from his shoulders.

Isa kept her back turned until she heard Robbie close the door behind him. She might not be able to stop her tears, but she certainly did not have to let him see them.

She grappled with her emotions, forcing herself to keep moving, to gather what was needed for the journey. It felt as if she stood outside herself, watching herself go through the movements as a normal person might, but she felt anything but normal.

Anger seethed through her, twisting and burning like a fiery serpent. Worse still, the pain in her heart beat at her. Heavy and throbbing with the knowledge of her loss.

She piled as much as she could onto the cloth, then tied the corners together, making a neat bundle for the journey to MacQuarrie Keep. That should do well enough for the two of them.

Crossing the room, she ran her fingers lightly over Jamie's sleeping face, tucking his hair behind his ear before brushing her lips over his forehead.

That Robbie would see to his welfare she had not the slightest doubt.

At the door she paused for one last look around her beloved home.

Robbie had been absolutely correct. She could not

ask him to risk his life in confronting Roland. Nor was she willing to put poor Jamie in danger again.

But there was nothing to prevent *her* from delivering the justice Roland Lardiner deserved. He'd taken from her the only family she'd ever had and she meant to make him pay for his crime.

Chapter 23

"Goddammit!"

Robert stood in the center of the quiet cottage, furious at his own stupidity. He should have known better. Should have guessed Isa was up to something the instant she gave in so easily.

But he hadn't. He'd allowed himself to be tricked because he'd wanted it so badly.

"Goddammit to hell," he fumed, stomping across to the table.

She'd left their provisions all packed and ready to go like she was fool enough to believe he'd leave without her.

"Robbie?"

He turned at the sound of the little voice, hurrying to the boy's side.

"Hush now, lad. Try to get yer rest. I'm going out for a bit to find Isa, and when we return, we'll all be leaving this place."

Faerie Magic be damned. Whether she wanted to or not, he intended to get her to safety if he had to tie her to the back of his horse.

Perhaps she had been just a wee bit hasty in her decision.

Isa stopped running and bent over at the waist to catch her breath, the energy from her white-hot fury beginning to wane. The betrayal she'd felt when she learned Robbie had withheld the news of Annie's murder had stoked the fire burning in her belly. A fire of hatred and the need for vengeance. Not that the anger had gone away, only that she'd had time for reason to kick in. Reason and the vaguely unsettling feeling that something important wasn't as it should be.

She straightened, and looked around to gauge her bearings, trying to determine how far she'd come. She'd specifically chosen to cut through the forest, avoiding the trail just in case Robbie tried to look for her, but that made it more difficult for her to judge her progress.

Not far, she'd guess.

Standing here looking around like a lost sheep certainly wouldn't get her where she was headed. Wiping a hand across her perspiration-slicked forehead, she pushed back the damp curls that tickled her face, squared her shoulders and started out again, at a slower pace this time.

One foot in front of the other.

"One, two, one, two," she murmured, keeping time with her footsteps.

Her father had taught her to count, and in languages other than her own.

"*Unum, duo . . .*" she said aloud, recalling how lovely the Latin had sounded rolling from his tongue as he'd read to her.

"*Alpha, beta.*"

She shuddered, remembering her dislike of the ancient Greek language her father had deemed so important to learn. There had been something about using letters for numbers that had confused her, even when she was older and her grandfather had gone over it, again and again, until he'd lost his patience.

Her footsteps faltered at the memory.

How could she have forgotten all the time he'd spent trying to carry out her father's wishes for her? Had she been so determined to separate herself from him because of his hatred for her mother that she'd locked away all those little moments where he tried to show her kindness? And only now, when it was too late, she remembered.

Pain seared her heart at the knowledge of her loss. Her grandfather had cared for her. The realization brought a fresh onslaught of sorrow and memories.

She'd been thirteen. When he'd accused her of not trying hard enough to learn the Greek she'd yelled at him, demanding that if he wanted her to learn another language he should teach her in her mother's language. His face had paled and he'd stormed from her room, and after he'd gone, she'd cried for hours.

The rains had lasted for days afterward, coming down so hard the bailey had been riddled with running water that looked like miniature rivers.

Her breath caught and she reached out to the nearest tree to steady herself.

That was it! That was what wasn't as it should be.

She turned to run home, screaming when she smacked directly in the wall of man standing behind her.

"Christ, woman," Robert panted, grabbing Isa's wrists to keep her from pounding her fists against his already aching chest. "It's me."

She looked up at him then, gulping in great gasps of air, her eyes wild.

When it became apparent she was calming, he let go of her and she backed away, but not before smacking his arm with her open hand.

"What in the name of all that's holy were you thinking, sneaking up on me like that?"

He hadn't sneaked, hadn't made any attempt to cover the noise of his approach. She'd been oblivious, and that had only served to spark his own anger.

"Do you never give any thought to yer own safety? I could have been anybody. One of Lardiner's men or even the man himself. You were blundering about out here like some blind woman when I found you."

Vacillating between anger and fear, he glared at her, making no move as she gathered her wits. Fear finally won and he reached out, pulling her to him, crushing her to his chest.

"Christ, Isa." He hadn't realized how worried he'd been until this very moment and now that he'd found her, unharmed, his stomach fluttered as if it might empty its contents right here on the forest floor. "Coming out here alone was an incredibly stupid thing to do."

"Yer right. I admit it," she said against his chest, making no attempt to pull away from him. "And I'm so glad you've come for me, Robbie. Everything's gone all wrong, and I dinna ken what to do anymore."

Her words were all he needed to hear.

"I'll tell you exactly what yer going to do. Yer coming with me, and when we get back to the cottage, we pack up Jamie and head for MacQuarrie Keep. And I'm no letting you out of my sight until we reach there, so dinna even think of trying something like this again."

"I promise," she whispered, dragging her hands down her cheeks to wipe away the tears.

He hated seeing her so upset, but time was clearly running out for him. If this was what it took to get her to agree to leaving her home, then so be it.

They made their way back toward the cottage in silence, his arm protectively around her shoulders until she dragged her feet to a stop, pulling against him.

Robert clenched his teeth to keep from yelling out his frustration. If she'd changed her mind again, he thought, he might lose his mind.

"We've no time to waste, Isa."

He nudged her forward but she ducked out from under his arm, turning to face him.

"Have you noticed what a lovely, calm day it's been? No a cloud or drop of rain in sight?"

The weather? The daft woman wanted to discuss the damned weather?

"It's a beauty," he ground out, catching up her hand and starting forward, all but dragging her behind him. "An ab-so-freaking-lutely gorgeous damned day. All right? Now let's get on with it."

Isa planted her feet and pulled her hand from his, crossing her arms around her waist as if she were going to be ill.

"That's just it. There should have been thunder and lightning, and the ground itself heaving up and breaking apart under our feet. I was that angry, Robbie."

"It doesn't matter." He reached for her again but she stepped back. "You've come to yer senses now and we're doing what we need to do." *Please, God*, he prayed, *let her have come to her senses.*

She scrubbed her hands over her face before clenching them together in front of her. "You dinna understand what I'm trying to tell you. This very morning, though it seems a lifetime ago now, you said we needed to talk. You were right, but that's because I've something I've need to tell you before you take me anywhere near yer family. Something I've no wanted to share. I'm no the madwoman I pretended to be for so long."

"We established that fact quite some time ago, did we no?" Robert did his best to tamp down his impatience. Obviously she was headed somewhere with this prattle, and obviously wherever that somewhere was, it was important to her.

"Aye, we did." She paused to take in a deep breath, lifting her chin defiantly before she continued. "But that's no to say I'm like everyone else. My mother was one of the Fae folk and, as a result, I'm possessed of a terrible magic I canna control. Or . . ."—Here she stopped, lifting her hand to stare at the duplicate of his Guardian Mark. "I *was* possessed of such a magic. But now . . ."

Her voice trailed away as she looked up at him. Her expression so lost, so frightened and unsure of herself, it dug into the small places of his heart and made him feel small and powerless.

Once again, he gathered her into his arms, holding her tightly to him. "Tell me of this magic, Isa, and of what's happened to it."

"That's just it. I dinna ken what's happened—only that it's gone and that I feel somehow less without it."

He nodded and tucked her back under his arm, gradually urging her forward, one step at a time, as she continued to speak.

"Before this morning, before this"—she held up her hand as if to show him the mark—"it was as if the weather, as if all of Nature herself, were somehow tied to my emotions. When I was sad, it rained. Happy? Bright, sunny, warm days. And if I were afraid, or worst of all, angry, it was as if hell had been released from the very clouds."

So it was true. He felt as if his heart paused in his chest, just long enough for him to have to work at that next breath. Was there no part of his life the Fae hadn't penetrated?

His mother said the Fae had predicted his birth while she herself was yet a child, and, for a fact, he knew they would have a hand in his death soon.

Confirming that Isa was one of them simply tied the whole of his life up into one tidy little package of Faerie interference.

Yet, in spite of that, he couldn't hold them to any blame. All things considered, who was he to question the workings of the Fae? If not for them, he wouldn't have had a second chance at life.

Wouldn't ever have met Isa.

Wouldn't have discovered his Soulmate, no matter how few the days he was destined to share with her in this lifetime.

And *that* was the true crux of the pain he suffered at this moment. Though he'd danced his way all around it for days, there was no denying it any longer.

Isabella was his Soulmate.

Everything that had happened made sense once he accepted that single fact, from his having arrived twenty years later than he planned to the mark on Isa's hand. All of it, right down to the way he felt when he held her in his arms.

He'd taken the Guardians' Pledge to reunite the broken Soul Pairings, and in doing so, he had enabled the Magic to direct him to his other half. That she might never accept the truth of it was beyond his control, beyond even the Magic's control.

And though they'd be separated soon, he now had no doubt that one day, one lifetime, they'd be together again.

His arm tightened automatically when she pulled to a stop again.

"What's that?" she asked, looking up at him, wrinkling her nose. "Do you smell that?"

"Aye. Fire."

They started forward again, their speed increasing until they ran. Robert took the lead, with Isa trailing farther behind as they raced through the trees.

He spared only a moment to wondering whether Isa's hand tingled as his arm did now, whether she realized yet to pay attention to that feeling. No time to let himself be distracted. He blocked that thought as he blocked the pain burning through his chest. His mind focused on the cottage where he headed and the small boy he'd left sleeping there, and he pushed himself to run harder.

Smoke drifted through the trees toward them. Sharp and acrid, it stung the back of Isa's throat as she gulped in air. Her chest and legs ached from running but she couldn't stop. Robbie's long legs had left her too far behind already.

Up ahead, where the trees gave way to her little piece of cleared forest, Robbie stopped. One hand clutched to his chest, he bent from the waist, obviously catching his breath.

As she drew close, he held up his arm, apparently signaling something.

Stop? Keep silent? She had no idea. And looking beyond where he waited, she lost any interest in trying to figure it out.

Her cottage, her wonderful, lovely cottage, was burning, flames leaping up into the sky from what had been her thatched roof. The same roof she'd repaired herself just last summer.

"No," she whispered, her feet moving her forward as if through a haze.

Her home. Her animals.

Oh God!

"Jamie!" she screamed, rushing forward, swerving to avoid Robbie's outstretched arm. "Jamie!"

She ran, powered by a burst of fear-induced energy coursing through her limbs. Out into the open, racing over the uneven ground to the stream, she plunged in. Oblivious to the water pushing at her body, she crossed and scrambled up the other side, not stopping until she neared the inferno that had been her home.

Lifting her arm to shield her face from the heat, she took a step back from the horror, her legs struggling to hold her weight.

Nothing. Nothing could survive that fire.

Vaguely, as if from another place, she heard Robbie calling her name, but she couldn't tear her eyes away from the flames.

It was so wrong for this to have happened to poor, wee Jamie. Fire. Why did it have to be fire?

Yelling came from all around her as she sank to her knees, unable to stand any longer. Men she didn't recognize, brandishing swords and angry faces, circled around her, but she couldn't bring herself to care about any of it. Not the men, or the heat from fire—not even the smoke that clogged her lungs. None of it mattered.

Until she thought of Robbie, and by then it was too late. Rough hands held her pinned to the ground with her arms wrenched up behind her.

She could see him, battling his way across the open ground. He fought magnificently, pulling one man from his mount and leaving his body crumpled in the grass as he ran toward her. The late-afternoon sunlight flashed brilliantly from his blade as it sliced a path through the next two men. The glorious tales of her father's battles that her grandfather had told her when she was small pushed their way into her memory, and for a short while she had hope.

In the end, though, there were simply too many of them. Too many men, both mounted and on foot, all converging on Robbie, burying him under their weight.

Isa squeezed her eyes shut, waiting for whatever might come, wanting nothing more than to have it done with. These beasts who called themselves men had trapped little Jamie in the blaze, and now they'd taken Robbie to the ground. What they did to her after those horrors didn't matter. They'd already destroyed all that she held dear.

"Drag him over here next to the madwoman."

After their actions here this day, they dared call *her* mad?

She fought against an uncontrollable laughter bubbling up from her chest. Tried so hard to hold it in, all to no avail. It burst forth, surprising her when it sounded more like broken sobs.

"No, Isa. Dinna cry, love." Robbie's voice, no more than a ragged whisper.

Two men held him to the ground next to her when she opened her eyes, his face streaked with dirt and blood and soot. Beaten, battered, but he lived.

"How do you want it done, Shaw?"

The question came from somewhere behind Isa. She tried not to think about what the words meant. Robbie's gaze held hers, even when one of their captors placed his boot on the side of Robbie's head, pushing his cheek to the ground.

"Take their heads. They'll serve as Lardiner's proof."

"Close yer eyes, love," Robbie whispered, struggling against the men who held him even as the foot ground into the side of his face.

She did as he said, wishing she could but touch him one last time as she heard the sound of steel being drawn behind her. If only the magic she had hated for so long hadn't deserted her now that she really needed it.

"Stay yer swords!"

The order rang out over the thunder of approaching horses.

"It's a grand mistake you make here, lads. Yer new laird is no likely to appreciate having his bride delivered without her lovely head, now is he?"

"I dinna ken who you be," the one called Shaw responded, "but we act on the orders of our new laird."

"No, I dinna think you do."

The pressure on Isa's arms lessened and then she was on her feet. Her eyes flew open when an arm encircled her waist, and her feet left the ground as she was lifted up to sit in front of one of the riders.

"And as to who I am?" The large man settled her against him on his mount. "Patrick MacDowylt, brother to yer new laird. Bring him." He motioned toward Robbie before tugging on his reins to turn his horse back in the direction of Castle MacGahan.

Chapter 24

"Where have you taken Rob—" Isa stopped herself, glaring at the man who so arrogantly occupied her grandfather's chair. "What have you done with MacQuarrie?"

"Dinna fash yerself over yer guardian's well-being, lass. Lardiner is seeing to his accommodations. Ah!" Malcolm MacDowylt looked past her as the door opened. "And here's our ever-helpful friend Lardiner even now."

Isa sat on the edge of a small chair the man called Patrick had pulled up in front of the MacDowylt before returning to his brother's side. Though they'd not bound her hands or feet, she felt every inch the prisoner as she surveyed the faces of the people in the room.

Several warriors—all MacDowylt's men, no doubt—crowded into the chamber. One fellow she'd seen before. Roland's man, Shaw, leaned against the back wall. And Agneys, perched daintily on a chair on the far side of the room, watching everything with her usual air of disdain.

Isa worked at gathering her scattered thoughts. Robbie lived. They'd brought him here as captive, but he lived. All was not lost.

Roland strode into the room, sparing her one of his greasy sneers as he neared. Before he reached the MacDowylt's side, Patrick stepped forward, his hand on an empty chair across from Isa, clearly indicating to Roland he should be seated.

"Good." Malcolm steepled his fingers on the table in front of him. "Now that we're all here, perhaps we can settle this matter."

"We've no a need for the half-wit to be present," Roland snarled. "I can have my man, Shaw, see to her."

Shaw seemed to shrink in his spot near the wall, glancing to the men on either side of him, their hands lying loosely on their weapons.

Malcolm shook his head. "I dinna think that would be our wisest course of action, eh, Isabella?" He turned to her, a grin splitting his face. A grin that didn't touch his eyes. "In fact, Isabella's our guest of honor. Which is only fitting for the woman I'm to wed, is it no?"

"You canna do that! There's no a reason for it. You ken my own Agneys carries the old laird's heir. If yer to wed any it should be her," Roland blustered.

Isa could imagine nothing more repugnant than to be on the same side of an argument as that slimy bastard, but in this case she agreed.

"I've no intention of being yer wife, MacDowylt."

Hands clasped in her lap, Isa waited for the silence to draw out as inspiration struck. "I . . . I've already given my vows of marriage. To MacQuarrie."

"Vows dinna mean so much if yer a widow," Roland snapped.

"They also dinna mean much coming from a fickle, murdering whoreson like yerself," Isa retorted, forcing herself not to think on that *widow* remark.

Roland lunged from his seat, his arms outstretched, but two of the MacDowylt's men stepped in front of him before he'd taken a single step, encouraging him back into his chair.

She wouldn't be stopped by his anger. "Yer a child-beating bastard and you murdered my grandfather," she accused, pointing a shaking finger his direction. Whatever was to come, she meant to make sure everyone heard what horrible deeds lay on Roland's hands, whether they believed her or not.

Malcolm sat back, turning his steely gaze on Roland. "These are serious accusations. Is this true, Lardiner?"

"She lies," Roland answered through gritted teeth. "I told you she was mad."

"So you did." Malcolm nodded, turning back to her. "I dinna suppose you've proof of yer charges? A witness, mayhaps?"

Isa shook her head, struggling to speak around the lump that formed in her throat. "There was one. But Jamie, the child who saw what Roland did to my grandfather, slumbered in my cottage when those men put it to the torch." More words refused to come and hot tears streaked unbidden down her cheeks while silence filled the room.

"My, but isna that convenient?" Roland's sarcastic tone grated on Isa's ear. "You claim there's only one witness to yer sack of lies but you canna even produce him. You see? You canna believe the blether of a madwoman, MacDowylt."

"Perhaps it is as you say, my friend." Malcolm stroked his chin as if deep in thought. "But I'm of a mind to hunt for the truth in this matter before I make my decision. Until that time, I think it best we confine you all to yer chambers."

With a flick of his wrist, his men closed in, waiting.

"Me?" Agneys sounded indignant in her surprise. "Yer thinking to hold me in my chambers as well?"

"Everyone for now."

Isa rose to her feet, jerking her arm from the grasp of the man who'd offered assistance as she stood.

"Except Isabella. I'd ask you to stay for a moment, my lady. We have a private matter to discuss."

The guards on either side of Isa took their leave and she dropped back into her seat, waiting while Patrick crossed the room and closed the door behind the others.

"In this chamber, Isabella MacGahan, between the two of us, with my brother Patrick as witness, I'd ask that we set aside our personal strategies in favor of honesty. Can you agree to that?"

Isa paused, choosing her words carefully. "I see no point to be made in being dishonest with you."

Again the man steepled his fingers in front of him. "You expect me to believe that? Yer obviously not what you represented yerself to be the last time I saw you. And if you'd lie about that . . ." He left his words hanging in the air like he'd thrown down a gauntlet.

"My disguise was my protection. When I presented myself as that creature, no one bothered me."

"Except me." Malcolm stood and began to pace, at last stopping directly in front of her chair. "We have a problem to solve, you and I. I mean to have these lands for my clan in payment of a MacGahan debt. I'd prefer to accomplish this goal without the need to raise a sword, but as there's no a male descendant and you are the named heir, it seems we must come to some agreement."

Isa sat back in her chair, wishing she had Robbie at her side to advise her now. She knew nothing of clan politics, only that the responsibility of the decision Malcolm required weighed heavily on her shoulders.

"Why me? Agneys is the laird's widow. Why do you no just wed Agneys? Wait for the birth of her bairn and name yerself his guardian."

The smile that broke over Malcolm's face this time was genuine, lighting his eyes and carving years from his face. "Ah, Isabella, yer too trusting by far, lass. No, I'm afraid that taking you to wife is the only way to rightfully lay my claim."

It was up to her. This man held Robbie's future in his hands and her response to him now would determine what he chose to do with that future. What would her father have done in her place?

Probably not what she was about to do. Then again, her father wouldn't have been in her position—needing to save the man she loved.

"As you say, in the past I may no have been completely honest with you. But you can believe this: I've no desire to control anything. I want only to be left alone. If you'll but free Robbie, I'll happily declare these lands yers and leave this place to yer care."

"So you say. But what's to stop this Robbie, yer . . . uh, yer *husband*—from coming back later with men of his own to challenge me for what he sees as rightfully his?"

Isa wet her lips, feeling her face heat as she stalled, trying to determine just how much truth she wanted to share with this man. A few long moments of silence and she made her decision. MacDowylt held the power and she had nothing to gain in deceit.

"He willna do that because he has no right to anything here. As you seem to suspect, I lied to you. We've taken no vows. Robert MacQuarrie has sought nothing but that I should leave this place so that he could see to my safety as he promised my father he would. If you'll allow us to go in peace, I'll give my wedding vow to you in front of the entire clan."

"I'm no as blindly trusting as you are, Isabella." He made no attempt to disguise his skepticism.

"Oh?" It wasn't bad enough he didn't believe her, but now, for a second time, he'd all but called her stupidly naïve. "Is that so? Well, from what I've seen, yer no great judge of character yerself, naming one such as Roland Lardiner yer friend. It's Roland who murdered my grandfather. He who beat the poor child who'd witnessed the act and he who ordered my home put to the torch with wee Jamie inside. There's some friend for you. I'd no be turning my back on him if I were you."

In the silence that followed Isa's tirade, her own ragged breathing sounded loud.

"This child you speak of." Patrick's voice filled the stillness. "He was a small lad with a disfigured face?"

Isa nodded, biting the inside of her trembling lip while she strove for her self-control. Though she hated the thought of crying in front of these men again, the hot tears filled her eyes as she thought of poor, sweet Jamie.

A look passed between the MacDowylt brothers— a look Isa couldn't interpret other than to know it appeared as though the two men shared a single thought. With a respectful nod of his head, Patrick turned and hurried from the room.

Malcolm strode back behind the table, retaking his seat as one of his men entered and stood beside Isa.

"I'll give yer words consideration, my lady. For now, I'll have to ask you to keep to yer bedchamber."

Isa rose unsteadily to her feet, allowing MacDowylt's man to support her arm this time.

He'd consider her words, but would he believe them, or would he decide Robbie posed too great a danger to be set free?

Chapter 25

"I, Isabella MacGahan, take you to be my husband." Though it was shock to hear them in her own voice, the words had come out, just as she'd been instructed to say them. She hadn't choked on them or forgotten a single one.

Assembled in the great hall before as many of the castle inhabitants as they'd been able to quickly round up, Malcolm MacDowylt had spoken his own vow only moments before.

Numbly Isa noted that neither Roland nor Agneys were among the onlookers. Nor Robbie.

"It is done." Patrick's words were greeted by a few scattered "Huzzahs," but for the most part, the spectators seemed more confused than anything else.

Exactly how Isa felt.

The marriage, though irregular, was binding in every way. They'd given their vows in the present tense.

Though she had never really believed she would wed, when she'd allowed herself to dream of a wedding day, she certainly hadn't imagined it as this quick, detached business transaction. Once she'd agreed to MacDowylt's demands, his man had escorted her to her bedchamber. She'd hardly had enough time to wash her hands and face before there'd been a knock at her door. They'd whisked her downstairs and into the great hall, still wearing the same filthy, smoke-streaked gown she'd donned that morning, as if they feared she'd change her mind if she had any time to think on it. A few mumbled words and it was over.

She was married.

Now Malcolm and Patrick ignored her completely, discussing the need for new fortifications as they led her up the stairs and toward her bedchamber.

Her husband. She had a husband.

Isa could hardly believe what had happened, feeling almost as if she were walking through a dream.

At the entrance to her room, they stopped, and Malcolm entered the room ahead of her, holding her door open. He still spoke to his brother as he waited for her to pass inside.

"And what of MacQuarrie?" she interrupted. "Will you allow me to see him now?"

Another of those annoyingly inscrutable looks passed between the brothers.

"I'm afraid that won't be possible. He'll have to remain in the holding cell where Roland placed him for now."

Malcolm stepped out of her room, pulling the door to shut it behind him, but Isa jammed her foot into the opening.

"What?" he asked, frowning in irritation as he stepped back into the room.

"I've held to my end of our bargain, MacDowylt. I've given you my vows. Now it's time for you to keep to yers and allow me to take MacQuarrie and leave here."

Isa took it as a bad sign when Patrick backed away, giving them a measure of privacy.

"I'd ask you to consider my current situation, Isabella." Malcolm took her hand, leading her over to a chair by the fire. Only when she sat down did he continue. "As the new laird of the castle, I canna very well allow my wife to go running off around the countryside with another man."

"But we had an agreement." He had no right to do this!

"I agreed to nothing. You offered to wed in return for my allowing you to leave with MacQuarrie. I told you I'd consider yer words. Under the circumstances, I found yer terms unacceptable. Therefore, I decided we would proceed under my terms instead." Hands clasped behind his back, he strolled to the door.

He'd tricked her?

"*Yer* terms? You gave no terms."

"But I did. I told you we must wed and that is what we did. That you chose to believe anything else is no fault of mine. I did say that you were far too trusting."

Isa opened and closed her mouth soundlessly, her mind trying to catch up with the helpless frustration she felt.

"You let me go through with that . . . that sham of a marriage believing you'd let us go, and you without the slightest intention of doing so?"

"It's no a sham, Isabella, as well you ken. It's legal and binding what you've done. What we've done. And now, as laird, I've matters requiring my attention. Good day, madam."

Isa ran across the room but arrived there too late. He'd already shut the door and dropped the brand-new outer bar into place.

"Damn you, Malcolm MacDowylt!" she screamed, dropping her forehead against the wood.

Wait.

What had he said about Robbie? That he'd have to remain in the holding cell where Roland had placed him?

Castle MacGahan had no holding cells. Where could . . .

No!

Surely not even Roland would have tossed Robbie down into that horrible, long-abandoned dungeon.

"Perhaps we'll meet again in hell, MacQuarrie."

Robert replayed Lardiner's parting taunt over and over in his mind as he tried to form his next logical move.

Cold, hard stone bit into his back and head where he leaned against the wall, but he didn't change his position.

Roland hadn't bothered with a ladder. His men had simply pushed Robert into the hole. Thank the saints for all the training Coryell Enterprises had put him through. He'd tucked for the fall by sheer instinct, dropping like a stone. When he finally managed to stand, he'd reached up, unable to feel anything above him with his fingers, which told him the depth was well over seven feet.

After that, just finding the wall in the infinite black of this hole had taken all his energy.

All he could manage for the moment was to breathe through the pain in his chest and the one in his heart.

Fear, despair, frustration. He recognized their ugly feel. Not fear for himself but for Isa. Despair over his inability to protect her. Frustration that the wound in his chest had weakened his body and sapped the strength he'd needed to fight these bastards off.

From his perspective, *this* was hell.

It seemed clear from Lardiner's comment that they intended to leave him in this hole until he rotted. The memory of the castles he'd toured a couple of years ago with Jessie came back to him. There'd been one place where the proprietor had handed them a flashlight to look down through a metal grate into the dungeon below, pointing out the bones that had been unearthed there. They'd laughed at the time, making some joke about gullible tourists and cow bones.

It didn't seem so funny now, considering that it would be his bones illuminated in the dull glare of tourists' flashlights in seven hundred years.

Enough!

He couldn't let himself sink into that trap. It would be all too easy to simply give up. He wouldn't allow that. Instead he needed to keep his mind active, focusing on the facts at hand.

The stench of ammonia stung his nostrils, but whether it came from prior occupants or too many rats he couldn't say, and didn't really care.

He did care that Isa was somewhere above him in the castle, likely in danger. The thought of her alone, grieving for poor Jamie, tore at his heart.

If he'd only taken the boy with him to hunt for Isa, he'd still be alive.

If he'd paid closer attention to what Isa was up to instead of blindly accepting her word, they might have gotten away before Lardiner's men arrived.

If he'd simply forced her to leave that first day . . .

"If, if, if," he muttered, his own voice echoing back to him in the darkness more reassuring than the sound of his labored breathing. Clutching his hand to his side, he scooted into a less uncomfortable position.

He hadn't done any of those things and now they all paid the price for his lack of action. That was the bottom line.

And all that mattered? Figuring out how he'd get out of here and find Isa before it was too late.

Both of which he fully intended to do, just as soon as he could gather his strength.

Malcolm MacDowylt stared into the fire, an untouched cup of fine Scots whisky at his left hand.

His mind must be clear this night if his plans were to meet with success. Though he'd claimed his right as laird this afternoon when he and Isabella had exchanged their vows, much remained to be done to clear that path in fact. There were too many small details any one of which could slip through his fingers at any moment.

"Colm?" Patrick stepped inside the laird's solar, a satisfied grin covering his face. "All's in readiness as you ordered."

"Yer certain the lad overheard you? And that the men understand their instructions?"

"Aye, it's all as you said."

"I want the men leaving no stone unturned here. I need to learn every dirty secret these walls have to share. Do they ken how important their task is?"

"Yer men are well aware of their assignments." Patrick shook his head and pulled the door wide open, making no attempt to hide his irritation. "For the love of Freya, Colm, show some trust."

His brother was right. They each had their own tasks to accomplish this night. Pat had carried out the first part of their plan and now it was his turn.

Chapter 26

⁓

A knock at Isabella's door pulled her back to reality.

"A moment, please," she called, pushing herself up to stand, her leg useless and without feeling from having been tucked under her as she sat for so long.

Exactly *how* long she'd sat, staring into the fire, she couldn't say. But since the sun had long since set, hours had to have passed while she brooded uselessly.

Her stomach knotted as she limped to the door, her dead limb waking with a fierce prickling. What more could MacDowylt want of her? She'd already given him everything she had—her vows and with them the whole of Clan MacGahan. Surely he wouldn't expect her to actually perform the duties of wife.

The thought stopped her in her tracks and another knock sounded at her door.

"I'm coming," she hissed, leaning over to rub her hand up and down her calf.

Malcolm had said nothing of the sort earlier, nothing to give her any reason to suspect such an action on his part. On the other hand, he'd allowed her to believe he'd let her take Robbie and leave when he'd intended no such thing.

The new laird of the MacGahan was in for a battle if he expected to take *her* to bed.

With a deep breath, Isa straightened her shoulders and strode to the door, ready to give the MacDowylt upstart a piece of her mind as she flung open the door.

"By the saints!" she grunted as the little body slammed into hers, arms tight around her middle.

"Jamie!" She knelt, pulling the child away from her to look into his face, not believing it could actually be him. "How?"

"We have to hurry, Isa," he said, grabbing up her hand and pulling.

"Wait." She ran her fingers lightly over his scraped and bruised cheek. "I thought you were in the cottage when . . . I dinna ken how this has happened. I watched it burn to the ground."

Jamie nodded, pulling at her hand again, urging her to her feet. "After Robbie left to find you, I was hungry. I was at the table when I heard the horses coming so I went outside and hid in the stable. When the fire started, the animals ran out because . . ." Here he stopped, shrugging his little shoulders apologetically. "Well, I forgot to close the gate, but it's a good thing this time, is it no?"

"It most certainly is a good thing this time, dearling." She gathered him in her arms, holding him close until he pushed away.

"We've no time for that stuff now. We have to go." Again he took her hand with his little one, pulling at her.

"Wait. Go where? And how did you get here to the castle?"

"The MacDowylt's men brought me here. That big one found me in the forest. Me and Robbie's big horse. The same man that stopped Master Roland when he was so angry with me. He handed me off to one of his men and he brought me here to the castle and put me in the MacDowylt's own chamber. And they talked to me like I was one of them and then they gave me porridge, Isa. Very good porridge."

Against her will, Isa's impression of the MacDowylt improved just a bit. That his men had rescued Jamie and treated him well had to say something for the man.

"And just where is it yer so anxious to take me?" she asked as the child tugged at her hand again.

"To rescue Robbie, of course."

Oh, for the simple thoughts of a child. "I dinna see how that would be possible, Jamie. The MacDowylt has named himself laird and has his men in place everywhere." There was even one in the hallway outside. She'd seen the man when Malcolm had left her here. "How did you get past the guard to get in here?"

"That's just it. That's why we have to go now. The one that saved me and another man, they were talking in the room while I ate. They dinna think I listened, but

I did," he boasted. "All the guards save the ones on the front gates have been called to the great hall to meet with the MacDowylt himself this night. The guards and all the castle staff. The man said he worried that their prisoners might escape through the side exit, the one we use to get to the fields, but he said the MacDowylt himself had ordered it to be so and that it should be no problem because the prisoners wouldna ken there were no guards about."

Isa paused for only a moment. It seemed too good to be true, but she wasn't going to question her luck. As Jamie said, they had precious little time and this could well be their only chance.

Allowing him to pull her forward, she scanned the hallway in both directions. Empty, just as Jamie had said it would be. As quietly as possible, she ran with the child, to the end of the hall and down the stairs.

At the first floor, she peeked around the corner of the stairway, holding her breath in anticipation of some large man with an even larger sword waiting there. None to be seen, but she could hear the sounds of voices coming from the direction of the great hall, confirming what Jamie had overheard the men talking about.

"Come on," she whispered, leading him toward the old storage room and the dank, dark little steps she remembered finding as a child. The passageway to the dungeon.

Her grandfather had warned her to stay away from the pit and told her it had seen its last use before he was born—that his own father had sealed it shut and shut it would stay as long as he lived.

Obviously if Roland had no problem with murdering her grandfather, he'd have no problem reopening the nasty dungeon pit.

The shortest route to the storage room lay through the kitchens, and as they stepped inside, Isa found herself slowing down, amazed at the stillness.

"Do you ever remember finding the kitchens with no a soul in them? No even one person to tend the fires?"

Jamie shook his head, tugging at her hand again. "It's as the MacDowylt ordered. Hurry, before they finish and return."

As he said, there was no time to linger.

Isa snatched up a lantern hanging by the fireplace and lit it before heading back into the tiny cubby where they'd find the entrance to the storage room. Together they lifted the heavy wooden door and climbed down into the dark.

She paused at the bottom of the steps, trying to get her bearings. It had been well over twenty years since she'd been down here.

"This is no place for a wee lass to be playing," her grandfather had said when he'd found her peering into the black abyss of the dungeon. If you fall into the pit, you'll be stuck until someone comes down and hears you calling. It's too deep for even a grown man to climb out."

She'd done as he asked and left this place at the time, more because of the forbidding black depths she'd seen and the hideous smell rising up through the bars of the metal grate.

The smell. That was the key.

"Sniff the air, Jamie. We look for a stench something like a garderobe.

"I ken what you search for, Isa. It's over here." Jamie ran into the dark, away from the glow of her lantern, his awkward limp exaggerated by the shadows. "Look," he called excitedly. "I've found it here but I canna move the barrel that blocks it."

Following the sound of his voice, she reached the spot and set her lantern on a nearby crate.

"Bollocks," she muttered, putting her shoulder against the large barrel. What was she going to do now?

God, but he hated dark little holes.

Robert tried to lick his lips, but his tongue felt glued to the roof of his mouth, sticky and heavy. Lack of food and water were making themselves felt. That and the ever-worsening wound in his side.

He should have eaten last night instead of wandering out to stare off into the night. Ah, but that had led to Isa coming out to find him, and for the night they'd shared he'd gladly starve to death.

No! He was a long way from starving. He'd done without food for far longer periods of time. Food and water. He wasn't about to give up now.

He needed to stand, to move around through the black. That should convince him his cell was larger than it seemed.

Using the rough stone wall for support, he dragged himself to his feet while holding his chest, panting as he did so. He moved slowly, one heavy step after another, finding no corners. That told him he was either in a space so enormous he'd not yet traversed one wall or, more likely, he was in a round hole.

From the feel of the wall, this place had been hewn directly from the rock, giving even more credence to the round hole theory. In spite of that, he knew there had to be openings of some sort in here somewhere. He'd heard the scurried scratching of small animals. Rats, likely. Filthy, disgusting, disease-carrying rats.

"At least I've no call to fash myself over that," he muttered, continuing to follow the wall around. From the burn and swelling in his old wound, he knew it wouldn't be diseased rats that would bring about his death. No, he could thank the Faerie Magic for the fate awaiting him. A fate he didn't intend to give in to until he'd found a way out of this place and delivered Isa safely into the care of his family.

More scratching, a scraping from somewhere in the dark. Cocking his head to the side, he listened intently, but heard nothing more. The silence pounded at his ears, and he felt as if the walls were pressing in on him.

Had to keep moving. Had to keep up the pretense of more room than he knew what to do with.

The dark confined space had obviously disoriented his brain. It had sounded as if the noise came from the ceiling, but rats didn't live on the ceiling. That was impossible.

Unless he were already hallucinating. Or his cell mates were bats.

Or Faeries.

And where were the damned Fae when he really needed them? "No a fucking Faerie to be found down here," he yelled into the darkness, stumbling to one knee with the effort.

As if in answer to his angry call, a pale yellow light seemed to flicker into the darkness, from above, directly ahead of him.

Now wouldn't that be just his luck? To piss off some wandering Faerie.

As if there were anything left they could do to him.

"Take yer best shot, you Faerie bastards," he called, lurching toward the light.

"Robbie? Are you down there?"

Isa? He shook his head, struggling back to his feet. Not possible. She was prisoner somewhere in the castle proper.

"Robert MacQuarrie!" the disembodied Isa demanded. "I ken you have to be down there. I hear you moving about. Answer me, dammit!"

"Isa?"

He stumbled toward the light, looking directly up into it. Her face, her beautiful face hovered above the grated opening.

"Isa?" He whispered this time, fearful of speaking out loud lest the apparition disappear.

"He's there! Help me get this open."

"Look, Isa. There's a rope just up there."

He'd swear that was little Jamie's voice. Now that was impossible. He must be hallucinating because Jamie had been burned alive in that . . .

His throat tightened and he fought for air, feeling as if he might be reduced to blubbering like some dainty girl at any moment.

That infernal scraping sound again.

He looked up to see the grate disappearing as it was dragged away from the opening.

"Stand back so I dinna hit you with this. I've tied it off on this end, but you'll have to climb. Please tell me you can climb, aye?"

For Isa? Anything.

Whether this was hallucination or reality no longer mattered. He was going for it.

He pulled on the rope, testing, hoping it would hold his weight. Then, one hand after another, he lifted himself up the long rope, ignoring the searing pain in his chest.

When he reached the top, hands grabbed at his clothing, helping him over the edge. For a long moment he lay there, catching his breath.

"Come on, Robbie, on yer feet. We've no time."

He pushed to his knees and looked up. There before him, like angelic visions, Isa and Jamie waited.

Had he died in that hole?

Allowing them to help him to his feet, he decided not to look back down. Just in case.

He reached out and pulled Jamie to him, hugging the boy tightly. "How?" he asked, looking over at Isa.

"Later," was all she said, her face pinched with anxiety as she urged him forward.

His legs didn't seem to want to cooperate, and it was all he could manage to drag himself up the narrow wooden steps and out into the kitchens. By the time they made it across the big room and out the door, he was panting with the effort. Isa situated herself next to him, and draped his arm over her shoulder, helping to support his weight. He didn't want to lean on her, but he could think of no other way.

Too slow. They'd never make a successful escape like this.

They'd made it outside the castle and were near-ing the little gate that led out to the fields when Jamie veered off to one side.

"This way, Jamie," Isa panted, shifting his arm on her shoulder.

"No, Isa," the child called, limping steadily away. "Bronco's tethered out here. I heard the men say so."

"Bronco?"

"My horse." Robert had told Jamie about raising Bronco from a colt while they'd worked together on the fence. "I'm a hard-core Denver fan," he added with a chuckle, though even he'd be forced to admit his com-ment lost any trace of humor ending in that wheezy grunt. Damn, but his chest hurt.

"I've no idea about this 'hard-core,' but yer hard to understand, I'll say that for you," she muttered in re-turn. "Now why do you suppose they'd have left yer animal all alone, way out here?"

Before he could even consider her question, Jamie returned, leading Robbie's horse along behind him.

It took a few extra moments, and an argument with Isa about her walking while he rode, but soon enough both he and Jamie sat on Bronco's back, with Isa lead-ing them through a deserted side gate.

With a little more of this kind of luck, they might even have a chance.

Chapter 27

At this rate, they didn't stand a chance.

Isa winced as she stepped into yet another hole on the rutted road, twisting her foot once more. It had happened so many times as they made their way through the night, she'd given up counting. She was certainly no stranger to putting in a hard day's work, but the distance they'd traveled so far had taken its toll. Her shins ached and the muscles in the backs of her legs felt as if they'd knotted themselves into hard little lumps of pain.

She'd been so grateful to see the sun rise this morning, lighting her way at last, she'd come close to forgetting how tired she felt.

Glancing back at the horse she led, she almost wished it were still dark. Jamie's cheeks were stained a feverish pink, his small head bobbing with each step the animal took. Without a doubt, the child was asleep sitting up.

And Robbie! She couldn't begin to imagine what kept him upright in the saddle.

An involuntary shudder ran through her body. She'd promised herself that as soon as the sun came up she was stopping to have a look at the place he clutched on his chest, but from the circles under his tightly closed eyes and the sweat on his brow, she feared she'd not be able to get him back up on the horse if he once climbed down.

Again she stumbled, her legs numb with fatigue, the pain of her hours on her feet creeping up into her lower back.

"You need to rest, Isa." Robbie must have caught her looking back at him. "And I need off this animal before I fall off. There's tree cover over there."

She thought to protest, but he was already swinging his long leg over the back of his mount. He hit the ground with a grunt, doubling over.

Dropping the lead she held, she ran to his side and slid under his arm on his good side. Together they managed to get him to a grassy area and she helped him to sit up against a large tree.

Jamie slid off the great horse right into her arms when she tugged on his leg, and she wondered if he even woke up. When she laid him on the ground next to Robbie, he curled onto his side, all without ever opening his eyes.

She led the horse over to where they sat and looped his lead around a bush before dropping to her knees by Robbie.

"Move yer hand. I want to see what those bastards did to you."

He shook his head to deny her but didn't resist when she pushed his hand away and tugged his shirt up.

"Holy Mother," she whispered before she thought, glancing to his face guiltily when she realized she'd spoken aloud.

"That bad, huh?" His eyes were closed so she had no means of guessing what he was thinking.

Bad? It was the worst thing she'd ever seen. Like a wound freshly closed, the skin was swollen and bruised, with what looked like a newly formed scab covering a jagged cut between his ribs. Heat from the wound assaulted her fingers, hovering over the site.

When she looked up again, he was watching her intently, his expression telling her more than she wanted to know. If she could only fill the silence with her talk, she wouldn't have to hear the words she could see in his eyes. If she didn't allow him to say it, it still wouldn't be real.

"We've come such a long way this night. We passed the crossroads hours ago, so we're doing just fine. After we rest for bit, we'll start out again. I'm sure we'll find water soon, and we can wash that wound properly," She would have continued, but he covered her hand with his palm and the mark on her skin came alive, stealing whatever thoughts she might have expressed.

"It's time to face the facts of our situation. The wound is growing worse. We need to go over what yer to do if I should lose consciousness, aye? No matter what happens, you must give me yer promise that you and Jamie will get to MacQuarrie Keep. "

"Of course we'll get there. Together. All three of us."
They had to. She couldn't bear the thought of anything
else. "With you to lead us."

"As far as we have yet to travel, there could very well
come a time when I willna be able to lead. With one of
us walking, our progress is slow and Bronco canna carry
all three."

Desperation clouded her thoughts but fueled her
tongue. There must be a way. "In that case, you go on
ahead with Jamie. I'll wait here. You can come back for
me."

He made a clucking noise with his tongue that reminded her of her chickens at their feed.

"Surely you ken I'd never leave you behind. No for
any reason. As you say, we'll go on together, but you
must be prepared for whatever is to come. Just in case."

"Dinna say that!" she ordered sharply, covering her
mouth with her hand when Jamie's body jerked in response to her words.

Robbie picked up a stick and began scratching in
the dirt next to his leg. "I'm drawing you a map. You'll
need to memorize it exactly for when I canna direct you
there."

"Dinna you even think of such things." Surely he
wasn't giving up. She wouldn't let him. "We will make
it there together. All of us. We'll find help. We'll make
it to a village and find a healer."

Robbie leaned his head back against the tree and
closed his eyes, as if holding his head up took more effort
than he could manage. "I've traveled this way recently,
remember? We're too far from any village to count on
help. It's reality we must deal with now. Study the map

I've drawn. It'll be you who must find the way if I'm no able. It's time to use yer logic, no yer emotions, love."

"If no a village, then someone traveling on the road. We *will* find help." They had to. Logic be damned. She didn't want to hear anything else.

He lifted his hand, stroking the back of his fingers down her cheek before covering her hand with his again. "As much as I want yer words to be true, Isa, as much as I might wish for someone to come along to help us, you need to deal with what is, no what you want things to be. Make yer peace with that now. Our fate will likely be in yer hands before our journey is ended. You must be prepared for that."

Beside Robbie, Jamie sat up, rubbing his knuckles against his eyes. "Are we almost there?"

"No," she and Robbie answered simultaneously.

"Are we lost?"

"Of course we're no lost," Isa answered quickly, see-ing the fear on the child's face. "We've only stopped to allow Bronco a wee rest. We'll be back on our way soon, dearling, but for now, perhaps you'd best try to sleep a little more."

Sleep was the only answer she had at the moment. Sleep so he wouldn't remember how hungry he might be. Or how thirsty. Or how much pain he must be in with his own injuries. Sleep so he wouldn't ask the questions she couldn't answer.

"Are they going to travel with us?"

Isa slowly turned her head to look in the direction Jamie pointed. In the distance and closing, two wagons rumbled along. And now that she listened, she could hear the metal rattle that accompanied their passage.

"Tinklers," she breathed, pushing up to stand. "Thank the saints. Robbie, look, it's those Tinklers."

Robert opened his eyes, blinking in disbelief as Isa ran down the road toward the approaching wagons. Though he hardly had the energy to smile, he couldn't remember a time more deserving of great blustery guffaws of laughter. How like the Fae. Bring him right up to the edge and then dangle the carrot in front of him, even though they all knew the Magic would have its own way in the end.

Still, he felt grateful, in spite of what would likely be. The arrival of the Tinklers offered hope to Isa and to him as well.

Perhaps they would be willing to help them reach MacQuarrie Keep. If he could see Isa and Jamie safely there, he would have accomplished all he'd set out to do.

When he blinked, they had gathered around him, though he felt as if he'd only closed his eyes for a second. William Faas supported his head, holding a cup to his lips.

"Easy, friend," William murmured.

As if he'd forgotten how to drink, the water trickled from the sides of his mouth and down onto his neck like little rivulets of ice on a burning pavement.

"He's a fever." A soft, feminine voice. William's wife, Editha, and another woman leaned over him, but he wasn't sure which of them spoke. And then the cool air hit his chest as his shirt was lifted.

A gasp accompanied the gentle touch to his chest.

"I might could slow the progress of yer wound, but I canna heal such as this." The older woman spoke, her dark eyes capturing his. "It reeks of an old magic, aye? Only a more powerful magic could counter this. Perhaps a born healer could do it, but no a taught one such as meself."

A born healer.

"Leah." He spoke the name without thinking. Was the magic that threatened to end his life also showing him a way to survive? Leah possessed the gift of healing. He'd seen the power of her gift when she'd saved Jesse after he'd been shot. With her help, he just might stand a chance of making it through this.

"Who's Leah?" Isa knelt at his side, her cool, sweet hand brushing the hair from his face.

How could he explain Leah without compromising the safety of his young charge? Only one way.

He'd chosen the young girl's role himself as a means of guaranteeing her safety in this world, and denying it now could endanger her future. His responsibility to protect Leah was equally as great as his responsibility to protect Isa.

"Leah is my daughter. A born healer. She's at MacQuarrie Keep."

Isa's fingers faltered the moment he uttered the words. "Yer daughter?" she repeated. "You made no mention of a daughter before."

"It's a long story."

"Perhaps you'll see fit to share it later," she murmured as she rose to stand, moving out of the way to allow the two men to lift him to his feet and help him into one of the wagons.

Chapter 28

⁓

A daughter.

The lurch in Isa's stomach had nothing to do with the wagon's movement down the rutted path. No more than the heat or the cramped space might have to do with the pain in her heart.

A daughter waiting for Robbie at MacQuarrie Keep implied a wife waiting as well.

How could she ever manage to face that woman, his wife, after what she'd shared with him?

Unless . . .

Perhaps there was no wife. He'd never once spoken of one.

Isa might be willing to delude herself but her conscience had no desire to allow that.

He's never spoken of a daughter, either.

And yet clearly he has a daughter.

He had made mention of a family often enough, but she had never stopped to consider that to mean a daughter and a wife. No wonder he had been so insistent that she accompany him to his home. He'd wanted to return to his *family*.

His daughter and his *wife*.

Isa curled into a ball, turning away from the child sleeping next to her. She buried her face in the woolens Editha had laid out for them to rest on, hoping their fragrant thickness would absorb her tears.

If only she could join Jamie in slumber so she wouldn't have listen to her own horrible thoughts any longer.

The fantasy she'd allowed herself to construct, the cozy home with Robbie and Jamie and maybe even a baby one day—none of it would come to pass now.

He'd hidden a daughter and a wife from her.

Even in her misery, her conscience wouldn't let her be.

Who was she to hold him accountable for keeping secrets when she hadn't bothered to tell him her own? They'd walked for hours together on that long road. She'd had nothing *but* opportunity to tell Robbie what she'd done.

And who was she to blame him for shattering the fantasy she'd never had any right to create from the beginning? She herself had done that by her own actions. Even if no wife waited for Robbie at the end of their travels, it made no difference.

A husband waited for her back at Castle MacGahan.

Her husband.

The bone-jarring movement of the wagon rolled to a

stop, the lack of motion unsettling after so long a ride. As discreetly as possible, Isa wiped her eyes and then pushed herself up to sit. She might as well make herself useful because she certainly wasn't going to get any more rest.

Beside her, Jamie stirred and opened his eyes. The bandage Esther had applied to his cheek earlier hung askew and Isa could see at once that the child's injuries were worse. The skin was swollen and red.

"Have we arrived?" he asked, his voice hoarse with exhaustion.

"I dinna think so. No yet. I'd guess we're stopping for the night, lad."

"I'll see." Jamie turned over, crawling on all fours to the flap, where he slid out feetfirst.

Isa followed more slowly, heading for the second wagon the moment her feet touched the ground.

Robbie lay in the second wagon.

"Mistress Isabella."

The man who'd called her name, Ralph Faas, William's older brother, hurried toward her. It was his wife, Esther, who had done all she could do to treat both Jamie and Robbie.

"William asked me to tell you no to stray too far from the wagons because we doona stop for the night. We're only going to water the horses and give them a few hours' rest before we start out again. My Esther says yer Guardian canna afford the delay of a full night on the road."

Isa's thank-you was lost on Ralph, who'd already turned his back, heading off to tend to the animals.

As she reached the second wagon, Esther was climbing down.

"That was a long ride," she sighed, sending a tired smile back up toward Editha, who crouched at the opening, her small son in her arms. "I'll hurry back to watch over Sean for you so you can have a stretch of yer legs as well."

"I'll watch him for you. Go ahead with Esther," Isa offered, her arms fairly itching to hold the little boy.

"Are you sure? He sleeps at the moment, but he's rare fussy with his back teeth coming in. Only being held seems to help him sleep."

"I'm sure."

Editha moved to the side of the opening, allowing Isa to climb inside before handing over the sleeping child. With a grateful smile, she left them.

The interior of this wagon was exactly the same as that of the other, packed with goods to sell and provisions to keep the families going on their travels. A pallet was tucked into the front, identical to the one she and Jamie had slept on.

Robbie lay very still, his chest bare save for the great bandage swathed around his ribs.

Isa made her way over to him, balancing the sleeping toddler against her shoulder as she stretched out her hand to feel his forehead.

The skin under her touch was hot and clammy. Though Isa made no claims to any knowledge of healing, she was sure this wasn't a good thing.

The child in her arms slept soundly, his little mouth slightly open even after she'd managed to situate herself onto a spot on the floor next to Robbie.

She leaned her face down to the child's, delighting in the soft feel of his sweet breath tickling her face.

Tracing a finger lightly over Sean's cheek, she marveled at the soft, smooth texture of his skin.

"Quite a picture, you with that babe in yer arms. Like a natural mother, you are."

Isa started, looking up to find Robbie's eyes fixed on her.

"I thought you slept," she whispered, mindful of not waking the child. "How do you feel? Is the poultice helping?"

Esther had combined a variety of herbs and powders such as Isa had never seen before into a pasty mix that she had smeared across Robbie's wound before wrapping it tightly with a bandage.

He completely ignored her question.

"Jamie came in to see me moments ago. His injuries are no healing properly. His face shows signs of infection, and since we've no medicine, you must promise to have Leah see to him first."

He was panting as he finished speaking, as if so many words had taken more than he was capable of giving. Words that obviously came from the brainsickness of his fever because they made no sense.

"Promise me," he hissed, trying to pull himself up to one elbow.

"You have my oath on it," she answered, fearful he'd injure himself even more if he kept this up. "I'll have yer . . . yer Leah see to Jamie first." *Daughter* had stuck in her throat, as if her heart would not allow her to form the word.

"Good," he sighed, lying back down as if satisfied with her answer.

For long moments it was silent in the wagon save for

the baby's gentle snore and Robbie's labored breathing.

"When we reach the keep, there's one more thing I need you to do for me."

His voice breaking the silence startled her. She'd been so sure he'd slept, she hadn't realized he was simply gathering his strength until he lifted his head, his eyes glassy in his determination to speak.

"Anything, Robbie. But you must save yer strength now." She reached out a hand to him and he grabbed on, holding much tighter than she would have expected him to be capable of.

"You and Jamie are to have a home there, Isa. No matter what happens to me, you ken? Yer to stay there where you'll be safe. When you find my mother. Tell her yer my wife, aye? They'll look after you there."

"You mean you dinna have a wife waiting for you?" She wanted to bite her tongue, but the words were already out there, spewed from her mouth before she had time to censor herself.

"No wife," he panted, his head dropping back to the cushion, his eyes closed. "Only you."

"But what of yer . . . daughter?" She forced herself to say the word, somehow made less painful by the knowledge there was no wife. "Why have you no told me of her?"

"Leah's story is her own, no mine, to be told or no as she chooses."

How could his daughter's story not be his? Isa started to ask but Esther returned, with Editha following her.

The first woman carefully climbed up into the wagon so as not to spill any water from the pot she carried. When she reached them, she dipped a small cloth into the water and wrung it out before placing it on Robbie's forehead.

Editha took the peacefully sleeping child from Isa's arms before sitting down beside her.

"You'd best stretch yer own legs for a bit, Mistress Isabella. The last part of our journey will carry us through the night with few stops, but William says by morning we'll reach MacQuarrie Keep."

Isa nodded, and climbed down from the wagon. She wandered over to the edge of the stream, scanning the area for Jamie's whereabouts.

She found him at last, sitting on the bank, throwing rocks into the water with Ewan, Ralph and Esther's son.

A wave of guilt washed over her as she watched the child. He needed to know what had happened to his grandmother. But not now. She couldn't face breaking such horrible news to him after all the trauma he'd suffered. She couldn't bear to add to his burden or to see him even sadder. Once they reached Robbie's home, after both Robbie and Jamie were healed, there would be time. She and Robbie would tell the child together.

A shiver ran down her spine, the shock of realization slamming into her. Perhaps Robbie had felt this same way when he'd chosen not to tell *her* of Annie's murder?

No wonder she'd fought unsuccessfully for years to learn control of her emotions. How could she hope to control what she felt when she was so blind to the feelings of others?

As she watched, Ewan brought more rocks over to where Jamie sat, as if he realized his young companion hadn't the strength to gather them for himself.

Odd how these people, these tinklers who were scorned everywhere they went, had accepted them so easily and had shown them such kindness. She only hoped they would find this same sort of acceptance where they headed.

Jamie and her both.

Chapter 29

~

When Robert had referred to his home as MacQuarrie Keep, Isa had expected something much smaller than this imposing structure with the waters of the loch lapping at its back.

She lifted her hand to shade her eyes against the early morning sun, growing more frustrated by the minute as William argued with the guardsman on the wall denying them entrance.

"We've no need for tinklers here. Be on yer way!" the man yelled down for the third time.

Bollocks on this.

Isa pushed past William, her temper taking the lead.

"I've come to see Leah MacQuarrie," she yelled up at him. "I've her father in this wagon and he's hurt. If yer no going to open these gates, then get yer lazy arse down the backside of that wall and get her up there."

The guardsman stood for a moment as if he couldn't quite believe what had just happened.

"Do it now, you witless worm!" she screamed, stomping her foot to emphasize her point.

Not very ladylike to be sure, but she had a dying man and a sick child to consider, so whoever wanted to could criticize her later—she simply didn't have time for them right now.

"Well done, my lady," William whispered, arriving at her side as the chains holding the portcullis began to scrape against the stone.

"Enter," the guard yelled down, and from his tone, Isa was quite sure the man was none too pleased.

Isa ran along ahead of the wagons, surprised to find two women hurrying across the bailey toward her, one young and one considerably older.

"My apologies, my tinkler friends," the older woman said, taking Isa's hand in hers. "I am Margery MacQuarrie and I bid you welcome. The young man on the wall hasn't been with us long enough to have learned we never turn tinklers away. He said you have my son with you?"

Robbie's mother.

She was supposed to tell this woman she was Robbie's wife. She'd agreed to his request to do so. The words were on the tip of her tongue. But they weren't the words that came out.

"Aye, he's badly hurt and in need of special care."

The women asked no more questions, neither of them. They simply ran to the wagon where William and Ralph were helping Robbie to the ground.

"What have you done to yerself this time, lad?" Margery exclaimed, running to her son. "Hugh! Get those men over here to help. Leah! Come with me. We'll take them to Robbie's chambers."

Isa stepped back, feeling suddenly out of place. She considered climbing back into one of the wagons until a small, hot hand slipped into hers and she remembered her promise to Robbie.

"Come on, Jamie," she urged, pulling the boy forward. "Wait. Leah?"

The girl slowed, turning back to look at her with obvious suspicion in her eyes. "Yes?"

"Yer father made me give an oath to ask you to have a look a Jamie's injuries before you treated his own." She pushed the boy in front of her and toward Leah.

"Before I . . ." Leah's words trailed off. "Oh no. He did *not* think I was going to . . . well, of course he did. It is Robert, after all. I should have known." She came to a full stop and her head dropped as if she studied the ground at her feet.

What was wrong with the girl? Did she not want to help her own father?

"Esther, the tinkler, said Robbie's injuries were beyond her abilities. She said his only hope was a born healer. Robbie . . . yer father, that is . . . said you were one such."

Jamie backed up against her as if he sought to hide in her skirts and she put her arms around the trembling boy, rubbing her hands on his shoulders to comfort him. To comfort herself.

Leah's eyes darted toward the hand on Jamie's shoulder, and for a moment Isa thought she wasn't going to reply.

"You're Isabella, aren't you? You're the one he came back for."

Of all the things Isa expected to hear, that wasn't one of them.

"Leah!" Margery called from the top of the stairs.

"Coming!" Leah yelled back. "Come on, you and the kid, both. We'll sort this all out upstairs."

One thing was certain. Though Leah MacQuarrie might not favor her father's looks in the least, her speech was every bit as confusing as his.

Isa and Jamie followed the girl through the castle and up the stairs. By the time they reached the bed-chamber, the men who'd helped get Robbie into bed were coming out of the room.

"She says Robert wanted the boy taken care of first," Leah said to Margery as they entered.

"That sounds like something I might expect from my son," Margery murmured, flattening out the covers over Robbie. "And who are you that he'd give you this message to deliver?"

The look Margery turned on her was entirely no-nonsense. This was it, the opportunity for her to say the words Robbie had instructed. But how could she claim to be wife to Robbie when she had already wed another man? The words stuck to the roof of her mouth. She couldn't bring herself to lie to the woman.

"That's Isabella," Leah answered, placing a basin of water next to the bed. "*His* Isabella."

"Ah, I see. So yer saying Robbie wants us to have a look at yer young man there before we treat my son?" Margery asked, peeling the wrapping away from her son's chest.

"Exactly what I want. Leah's to see to Jamie first." Robbie's hand covered his mother's, stopping her movement.

"Yer awake!"

Isa all but ran to the other side of his bed, reaching out to touch him, but stopping as she remembered his mother and daughter looked on.

Robbie grasped the hand she'd withdrawn, pulling it to lie over his heart as he gazed into her eyes.

"It's no likely I could sleep through that joustling I took on the stairs, is it?" He tried for a grin but didn't quite make it. "Did she also tell you she's my wife?"

"She dinna share that with us," his mother answered.

"I thought as much," he said, tightening his grip on Isa's hand. "But now you ken the truth of it and you'll look after her, aye?"

"You can look after her yerself, lad, as soon as you've healed." His mother busied her hands, stopping at his Guardian Mark, tracing her forefinger over it.

"I'm no up to an argument, Ma. And you'll see to the boy's welfare, too. His injury looks to be infected." Robbie weakly tried to push himself up to one elbow, but his mother held him down.

"We'll see to him. Dinna fash yerself so, Robbie. Now let me finish with removing this bandage." Margery lifted the last of the wrapping from his chest, her fingers faltering as she exposed the wound. "Holy Mother," she whispered, her composure rattled for the first time.

The jagged wound centered between his ribs, a wide dark stripe, moist and puckered, as if the skin could barely hold itself together over the mark.

Isa struggled to find some sign of improvement. "Esther's poultice has taken the swelling down."

Robbie made a noise somewhere between a chuckle

and a cough, and shook his head. "It's no her poultice. It's regressing to where it was when it first happened."

"Oh crap." Leah pushed in front of Margery. "Let me see that. This is the big one? The one Cate took you back for? This is exactly what she and Mairi were afraid of, isn't it?"

"Leah!" The warning in Robbie's tone was clear, though what he warned his daughter of Isa had no idea.

"Fine," she answered, her irritation clear. "Well? Is it?"

"It is. I ken you've renounced what you are, lass. Still, I've no choice but to ask for yer help, though I'll understand if you refuse."

Leah crossed her arms under her breasts and paced away from the bed, a stain of red mottling her neck and face.

"Dammit, Robert. After what you did for me? How on earth could I refuse? You wouldn't be like this if it weren't for me. Okay. Everybody out. If I'm doing this, I need some peace and quiet to work in."

Isa sat on the cold floor in the hallway outside Robbie's bedchamber, her head leaned back against the stone. Jamie curled in her lap, his skin hot and fevered to her touch.

There was so much she didn't understand, not the least of which had to do with Robbie's relationship with his daughter. The girl even called him by his given name rather than Father.

Margery approached, pacing up and down the hallway as she'd done since Leah had shuffled them all from the room what felt like hours ago.

"I canna imagine what in the name of all that's holy can be taking the lass so long to—"

The chamber door opened, interrupting Margery's rant.

Leah leaned against the doorframe, her face damp with perspiration. "It's no good. Whatever magic has hold of him, it's stronger than anything I can do. Isa, he wants you with him."

Isa lifted the groggy child in her lap to his feet, and Margery took hold of the boy's shoulders as Isa stood and hurried to Robbie's side.

One touch of his forehead told her the fever burned in him, and she wrung out a cloth from the basin next to the bed, gently placing it over his skin. His eyes opened and he gave her a weak smile.

"It's as I feared. The Fae Magic will have its way with me, but as soon as Leah has rested, she's promised, she'll see to Jamie."

Fae Magic?

"What do you speak of?"

His eyes had closed and his breathing slowed. He slept again, so she wouldn't wake him now, but that didn't mean she wouldn't insist on an answer when he did awaken.

What reason could the Fae possibly have for doing something like this to him? It was much more likely that in his fevered state he had mixed the stories of her involvement with the Fae into what he suffered.

The very idea wracked her with guilt.

A muffled scream from behind her drew her to her feet in an instant.

Jamie lay prone on the floor with Leah's body draped

over him. His body shook with spasms as if he were possessed of some horrible demon trying to shake his limbs from his trunk.

Leah's body shook as well, but her hands were held tightly affixed to either side of the boy's face.

"Let him go!" Isa yelled, throwing herself at Leah, trying to pull the girl's hands from Jamie, to no avail.

When she tried to shove Leah away, the girl's head lolled to one side and her eyes rolled up. Clearly she no longer had any control over her actions.

In the next moment, right before Isa's eyes, the side of Leah's face began to redden and pucker, the skin bubbling and crawling, forming itself into a hideous parody of Jamie's scars.

"We have to stop this," Margery cried breathlessly, falling to her knees next to them, digging at Leah's fingers as she tried to break the horrible writhing connection between the two.

A high-pitched hum whined around Isa's head, and a pressure pounded at her as if the room were too full of air. The hum grew in both volume and power, and Isa could feel the sound rumbling and vibrating in her chest. She could swear a shaft of green light pierced Leah's hands where they joined Jamie's head, and then the light shattered into a million shards.

As the light shattered, both she and Margery were thrown across the room like rag dolls, landing several feet away.

Isa lay on her back, gasping for air.

Jamie! She had to get to the child to protect him.

She fought down a wave of nausea before rolling to her hands and knees. Another moment to gain her balance, and she slowly crawled back toward the crumpled pair in front of the fireplace.

The silence surrounding them now was almost more painful than the noise had been earlier, and she fought the urge to cover her ears against the roar of the silence.

Isa pulled Leah's limp body off the child's, pausing only long enough to see that though the girl's face and neck were as scarred and disfigured as Jamie's, she still breathed.

Too frightened to cry, she grabbed Jamie's arms and dragged him into her lap, clutching him to her before leaning away to check his breathing. His small face was so peaceful, his lips barely open, and just as she had when holding little Sean the day before, she turned her cheek to him. The soft, sweet breaths pulsed over her face and then, knowing he'd survived whatever had just happened in that room, she felt the tears prickling at her eyes.

"He's alive," she said aloud, to no one in particular, her fingers trembling as she pushed the tangled hair from his perspiration-slicked face to see if he'd suffered further damage to his injuries. Only then did she fully realize what Leah had done.

Jamie's face was perfect. All of it. The skin as smooth and soft and pink as little Sean's. Not a scrape, not a mark, not a single trace of the scars from the fire that had ravaged the boy's body.

Like a madwoman, she dug at his clothing, freeing his little chest and his legs. Annie had told her long ago that the entire side of Jamie's body bore the same scars as his face. It was the cause of his limp.

But now, the whole of him was smooth and perfect, as if he'd never suffered a single injury in his life.

Disbelief held her captive. Amazement kept her stroking his beautiful unmarred cheeks. How long she stared at Jamie's face she had no idea, but gradually she accepted that he was unhurt in any way and merely slept, albeit a deep sleep. As carefully as possible, she laid him back on the rug and moved to kneel beside Leah.

The marks on Leah's face looked like fresh, puckered blisters, the outline of the damage still vibrantly visible. It was as if she had taken on the damage that had been Jamie's only moments before. As Isa watched, the scars morphed and twisted, then amazingly began to fade, as if Leah healed right before her eyes.

The girl groaned as Isa touched her skin, but she didn't open her eyes.

"The lad?" Margery pulled herself up to stand.

"Sleeping." Isa answered. "Completely healed and sleeping. Leah, too."

Margery nodded, touching her fingers to a large bump on her forehead. "Well, that was an experience, was it no? If you'll wait here with our charges, I'll have someone come take them both to their rooms so they can rest in comfort."

Isa nodded, not moving from her spot on the floor as Margery bustled out of the room.

Though she had no idea exactly what it was they'd just experienced, she had not a single doubt it entirely involved the magic of the Fae.

Even now she could smell its familiar scent in the air.

One thing had become absolutely clear to her in the past few minutes. She wasn't the only one in this keep with Faerie ties.

Chapter 30

⌒

*I*sa lifted the compress from Robbie's head and doused it back in the water, her spirits spiking up. His forehead had cooled and the fever seemed to be gone, though she had a concern that his face seemed paler than before.

Perhaps it was only the candles that made it seem so. Margery had been in earlier to light them, one on either side of the bed. Fine creamy beeswax candles, not those made of tallow, so there was no bitter smell in the room.

Leaning back over him, she fussed with his covers, checking the bandage to see if the spot on it had grown any larger. A few hours earlier, blood had begun to ooze from the wound—not much to be sure, but blood nonetheless.

She touched her lips to his forehead, breathing in the scent of him as she did so.

"Sweet dreams, dearling," she whispered, surprised to find him watching her when she drew back. "Yer awake."

"I'd never sleep through my own wife's gentle kiss."

A pain lanced through her heart with his words. Now was the time for her to tell him. To confess to having wed Malcolm MacDowylt. But coward that she was, she couldn't make herself say the words. Instead she touched her lips to his.

His eyes fluttered shut and he dozed again, so she settled herself back on the stool next to his bed, his hand cradled between her own two.

A light touch on her shoulder and she nearly jumped from her seat.

"Sorry." Leah dropped to the floor next to her. "Is the little guy okay?"

Little guy?

"Oh, Jamie? Yes, he's magnificent. I dinna ken a way to thank you for what you've done for him."

"I'm really glad he's okay. I only wanted to help with the infection in his cheek, but I was so tired after trying to heal Robert, I lost control and the Magic took over."

"And you've recovered as well?"

Leah's face seemed to glow tonight, shining with radiant health as if this morning's events had never happened.

"I'm fine now. What about him?" She pointed to Robbie. "How's he doing?"

How is Robbie doing? He's dying.

She might allow the traitorous thought to ramble around in her mind, but she'd never give voice to the words. Especially not to his daughter. She needed to be strong for Leah. In spite of the years that had passed, she remembered all too vividly how it felt to lose a father.

"Yer father's fever seems to be gone, but now it seems the wound is beginning to bleed." In spite of her resolve, her voice cracked as she spoke, and she covered her mouth with one hand as if she could hold the hurt inside.

"You love him, don't you?" Leah put her hand up on Isa's lap, patting her leg. "I'm so very sorry I couldn't help him. I honestly tried, but I'm just not strong enough to turn back the Faerie Magic that has him in its grip."

"What Faerie Magic?" This was the second time she'd heard that term, and this time it was no fever-sick man who voiced the words.

Instead of an answer, Leah posed a question in return. "You know about the Faerie, don't you?" She ran her finger over the back of Isa's hand as she spoke, tracing the mark that had formed there.

Isa found no point in denying it. "I'm told my mother was Fae. She left us before I was old enough to remember her."

"Yeah," Leah agreed, her voice sad. "Whatever else those Faeries might be, they're especially good at deserting their families, that's for sure."

"What does this have to do with the magic you say has stricken Robbie . . . yer father?"

"Okay. I'm going to be totally honest with you here, but you have to promise me you won't freak out or anything. Promise?"

"Freak out," Isa repeated slowly, having no earthly idea what the girl meant. "I will try not to do this thing."

"First off, Robert isn't my father. He brought me here to protect me from some really bad guys." Here she stopped and shook her head, tears shining in her dark eyes. "Really bad Faeries, as a matter of fact. The father/daughter thing is just the cover story he came up with. But his parents have been so great to me. They've accepted me as their granddaughter, and for that I love them to pieces."

Isa stared at the girl, concentrating to follow Leah's strange pattern of words, trying her best to follow the girl's story.

"Here's the thing. About nine years ago in actual time, and don't even ask about that yet because it will all make sense in a minute or two, Robert got in this god-awful battle to save a friend, and he ended up getting a sword between his ribs for his effort. That friend used Faerie Magic to take Robert into the future, to a time where doctors had the tools to patch him up and save his life, because if he'd stayed here, he'd have been a goner. So—flash forward there he is in the future, doing fine until he agrees to bring me back here, back to *his* time, to save my butt. Only problem is, he isn't supposed to be alive in this time, and it looks like the Faerie Magic is determined to set things straight." The girl finally paused her nonstop rant to take a breath. "Make sense?"

Isa shook her head. Sense? Not at all. "Yer from this future Robbie was taken to?" she asked at last, her voice sounding hesitant to her own ears.

"Yes. And even though he knew this might happen, he decided to act as my Guardian to bring me back here because, way back when, he'd promised a dying friend he'd look after this guy's little girl, but first those guys almost killed him, and then the whole time thing got totally messed up, and now you're not a little girl anymore. In fact"—she smiled sadly—"you're his wife now. And he's . . ." Her words trailed off and she squeezed Isa's hand.

Leah's story boggled her mind. If not for the things she knew to be true, the things she'd experienced in her own life, she wouldn't have believed a word of it. Not even the words she could understand.

But she did believe, and knowing the truth of his story made so many things he'd said and done so much easier to understand. Still, honesty deserved honesty.

"I have something I must tell you as well. As yer no his daughter, I am no his wife." Isa kept her voice low, hoping to control the emotion buffeting her in waves. "No that I wouldna give all that I am to be such. Thinking to secure our release from the man who'd captured us, I spoke my vows to him in front of my clan. I'm no free to be Robbie's wife. No ever."

Leah rose up on her knees and put her arms around Isa, hugging her. "Don't cry, Isabella. You are his wife as far as he's concerned. That's all that matters right now."

All that matters? Hardly. If she understood Leah's story correctly, the man she loved lay dying before her very eyes and it was as much her fault as anyone's!

"He came back because of a promise to look after me." She drew on Leah's earlier words to help it all make sense.

"Uh-huh," Leah confirmed, sitting back down on the floor.

"Came back though he knew it might cost his life."

The girl nodded her agreement to that statement.

"Came back from a future time where he was perfectly healthy."

"Yes."

Isa felt as if there was something important just waiting to be plucked from the line of logic she'd followed, but it eluded her. Her tired mind struggled to find the missing piece, and then the pieces snapped together like the foreign puzzle box in her grandfather's solar.

She tried it one more time.

"If he can travel through time, and he's no in any danger in the future . . ." she began, pausing as she considered the implausibility of what she was getting ready to say.

"We should send him back to that future where the Faerie Magic wants him to be." Margery finished her line of reasoning from the shadows by the door.

"How long have you been standing there?" Isa stood and turned to face Robbie's mother.

"Long enough to recognize what you say as truth. An excellent plan, my dear. Leah? How do we make it happen?"

Leah had risen to her feet as well, one hand supporting her against the chair. "I'm not one hundred percent sure. I only know that the women who sent us told us we had to think about the place we wanted to be. So I guess you have to think about where you're going."

"It takes those of the Faerie blood to invoke the magic."

Isa jumped at the sound of Robbie's voice and hurried to his side. One look at the growing red splotch on his bandage and she knew they had little time left.

"I am of Faerie blood. Only tell me what to do, Robbie." Anything. She'd do anything to save his life.

He held out his hand to her. "Come sit beside me. I'll tell you about my home and we'll imagine ourselves there."

Isa carefully climbed up onto the bed, cursing her clumsiness when she noted the flinch of pain on his face. "Tell me. Help me to see it with you."

"My home sits in a lovely valley in the mountains. It's a big ranch, with plenty of room for . . ." He paused, panting for breath, obviously in pain. "Room for little Jamie and all the children you'll give me."

Isa tried to envision his words, but his dream was too much fantasy even for her, despite how much she wanted what he described to come to pass.

"It's no working. There's nothing," she muttered, her frustration and fear growing by the second.

His eyes were closed, as if it took too much effort to hold them open, his face wrinkled as he gritted through the pain. "Cate warned as much. It took three of them to send us."

"And we've only two." Leah stood at the side of the bed, twisting her fingers together. "Try again, Isa. Keep trying."

Try what? Isa had no idea what it was she should be doing. Think on someplace she'd never even seen? How was she supposed to do that?

Only Robbie could see where they were to go, and he seemed to be drifting in and out of consciousness now.

"Stay with me, love. I need you to concentrate on yer home for us." Isa grabbed his shoulders, giving him a little shake.

When her hand covered the mark on his arm, a shaft of green light burst from between her fingers, shooting out into the room.

"Whoa," Leah breathed, leaning forward. "Tell me you saw that, Grandma Mac."

"I did," Margery replied. "Though I've no idea what it was I saw."

"It's those tattoo things!" Leah cried. "Robert's Guardian Mark. It's on the back of Isa's hand, too. When they touched, it sparked the magic."

"But no enough." Isa swept her hand over Robbie's forehead once again, desperate to come up with an idea. Any idea.

"Love you," Robbie groaned, "Need to say that before I lose . . ."

"Oh, Robbie." Isa put her face close to his, kissing his cheek. "Dinna you die on me, do you hear? I dinna want to live without you."

"Soulmates," he whispered. "I'll find you again."

"No!" Isa sat up on the bed, grabbing his shoulders, sparking the shaft of light once more. "I dinna want you to find me. I want you to stay with me!"

As the light died down the door burst open and Jamie ran inside.

"I saw a strange light coming from yer door."

"Not enough," Leah murmured. "Not enough! Of course! It's only two."

She reached into the neckline of her shift and jerked, pulling a broken ribbon from around her neck. A shiny black stone dangled at the ribbon's end she held out to Isa.

"Take this. Hold it in your hand against the mark on

his arm. You've two marks. This will make three. It's worth a try."

Isa took the stone, sparing only a second to look at it. Carved into its polished surface was the same mark that Robbie wore on his arm. The same mark as on her hand.

"Wake up, Robbie. Stay with me. You must see where you want to be in yer mind."

His eyes fluttered open. "Be with you," he muttered.

"Aye, with me, love. But in the future. In yer home where yer safe. See it in yer mind for me. Please."

She slapped the stone against his arm, holding on to it as tightly as she could. If this worked, it would be up to him where they might go, for her thoughts were centered on him.

An odd green glow began to pulse through the room, with strange little bursts of color sparking in and out.

"Isa!" Jamie yelled, as he nimbly slipped past Margery's outstretched arm, straight up onto the bed beside Isa, his little arms locking around her waist.

With her free hand, she grasped onto Jamie's wrist, filling her mind with a new vision. A vision of the three of them. Together.

The tingling along the back of Isa's hand intensified and she fought the urge to slap at the invisible creatures she felt crawling on her skin as thunder rumbled nearby.

The green light grew more brilliant, shrinking into a wavering sphere that enclosed the bed, and the sparkles of color multiplied until it looked as though there were thousands upon thousands of them shooting around inside the sphere. They dashed soundlessly against the wavering emerald walls and through Isa's body, picking up speed until she could no longer discern individual shapes but only streaks of color swirling around her head.

The myriad colors gyrated around them, faster and faster, and at last, as if hitting the peak of their frenzy, they merged, and the world around Isa turned to black as she felt herself being thrown through the air.

Chapter 31

❦

$\mathcal{A}$s the black lifted, Isa found herself flat on her face, her grip holding tight to her two men. She opened her hands, trying to flex her cramping fingers before she pushed herself up to sit.

Jamie's body lay against hers, one limp arm, the one she'd held on to as they tumbled, still draped over her leg.

She grasped him under his arms and dragged him into her lap, smoothing her fingers over his soft pink cheeks.

"Dearling," she murmured. "Open yer eyes."

"He only sleeps."

Robbie, his eyes smiling and alert, watched her, a smug grin on his face as he sat up straight. "You did it, love."

She froze for a second before reaching across the child in her lap to whip the blood-drenched bandage from his chest. It gave way easily, leaving a wet brown smear across his skin.

Skin marked only with a thin silver scar.

Isa ran her finger over the ancient wound, finding herself speechless for one of the few times in her life.

"I told you. You did it." Robbie placed his hand on either side of her face and, leaning forward, pulled her toward him until their lips met.

What began as soft and gentle soon became desperate, and they broke apart, each of them gasping for air.

"Let me get our lad settled." He scooped Jamie into his arms and climbed off what had to be the biggest bed Isa had ever seen in her entire life.

"Yer sure he only sleeps?" His breathing did sound like that of a sleeping child, but she hardly knew what to believe after all she'd seen in the past twenty-four hours.

"Time travel is hard on Mortals. He'll sleep for a good twelve hours or more and wake as hungry as a bear in spring." Robbie chuckled as he walked away from the bed carrying the boy. "Dinna you move from that bed, wife."

Wife.

If he'd intended to freeze her to the spot, he couldn't have chosen a better word.

Wife.

It rattled around inside her head and dropped into her heart like a heavy lump of lead.

Wife.

What she wanted most. What she couldn't have.

"Ugh! Let's get rid of that." Robbie returned, snatching up the bloody bandage between two fingers and walking through another door with it, continuing to talk even after he disappeared. "I was thinking as I put Jamie to bed, I can only guess it's the Guardian Mark we wear that brings us through the travel so alert."

Isa changed her position to try to see into the room where Robbie had gone and her knee hit on something hard. Reaching down, her fingers tightened around a small, oval object.

Leah's stone.

Without this, they'd still be in MacQuarrie Keep. *Without this, Robbie would be . . .* She couldn't finish the thought. After days of staying strong, her reserves crumbled and, like some dam they had broken through, tears coursed down her cheeks.

"What's all this? We're fine now, love. You've nothing else to worry about. No ever."

Robbie had returned, pulling her to him. He held her in his arms, stroking his large hand gently over her hair, making little shushing noises that only seemed to elicit more tears.

He was so good to her and she wanted to be his wife more than anything in the world. She wanted to bear the children he'd spoken of when he shared the vision of his home.

She wanted him, but she was already the wife of another man.

"It's no fine. It'll never be fine," she finally managed to blubber.

"Of course it is. You've brought us here to our home. Jamie sleeps like an angel in the other room. We're together. What more could you ask for?"

"To be yer wife," she sobbed, unable to stop the tears at this point.

"And you will be." He pulled back from her, wiping her cheeks with his strong fingers. "We'll have a fine wedding here on the front lawn. Cate and Mairi put on grand affairs. What? Why are you crying even harder now?"

"I already wed the MacDowylt," Isa blurted out. She wanted to ease into the news, but her mind and her mouth were working at odds with one another. "I said my vows to him in order to . . ."

"You dinna need to give that a second thought, love. I already know about it and why you did what you had to," he interrupted. "I heard you tell Leah the story. It's no in the least important now."

He wasn't listening. He didn't understand.

"I'm a married woman."

She blinked back her surprise, her tears drying on her face as he laughed! Laughed as if this horrible, horrible situation were something funny.

She tried to resist when he pulled her back into his arms, his chest still spasming with his chuckles.

"Oh, love, yer no a married woman. If anything, yer a widow."

Pushing away again, she studied his beautiful smiling face for some clue as to the madness that possessed him.

"A widow," she repeated. "And how would you ken that to be the case?"

"Because MacDowylt was a Mortal. A fine man, by my guess, based on the improbable spate of *luck* we encountered in our escape from Castle MacGahan, but a Mortal nonetheless. And I've yet to meet the Mortal who can live for over seven hundred years."

"Seven hundred . . ." The future. Of course. Leah

had told her Robbie had lived in the future. It was the whole point of what they'd done.

"Aye. My condolences, Mrs. MacDowylt, but yer husband's long dead." He touched his lips to her forehead and then her cheek. "Yer mine, Isabella MacGahan, as you were intended to be from the beginning of time. All mine."

He lowered her to her back, covering her with the warmth of his body, crushing his lips to hers.

Her mind soared to that wonderful place he took her when they kissed and her need for him crashed down over her, hot and heavy.

He lifted his head, obviously aware of his power over her, grinning like a madman.

"I've so many things to show you. So much yer going to enjoy. In fact . . ." His eyes lit up and his grin turned seductive. "Oh, I've a grand idea."

He backed away, off the edge of the bed. Standing beside her, he began to unwrap the plaid he wore around his hips.

"Grand idea indeed," she agreed, fumbling with the ties on her overdress.

"Arms up," he ordered, and when she complied, he pulled the layers of her clothing up over her head and tossed them to the floor. "Thankfully here you'll no be wearing so many things at once. It will make life much easier on both of us."

"Much easier," she agreed breathlessly, not giving any thought to what he blethered on about.

As easily as he'd appeared to lift Jamie earlier, he picked her up in his arms and started toward the room where he'd taken the bandage.

"What is this place?" she asked.

"This is the master bathroom."

Nothing in this chamber looked in the least bit familiar. A see-through box filled one side, and on the other a cabinet jutted from the wall, made of a fine, polished stone. Above the cabinet hung what had to be the largest, clearest, most wonderful mirror in the world. The largest one she'd ever seen before had been no bigger than the width of her two hands.

She felt her face heat as she looked at their reflection in that amazing mirror, a disrobed woman in the arms of an equally bared man.

He obviously noted her fascination with the mirror and set her on her feet in front of it. Standing behind her, he wrapped his arms around her, fitting his palms over her breasts and pulling her back up against him.

He dropped his lips to her neck, running his tongue from her collarbone to her ear while she watched his movements in fascination.

"Funny," he whispered. "I thought that piece of glass good for nothing but my morning shave. Until now."

He captured her eyes in their reflection and held them as he placed his hands on her shoulder and slowly slid them down her arms. Grasping her wrists, he lifted them above her head, draping her wrists over his shoulders.

Tiny chill bumps sprang up along the path he traced down her sides, his fingers so delicate, his touch feeling as if it rippled along her skin. From her breasts down to her stomach and back up again his hands skimmed along, igniting a pulse in her body that she felt to her toes.

His fingers traced the contour of her nipples, and she watched them pucker and harden as she felt her breasts grow heavy. It was as if the little circles he drew had the magic to change the very makeup of her body.

"I could look at you forever," he whispered, his eyes dark with his need.

Grasping her waist, he turned her and lifted her at the same time, sitting her up on the countertop facing him.

The mirror must have lost its fascination for him because he stared into her eyes as he slid his hands under her bottom and pulled her toward him. The movement spread her legs apart and he fit himself into that opening.

The cold smooth stone beneath her bottom was a stark contrast to his heat pressing into her, and when he took her breast into his mouth, a magnificent pressure burst through her body, demanding more.

She wrapped her legs behind his back and pressed against him.

A noise sounded from somewhere low in his throat, part chuckle, part growl. As if her movement was all he'd waited for, he grasped her hips and drove into her, pulling her forward to meet each of his thrusts.

When her release came, it felt as though every muscle in her body spasmed it's delight in unison. His release came almost immediately after, filling her as he clutched her body to his.

Her legs had become too heavy to hold up so she lowered them and they leaned there together, his head on her shoulder, each of them panting as if somewhere along the way they'd forgotten to breathe for several minutes.

"Nothing," she managed to say at last. "Nothing could be more wonderful than that."

He grinned, his manly pride obviously well pleased, and lifted her off the countertop and to her feet.

"As they say in this time, you ain't seen nuthin' yet."

Leading her to the clear box in the corner, he pulled open the door and turned a handle, sending water spraying out.

She didn't realize her mouth hung open until he dipped his head down for a kiss, darting his tongue into the opening.

"It's called a shower, and the water is hot whenever you want it."

She stepped inside and stood under the flow, warm water cascading onto her shoulders and down over her body. Surely this was heaven.

Or it was when he joined her under the spray of the water.

"You think yer going to like yer new home?" he asked, pulling her close to nibble on her earlobe.

"Without a doubt," she breathed, all but losing her train of thought. "This is what I would call the perfect home."

"Yeah?" He lifted his head and grinned at her. "It's what I'd call the perfect homecoming."

Home. Their home. Together.

He chuckled as he dipped his head for another kiss. "If yer sold on it now, just wait till you meet my dog."

Epilogue

⁓

1293

"You believe the man?"

Malcolm MacDowylt strode down the dark hallway at his brother's side. It was a legitimate question that Patrick posed.

"I do. The MacQuarries sent him with the message. They'd have no reason to tell us a falsehood and the rider says he looked upon the graves with his own two eyes."

It saddened him to hear of Isabella's death. And the warrior who had been her self-appointed guardian. Though their presence had been naught but a hindrance to him, he'd hoped that in engineering their escape he'd given them a chance for long life together. Apparently the injuries the warrior had suffered at the hands of Lardiner had been too great for him to survive.

"The lad as well?" Patrick's question brought him back to the present.

"Aye. The child dinna recover from the beating, I suppose."

"Bastard," Patrick hissed, picking up his pace.

Malcolm placed a hand on his brother's forearm. "He'll be dealt with. Keep yer anger in check, Paddy. We've a plan to carry out."

His brother nodded, keeping his thoughts to himself until they reached their destination.

"I only hope the worthless whoreson tries to run," Patrick muttered, pushing open the door for Malcolm to enter.

Malcolm didn't mind admitting, at least to himself, that the same sentiment had crossed his mind more than once in the last hour. His hands fairly itched to mete out some well-deserved punishment.

He nodded to the men who stood guard duty outside the room as he entered, stopping to verify all was as he'd asked.

Patrick had gathered everyone together in the laird's solar—*his* solar—before coming to get him. Roland Lardiner lounged in a chair by the fire, with two of Malcolm's best men on either side of him, of course. His lackey, Shaw, fidgeted in the corner, also guarded by two men.

The lovely Agneys had taken a seat near the wall, as far away from her father as she could get.

Malcolm opted to stand, Patrick at his left shoulder.

"I've called you here to share with you my decisions about yer future."

"You've no right to be passing judgment on me,"

Lardiner snarled. "As Agneys's father, I'm the rightful laird here. When she delivers the old laird's male child, it'll be me who sees to the lad's training and welfare."

"Truly?" Malcolm asked, managing to keep his voice light and pleasant. "Would you be seeing to his welfare in the same manner as you saw to the old laird's?"

"And what is that supposed to mean?" Lardiner asked, straightening in his chair

"Only that you murdered yer laird. Pushed him down the stairs, according to his granddaughter and her witness."

"Her witness?" Lardiner sneered. "A child she claims saw this happen. And her naught but a madwoman at that."

"Perhaps. But the lad survived the fire and told us of what he'd seen in his own words. And even had he not, since I married that madwoman a fortnight ago, I am forced to give credence to her word."

"You did what?" Agneys made it almost out of her chair before she caught herself. "My apologies for my outburst, my laird. I had not heard any rumor."

Lardiner glared, his eyes darting from person to person in the room. "And welcome to her you are. It will do you no good. When my Agneys delivers the old laird's son . . ."

Malcolm had had enough of this.

"There will be no son. No bairn at all, as a matter of fact. Yer daughter is no with child."

"You lie!" Lardiner yelled, attempting to rise from his chair but finding the hands of his guards holding him in his seat.

"No. You murdered yer laird too soon, Lardiner. And you'll have to answer for that. Murder's a premeditated breach of the king's peace. The justiciar ayres will meet in a few months. We'll make sure yer brought before them to answer for yer crimes."

"I had no part in what he did to our good laird," Shaw sniveled from his spot in the corner.

"No, I ken the truth of that." As he'd hoped, the rat was ready to turn. "But you had a hand in the other deaths, did you no?"

"There were no other deaths," Lardiner snarled.

"But there were. My good wife's guardian, beaten before he was thrown into the pit, I believe? He dinna survive that. His death is on yer head as well as yer master's."

"And the child," Patrick said roughly.

"Aye," Malcolm agreed. "The child who witnessed the old laird's murder. Lardiner beat the boy severely and then you—" He smiled at Shaw, but he felt nothing even approaching humor. "You tried to burn him alive in my wife's cottage."

"I dinna ken the lad to be inside. I heard no screams. I told Master Roland. I heard no screams." Shaw's voice became more frantic as he pleaded his case.

"And if you had, would it have made a difference? My own brother tells me you were about to put my wife and her guardian to the sword when he arrived."

The man looked around the room as if desperate to find a single ally. He would find none here.

"And the old woman here at the castle?"

"I had nothing to do with Auld Annie. That was Master Roland himself did that," Shaw offered up.

"Strangled her with his own two hands. I stood witness to that."

"Hold yer tongue, you fool," Lardiner yelled, once again being held down in his seat.

"You stood witness," Malcolm repeated, disgust turning his stomach at the murder of a helpless old woman. "But you did nothing to stop it."

"Yer as guilty as that one," Patrick all but spat at the man.

Malcolm held up a hand to stop his brother. All in good time.

"And he'll stand before the justiciar ayres for his crimes as well."

"You've a nerve," Lardiner yelled. "As if yer above murder yerself. Did you no threaten to bring yer army down on the whole of the MacGahan in order to take over these lands?"

"It's because of yer deceit we came here, Lardiner." Patrick delivered his accusation with deadly calm. "You came to us two years back, claiming to represent the word of yer laird. Offering money you never paid for livestock we supplied. In his name, yer the one offered us title to the lands if yer laird failed to make payment. Did you no think we'd track you down?"

"Enough." Malcolm was done with the men. "My men will accompany you both to Edinburgh on the morrow. You'll be turned over to the sheriff there to await yer trials. The justiciar ayres will deal with yer crimes. Get them out of here."

"And what of me?" Agneys asked quietly from her seat. "You ken I had nothing to do with my father's crimes. I even warned you of his plan against you.

Would you have me be yer wife's maid or will I be confined to my chambers for the rest of my life?"

Patrick made a noise of disgust low in his throat, but Malcolm forestalled any comment he might make with a touch to his brother's arm.

"Sadly my good wife did not survive her trek to see her guardian home to his family."

As he expected, Agneys's expression brightened and she popped up from her chair, heading straight for him. "That's perfect. We can go forward as we planned. None save the men in this room ken that I dinna carry the old laird's bairn. We can marry and yer child can be the rightful laird."

She had closed in on him, sliding her delicate hand seductively down his chest.

He grabbed her fingers, trapping them before they trailed below his waist, surprised she'd try this ploy with Patrick as witness.

"Can you no see my poor brother's in mourning after the recent loss of his wife," Patrick said. "As you should be for the loss of yer laird and husband."

"Must he stay?" Agneys asked, her pleasant façade cracking just a little as she placed her other hand on Malcolm's chest.

"Aye, my lady," Malcolm answered, peeling both her hands from his body and backing away. "I think it's for the best that he remain with us. And as to the plans you spoke of, they were yers alone and none of mine. I dinna require a bairn to name myself laird."

"He is laird by rights of his own," Patrick added.

"As you say." Agneys turned her back, crossing to

her chair and retaking her seat. "If you won't take me to wife, what will you do with me?"

He'd thought long and hard on this. Though Agneys was a beauty indeed, he'd tossed his lot to chance when he wed Isabella to ensure a clear succession. She, to his good fortune, had been an honest woman, true to her word. But he wouldn't risk his future to any female again. He didn't need to.

"You've a choice, my lady. I'm told yer father has family in England and yer mother's people are in France. I'll see to it yer delivered to whichever one you wish."

"France," she answered without any hesitation, and with a deep sigh she rose to her feet. "The young widow of an old Scottish laird, living in France? I could do much worse."

"Indeed, my lady."

It was Malcolm's guess that a woman like Agneys would do very well indeed.

Epilogue

~~~

"*D*id you see that catch?" Laughing, Robert clapped his hands and yelled his support. "No doubt about it, my Jamie has the makings of a fine running back, for a fact."

"Aye, but it was Dougie's arm that laid the ball right in the zone." Connor slapped his back as they both sat back down on the grass to watch their children at play.

"*Ooof!* That hit was hard enough to rattle my teeth," Ramos observed returning from the house and passing a cold beer to each of the other men. "After that hit, my money's on Rosie for first all-pro female tackle. We should put her up for rugby."

Robert smiled, stretching his feet out in front of him and scratching the head of the little dog at his side. It didn't get any better than this. Two of his best friends and their families, a holiday cookout, and fireworks in town tonight.

This was the life he'd always dreamed of.

"And who's watching the grill?"

He turned toward the sound of his wife's voice, a thrill running through him as he watched her picking her way across the lawn, a precious bundle held in her arms. He would never grow tired of watching that woman.

Cate and Mairi followed along after her, their arms laden with bowls and bags and whatever good things they'd spent their morning gossiping over in the kitchen.

"If you guys burn those burgers, yer going to have to answer to the footballers out there," Mairi called, peering down at the grill with a raised eyebrow.

"Dinna you touch that fire pit, lassie," her brother warned. "Grilling is man's work."

"Riiiight," Cate shot back, rolling her eyes and plopping down on the bench. "Men's work."

The footballers had picked up the scent of food and were headed toward the table. His own Jamie, followed by Connor and Cate's three children—all had played hard enough to build hearty appetites, though their youngest, Cory, a happy two-year old, had done little but run under the legs of the older three.

Robert glanced back toward the picnic table under the trees where his beautiful Isa poured cups of iced juice for the children.

When she caught him staring she laughed, placing a hand on the delicate basket at her side. By this time next year, there would be another MacQuarrie future footballer toddling around in the mix. His precious daughter, who he hoped would grow to look exactly like her mother. Though barely four months old, she already had the wild red hair. More strangely still, she'd been born with the Guardian Mark on her perfect little hand. No one, not even Pol, could explain how that had happened.

"Oh, I almost forgot to tell you." Cate paused to lift Cory from his feet and settle him on her hip. "Jesse called. He said to wish everyone a happy Fourth. He said he and Destiny had their own celebration this morning, complete with fireworks, though he suspects it might not have been the politically correct thing to do. Considering where they are and what they were celebrating."

"Are you joking?" Ramos responded with a laugh. "It's Scotland we're talking about. They'd gladly celebrate anyone's independence from England."

Robert chuckled along with the others, knowing his best friend, Jesse, had never been particularly concerned with political correctness.

But the man was happy and that was what mattered most. Robert had seen that with his own two eyes when he'd taken Isa and Jamie to Scotland for a visit several months ago.

As soon as she'd settled in, Isa had wanted to see for herself how her home had changed over the past seven hundred years, but it had taken a while to manage all the proper documentation for her and Jamie. Thanks to Coryell Enterprises and their backdoor connections, even the adoption paperwork officially naming Jamie a MacQuarrie had come through before their trip.

Jamie had taken the news of his grandmother's death like a stoic little warrior. Robert liked to think the boy's strange new life and his loving new parents helped ease him through the transition.

When they'd finally reached Scotland, Isa and Jesse's wife, Destiny, had hit it off as fast friends immediately, cackling together like hens as they shared stories about Leah, Destiny's sister. And when Isa gave Leah's stone to Destiny? Lord, but it had been a major piece of waterworks if he'd ever seen such.

He and Jesse had left them with their female bonding in favor of introducing Jamie to the Portal Jesse guarded and the Faerie world beyond. As a part of this new clan, the lad needed to understand all he would encounter.

The visit had been an emotional roller coaster for them all, and certainly it had raised new challenges they'd need to confront in the future.

Somehow MacQuarrie Keep, which had been a pile of ruins before he'd taken Leah back in time, was now a beautifully kept private home. Mairi had spent long days researching the records she could find, trying to determine what they might have done that had so altered history, but she hadn't yet uncovered the documentation that held the secrets they sought.

Neither had she found evidence of what had become of Leah or of her own cousins, the MacAlisters, though he knew her dogged determination. If any scrap of document remained, she'd eventually find it.

Pol had been none too pleased with that bit of news about the changes they couldn't explain, but he was hard pressed to say much since it had been at his own suggestion they'd gone in the first place.

"Robbie!"

His attention snapped back to the present at the sound of Isa's call.

"The bairns are hungry, dearling. Stop yer lying about on yer arses, the three of you, and get these burgers cooked."

Much might have changed, but not Isabella's fiery temper.

"That's right," Cate added. "It's getting late and the boys are looking forward to you guys having a sword practice before we go into town for the fireworks. You promised."

They had indeed.

Robert pushed up off the grass, grumbling and muttering in play, just as his two friends did. It was their job as the men of the house to appear put-upon, though everyone present knew how much they enjoyed their lives.

Flipping a burger on the grill, the sizzle and smoke rising into the air, this was the best of times.

Robert had enjoyed his visit to Scotland, but in truth, he couldn't imagine living anywhere but here. And his trip back in time had proven once and for all that right here, right now was where *this* highlander belonged. This was his home.

It had taken him almost a decade of self-doubt and

the near loss of his life—twice!—but all the wonder that he saw as he looked at the friends and family surrounding him left him with no questions.

This was what made this highlander's homecoming worth every minute of his life.

Go back to where it all began!

Turn the page for an excerpt from the first
Daughters of the Glen book,

THIRTY NIGHTS WITH A HIGHLAND HUSBAND

Available now from Pocket Books

Prologue

The Legend of the Faerie Glen

*L*ong, long ago on a beautiful spring day in the Highlands of Scotland, a Prince of the Fae Folk peered through the curtain separating his world from that of the mortals. There, deep in a glen Pol thought of as his own, he saw a beautiful young woman gathering herbs. He watched her for a very long time, until her basket was nearly full, and he knew he had fallen in love with this innocent mortal. His love was so great for this woman that he was able to slip through a crack in the curtain between their worlds. Pol appeared to the maiden in his true magnificence, making no effort to disguise himself, for he knew she must love him for what he was.

Rose had wandered deep into the forest that day, gathering her herbs, and she had become entranced by the serenity of the glen. When Pol appeared before her, his beauty stole her breath away, and she knew at once that this was her own true love.

Pol and Rose dwelt happily in their idyllic glen next to the little stream where first he had seen her. But after a mortal year together, Pol was forced to return to his own world, for in those days, far in the misty recesses of time, the Fae abided by very strict rules.

One of those rules governed how long one of their own could remain outside the Realm of Faerie. Once returned to his own world, Pol would be unable to pass through the barrier again for a full century. And though one hundred years was nothing in the life span of a Fae, Pol knew his Rose would be no more at the end of that time.

Rose returned to her family, knowing her prince was lost to her forever. At first Rose's father, the old laird, was ecstatic that his little Rose had returned to him, even hearing her fantastic story of the Fae prince with whom she had spent the past year. Soon, however, it became apparent that Rose was with child, and her father and brothers were furious. Not only was their Rose a ruined woman, but to their way of thinking she had been defiled by a devious, unholy creature of magic. They began to treat her not as their beloved daughter and sister, but as their most reviled servant.

Rose toiled in the hot kitchens from sunrise to sundown each day and suffered all manner of indignity, but she didn't care, because her heart was gone from her. Her reason for living had disappeared with Pol.

Meanwhile, Pol could only watch with growing dismay, unable to pass through the curtain separating their worlds, as his beloved Rose slipped farther and farther away.

Finally the day came when Rose delivered her babes—three strong, healthy, beautiful girls. But Rose, whose spirit was damaged by the loss of her one true love, did not survive their birth. Rose's father refused to look upon the faces of the infants and decreed that they should be taken deep into the forest and left for the Faeries to whom they belonged—or the wolves. He cared not which claimed the infants first.

The old laird himself led the small party deep into the forest. As fate would have it, they were in the very same glen where Pol had watched Rose for the first time. The old laird ordered the infants to be laid on the grassy forest floor near a small shallow stream. Rose's brothers, who had each carried an infant, laid the babes on the ground and remounted their horses in preparation to leave the glen.

Pol, watching at the curtain between the worlds, was livid with rage and wracked with grief. Not only was his beloved Rose gone from the world, but now her children, *his* children, were being cruelly abandoned. His tormented cry of anguish reached his queen, who, in a rare moment of pity, broke the rules and opened the curtain just enough to allow Pol to slip through.

The wind suddenly began to howl through the tiny glen and thunder rumbled ominously. The ground around the old laird's party heaved and shook, and the old laird himself was thrown from his horse to the forest floor. He and his sons watched in horror as boulders pushed up from beneath the earth in the very center of the stream, piling higher and higher, one upon another. There they formed a magnificent waterfall and a deep crystal pool where only moments before a shallow stream had flowed.

Pol rose slowly from the depths of the pool, choosing to play upon the individual terrors of the men by appearing to each of the mortals as that which they most feared.

"I am Pol, a prince of the Fae. And you"—he swept his arm to include the brothers as well as the father—"have incurred my wrath. Now you will pay the penalty." His gaze turned to the helpless infants lying nearby, all three strangely quiet and untouched by the tumult around them. "These are my daughters. My blood runs strongly in them." Pol moved to the infants, gently picking up each one in turn. "I name each of you for your mother, my beloved Rose. For all time, your daughters shall carry a form of her name to ensure that her memory will live on in this world forever. I give each of you my mark and my blessing. Know this glen as the home of your mother and your father."

Pol turned back to the old laird. "I charge you with the care and the safety of my daughters."

"Never," the old laird hissed. "They are yer abominations. You take them. Neither I nor my sons will shelter yer spawn at our hearth."

"Oh, but you will, old man, and you'll be grateful to do so."

The shape of the Fae prince shimmered and grew until it filled the entire glen, surrounding the old laird and his sons, weighing them down with the power and the fury of the being they had angered, blocking everything else from their view and their minds.

Pol smiled with evil satisfaction. Well he knew the weaknesses of mortal men. His voice rang in their minds, all the more terrible for not being spoken out loud. "Should you or any male of the family fail to nurture and protect my daughters, hurt them or allow anyone else to hurt them, prevent them from making their own choices in life, or deprive them of finding their one true love, you shall suffer my curse. You will bear no male offspring. Any sons already living will suffer the same fate. You will be unable to enjoy the intimate company of any female ever again. Your line will die out and your name cease to exist in your world."

Pol waited for the full impact of his words to sink into their minds. Then he continued. "My blessing on my daughters, and thus my accompanying curse, will carry forward for all time, passed from mother to daughter. As even the smallest drop of my blood flows in their body, so they will have the power to call on me and all Fae to aid them. My mark upon them and upon all the daughters of their line guarantees all men know the penalty they will suffer for harming my beloved daughters."

As Pol's terrible voice reverberated in the minds of the old laird and his sons, his form shifted and shimmered around the infants, enveloping them for the first time, and the last, in the emerald glow of his love.

The old laird still lay on the ground where he had fallen, trembling with fear. And although he could not see the infants through the green mist surrounding them, he could hear what sounded impossibly like children's laughter.

Just before the mist faded, each of the men present felt an ominous warning echo through his mind.

"Never forget."

Later, much later, the old laird and his sons crept close to the infants to find them sleeping contentedly, each one bearing the mark of the Fae prince. The old laird gently gathered up his granddaughters—for so they must now be to him—and hurried from the glen.

Pol's daughters grew and prospered and eventually married, having families of their own. In time to come, though many generations of the Fae prince's offspring traveled and spread to varied parts of the world, all the men of all the lines continued to honor the Legend of the Faerie Glen.

Chapter 1

The clatter of metal on stone rang through the air even as the goblet spun slowly to a stop on the floor where it had landed.

"Tantrums will no be helping you, laddie." The old warrior shook his head, warily eyeing his companion sitting at the far end of the great table. "You only waste good ale."

Connor MacKiernan glared at him. It was a look that had weakened the knees of many a strong man. "Nothing will help me now. I am as the weak, helpless fool, all my options closed save one." He dropped his head into the crook of his arm on the table. "I am a king's knight, yet my sword might as well be a woman's pretty feather for all that I can do." He spat the words as if they soured and burned his mouth. "I dinna want to involve Rosalyn. This is no my aunt's trouble, Duncan, but mine. I am to protect my family, no to place them in greater danger."

Duncan pushed back from the table laughing. "The Lady Rosalyn would, I wager, see things verra differently, Connor. Dinna she tell you her plan would make everything work out just as you need?"

"Aye." Connor lifted his head only enough to peer up over his arm. "And that's what worries me. There is no regular way out of this mess. You ken that as well as I do." He raised an eyebrow and leaned toward the older man. "She takes a terrible risk."

Duncan took a long drink from the tankard in his hand and shrugged. "So she'll use her gift." It was a statement of fact, not a question, and required no answer from Connor, who simply continued to glare at the older man. "It is what she does, laddie, as did her mother and her mother before her. She disna deny who she is." Duncan took another long drink and smiled. " 'Tis no good reason to waste such fine ale." Duncan strode to the far end of the table, placing his hand on Connor's shoulder as he sat down next to him. "It's no she disna ken the risk to her if she does this, Connor. It's that well she kens the risk to all of you if she does nothing. You must remain here with yer sister, laddie."

"Aye, it's my duty to see her protected and happy."

Duncan lowered his head, speaking quietly. "You ken there are men who would follow you. Men who would fight for you if you choose to oppose yer uncle. To take back what's rightfully yers. You do have a choice."

"And how many would die then, Duncan? How many innocents would be caught in the middle of that great battle? We've been over this many a time. I'm no willing to sacrifice the lives of so many of my people." Connor groaned, dropping his head back down to his arm. "It disna matter, Duncan. I've failed my family yet again. Rosalyn was right. In order to save Mairi without bringing death to my people, I hae no choice but to risk my aunt's use of the magic." He shook his head, sighing with resignation, and sat up straight. "Rosalyn bids us leave this night. She'll be down soon."

"She's down."

Both men jumped to their feet at the authoritative sound of the female voice coming from the entryway. A tall blonde woman, with a bearing equally as authoritative as her voice, strode toward them.

"Quit yer sulking, Connor. We've been all through this. You ken it's the only way out. I promise you, this will be the answer to all yer problems. Do you hae the trinket I requested?" Rosalyn MacKiernan smiled at her nephew, ignoring his glare much as Duncan had. Fully expecting his compliance with her earlier instructions, she held out her hand.

"Aye." Connor reached into his sporran and handed over a small velvet pouch.

Rosalyn opened the little bag and dumped the contents into her hand. "Oh, verra good, Connor. It's exactly the piece I had hoped you would choose." She glowed with happiness as she lifted the emerald pendant, light from the candles reflecting in the facets of the jewel. "I remember when Dougal gave this to yer mother. It was at the dinner when they announced they were to be married." Her soft blue eyes glazed over with memory for a moment as she began to turn away, but she quickly turned back. "Oh. I almost forgot." She smiled at her nephew then, in a way that always worried him. "I need a small something of yers." Again she held out her hand expectantly. Seeing his momentary confusion, she explained, "Something of yers, Connor. Something personal. The magic willna work without it." She paused and looked around the great hall. "I know . . . yer plaid. A piece of yer plaid will do nicely." At his frown, she sighed. "Just a small bit, Connor. Honestly, nephew, must you make everything a battle?"

Connor shook his head, knowing it would do him no good to argue. He tore a strip of material from the end of his plaid and handed it over to Rosalyn. "I trust that's the last thing you'll be needing of me, Aunt."

"Indeed it is."

Rosalyn paused and Connor could feel the forces of fate gathering around him.

"Weel, except for yer presence at the glen." She looked remarkably innocent for someone so devious.

Duncan choked and spit out the ale he had just taken into his mouth. "The Faerie Glen?" he managed to croak. "Och, I should hae guessed that was where you'd be wanting to go." He looked at Connor. "You may hae had the right of this, laddie. I'll go see to the horses." He paused and raised an eyebrow. "And just where do I tell the others we'll be headed? Yer uncle will ask them when we've gone, you ken?"

Connor considered this for only a moment. "Tell them we head to the port in Cromarty. We'll be back within a fortnight."

Duncan MacAlister, although easily twenty-five years Connor's senior, was closer to him than any man alive. The grizzled warrior had served Connor's father from his youth. Only Duncan could be trusted with the truth of their destination.

Duncan nodded. "Lady Rosalyn"—he bowed slightly in her direction—"I'll be in the courtyard awaiting yer readiness."

"I suppose it's the Clootie Well you'll be wanting?" Connor's ice blue eyes reflected his irritation. He shook his head in disgust. "I will regret this, I am sure," he muttered.

Rosalyn beamed at her nephew. "My things are at the foot of the stairs. You can take them out and see that Duncan has our horses ready. I'll join you shortly."

Watching Connor stomp out of the great hall, Rosalyn smiled. How like his father he was. Both of them handsome and strong, just as her own father had been. Both of them clung rigidly to ideals of right, wrong, honor and responsibility to the family. Both held themselves to standards higher than those against which they measured anyone around them.

Those lofty ideals had brought her older brother an early death on a lonely battlefield. She would do anything in her power to prevent that same fate for Connor. Knowing the sacrifices her nephew had already made for his family, and the burdens he carried, she loved him all the more. This one time, however, she wanted Connor to get what he needed.

She carefully tucked the strip of cloth from his plaid into the velvet pouch with the emerald necklace and tied the strings, smiling broadly. She had very special plans for that little piece of cloth. And for her nephew.

When they reached the Faerie Glen she would tap into the source of the power and say the words that would allow the magic to travel within the pendant, guiding it wherever it needed to go to find the very special one it sought.

Chapter 2

"*D*amn it. Why couldn't I do something, say something?" Caitlyn Coryell slammed her front door and threw her keys across the room, where they bounced off the wall.

This is just great. Now she was talking out loud to herself. Surely just one more thing for Richard to criticize. " 'Just who do you think you are?' That's what I should have said to Richard." Cate shook her head. "I should have said something, anything, to Richard." Instead she'd just let him usher her out, like she was a small child. Like nothing at all had happened.

Cate walked woodenly down the hall to her bedroom, kicking off her sandals and tossing all her packages onto the middle of her bed. She went back to the living room and flopped onto the sofa, pulling her legs up until she could rest her forehead on her knees.

"I'm so pathetic." *Maybe Richard is right.* Wasn't he always? Maybe it was all her fault. If she could just be more . . .

"More what," she mumbled, absently twisting the diamond ring on her left hand. "Not more. Less. Less like me." Cate heaved a deep sigh and sat up. "Less afraid." Afraid and powerless to make even the simplest decision.

I sound like a sulky little girl. She picked up the telephone and dialed.

The hollow echo of the telephone ringing sounded for the third time. *Pick up.* Jesse should be in his room by now. It had to be around midnight in Barcelona. She needed him to answer. Though she was close to all three of her older brothers, she was closest to Jesse. He wasn't just her brother; he was her best friend.

There was no reason for him to still be out. They had contacted the office this morning. The mission had gone well and the hostages were safe. The team should have been at the hotel long ago.

Fourth ring. *Come on, Jess. Pick up. Pick up. Pick up.* Cate paced anxiously across the living room, stopping to tuck a box of tissues firmly under her arm. She'd need them for the good cry she was planning later.

Fifth ring. "PICK UP THE PHONE!" Cate yelled desperately, just as she heard the answering click on the other end of the line.

"Whoa there, no need to . . . Cate, is that you? What's wrong?" Jesse's sleepy confusion was evident.

"Sorry, Jess. I was just being impatient. Nothing's wrong." *Unless you count finding my fiancé having sex on his desk with his receptionist the week before our wedding as something.*

"Well, baby sister, you dragged me out of bed at . . . what time is it anyway? What's going on?" That was more like her Jesse. He sounded annoyed.

Maybe calling Jesse wasn't the smartest thing for her to do but she had already started. "Richard said, that is, we sort of had a disagreement, and, well, I've been thinking about what Richard said, and . . . " Her voice trailed off as she vividly recalled the "disagreement."

She had thought to surprise Richard with a picnic lunch since he'd told her he was too busy to get away from the office and meet her. He was busy all right. And all three of them had certainly been surprised. The blonde on the desk had screamed and Cate had dropped the basket of food, lemonade darkening the pale, thick carpet after the glass container shattered.

Jesse's voice brought her back to the present.

"Answer me, Cate. What did he do? You say the word and I am so on the next plane home. I'll have my foot up his ass before he can even think of another thing to say."

At least Jesse was completely awake now.

"No, Jess, you know I don't want that." Not that her brother couldn't do it, with his black belts in God only knew how many martial arts.

She closed her eyes and watched it all happening again.

She had backed out of the office into the hallway, but couldn't seem to think to move from the spot outside Richard's door. This couldn't be happening to her. The door had opened and Richard had grabbed her arm, pulling her into the of-

fice as the blonde receptionist sidled past on her way out. She didn't even have the courtesy to look embarrassed.

"Why?" she had asked him, hating the hurt in her voice. "Why would you do this to me?"

"I wasn't doing anything to you, Caitlyn. It meant nothing. You know I'm under pressure with the new cases I've taken on. How many times have I asked you to have sex with me? If you had, I wouldn't have been forced to find my relief elsewhere."

"You're blaming . . . that"—she pointed to the desk, unable to find the words to describe what she'd seen—"that . . . behavior on your work?"

Richard had led her to the large leather sofa in his office, waiting for her to be seated before he perched himself on the arm. Always the perfect gentleman.

"No. If there's any fault to be placed here, it's yours. I'm a man with needs. I've made that clear to you."

Cate shook her head to banish the memory. On second thought, it might not be a good idea to share the whole scenario with her brother. "Besides, Richard says it's my fault anyway."

"That's bullshit. Richard's full of it, and you deserve better than him." Jesse always ended up here when they talked about Richard.

"All I need from you is, I need to ask you a question, and I need your promise that you'll be completely honest with me. Will you do that?" She might as well get on with this.

"That's what big brothers are for, Caty Rose. I excel at being honest, given the chance. Fire away."

"Richard says I'm not adventurous, that I'm stuck in a rut, doing the same things day after day, until I'm not even living life anymore."

"My fault?" she'd asked Richard. "How can your doing . . . that . . . possibly be my fault?"

Richard had given her that haughty look she'd seen him use on others in the past, the waiter who took too long to bring the wine or the sales clerk who didn't jump fast enough. "You live life like some kind of spinster. The only thing you show any enthusiasm for is Coryell Enterprises. I constantly have to take a backseat to your daddy's company and your work there."

"What my father and brothers do is important. They risk their lives to save people."

"I'm not saying it isn't important, Caitlyn. I'm saying that you treat me as if it's more important to you than I am. You have no adventure of your own. You spend ten to twelve hours a day running that office, coordinating everything that goes on there. You deal with some of the most powerful people in the world, but look at you. You're in a rut. You don't fix yourself up unless I remind you to. What am I supposed to think? How can I pursue a career in politics without a wife at my side who understands my needs? One who's willing to sacrifice for my career?"

"I'm adventurous." She'd desperately grasped at the only part of his censure she could, her stomach clenching in horror as he criticized her passion for her work, the one thing she truly felt she excelled at.

His cold laughter stung. "Really? Then prove it. If you have any adventure in you at all, you'll have sex with me right here, in this office, right now." He'd stood then, straightening his tie. "But you aren't up to that, are you? That's simply too out of the ordinary for Caitlyn Coryell."

Her fault. He'd said it was all her fault.

"Do you think he could be right?" She hated the wimpy, pleading note she heard in her voice.

There was a long pause on Jesse's end. "Okay, fine. You know I don't like Richard. I never have. How many times have I told you he's not right for you? You want honesty, well here it is. No, honey, you aren't adventurous anymore. Your last big adventure ended up with you ass over end flying off a horse."

She shuddered at the painful reminder. It had been so exciting to sneak out for a ride on her father's horse, at least for the first few minutes. What is it they say? It's all fun and games until somebody almost gets killed. She'd spent weeks recovering from that accident.

"But more important, Caty, is the change in you since you met Richard. The longer you've dated this guy, the more withdrawn you've become. You're so busy trying to be exactly what he wants you to be, you're like some 'Richard robot.' You should listen to yourself talk. You can't go more than five minutes without a 'Richard says' in your conversation."

Jesse was on a roll. "You fix your hair the way Richard wants, you attend the society functions Richard wants, you're forever starving yourself trying to lose weight because Richard wants, you wear the clothes Richard wants. Hell, you aren't even going to wear Grandma's wedding dress, and you and I both know you've wanted to do that your whole life."

"Richard said he only wanted the best for me, that he loved me." She barely noted that she'd referred to him in the past tense.

"I am so sorry to be the one to say this to you, but it's way past time someone did. Richard doesn't love you. Anyone can see it. If he did, he wouldn't be trying to change everything about you. You're great just the way you are. Richard only loves Richard. And the Coryell money. That and all the potential political allies he can meet through Coryell Enterprises. He's slime, Caty, and you need to drop him like a bad habit." Jesse stopped to draw in a ragged breath.

"He's simply an ambitious lawyer." She defended him now out of habit, though that wasn't really much of a defense for the man she was supposed to love more than anything.

"Lawyer or not, Richard is just plain slime of the earth. And, Caty?" Jesse waited until he knew he had her attention. "I don't really believe you love him either. I haven't seen you seriously happy since you agreed to marry this creep. I think you just want to be in love because you think it's supposed to happen now. But love doesn't happen on schedule. It sneaks up when you least expect it. You can't plug it into that little day planner of yours. You can't make it happen. You need to ask yourself some pretty serious questions about how you honest to God feel before that wedding next week."

"Okay, enough. Thanks for your honesty. I know you don't understand my relationship with Richard, I just . . ." She paused and took a deep breath. How could he understand? She wasn't sure she understood why she'd agreed to marry Richard. Or why she was still considering it. "So will you guys be finished up in time to get home by the end of the week?" He would know she was changing the subject, but she couldn't bear anymore right now.

"Sure." His deep sigh was clearly audible on her end. "You know we will, Cate. We won't let you down. So, I guess that means you're still going through with this?"

Still going through with it? That was the question she'd been asking herself for the last couple of hours.

After listening to Richard tell her how it was all her fault, how he forgave her, how he loved her, and how they needed to put this incident behind them, she had risen from his sofa without comment and crossed the office, dazedly stepping over the broken glass and the spilled basket that had been her carefully packed lunch. Lemonade had squished into her sandals as she'd opened the door.

"Don't forget the dinner tonight," he'd said as he strode toward her. "Remember there will be some very important people there, Caitlyn. Try to be ready when I come to pick you up. I don't want to keep them waiting. Oh, and why don't you put your hair up tonight? You look more polished that way." He'd kissed her on the forehead and ushered her out the door, closing it behind her as if nothing out of the ordinary had happened.

Was she still going through with it? She'd been too numb to think, too shocked to fully accept what had happened. Even now she avoided the decision, rattling off the first thing that came to mind in response to her brother's question.

"I finished my last prewedding detail today. I wandered into this little antiques shop in LoDo and found the perfect 'something old' to wear. I can't wait to show it to you. It's this beautiful old necklace. It looks like an emerald, although I know it can't be because I only paid ten dollars for it." Cate forced some lightness into her voice. "Oh my gosh, it's almost five thirty. I've got to get off the phone and start getting ready for tonight."

The senior partner of Richard's firm was giving a

dinner in honor of their upcoming wedding. If she were late, there would be such a scene.

"All right. But at least promise me you'll think about what I said, okay? It's not too late to change your mind. You don't have to go through with this. I'm not hanging up until you promise."

As if I'll be able to think of anything else.

"Don't worry about me, Jesse. And yes, before you get all upset, I promise to think about it. I love you. Give my love to Dad and the guys."

"Love you, too, baby sister. You remember to think about what you really want. Just because Mom and Granny were both married at your age doesn't mean you have to get married right now." Allowing no time for her to protest, he quickly continued. "We should be on our way home in a couple of days. We're just tying up loose ends here. But when I get home, we're going to continue this conversation, whether you want to or not." He hung up before she could argue the point.

She put down her tissues, deciding she didn't have time to spend on tears, and shuffled off to the shower, deep in thought.

Why couldn't she decide what to do?

On a daily basis Cate negotiated contracts, met with clients of her father's company, and compiled sensitive background information for negotiations or hostage rescue. She even handled the business side of Coryell Enterprises whenever government agencies contracted them for civilian covert operations. How could she possibly be so weak willed and indecisive now?

"Because that's business and this is personal."

Cate stood wrapped in a towel in front of her bedroom mirror, examining her reflection. She'd spent thirty minutes in the shower, trying to decide what was wrong with her. If she hadn't used all the hot water, she'd probably still be there.

"I'm not that bad. Maybe not model or movie star material, but not totally ugly. I'm smart. I'm good at my work. I'm not mean and I don't smell bad." Cate smiled ruefully at her image. "But I might be crazy, because I'm talking to myself again. Maybe this is what a nervous breakdown feels like."

It was then the thought hit, stopping her in her tracks. *Do I really, honestly love Richard enough to have a nervous breakdown over him?* No.

Such a simple word. *No.* And yet for the first time, it allowed her to see her situation quite clearly. No. She didn't love Richard that much. In fact, right now, she didn't even like him. Maybe that was why it had always been so easy to tell him she wouldn't sleep with him before they got married. Jesse was right. Richard was slime. But she couldn't lay all the blame at his doorstep. She had chosen to ignore all the things that bothered her about him because she should be in love by now. And Richard should have been the perfect one. He was tall, strong, blond, intelligent, and very handsome. He opened doors for her, held her hand, took her to the places she wanted to go. He had been attentive and affectionate. More important, he instantly took command of every situation and people flocked around him. He had power over any circumstances, always smooth and in control. Not only was he everything she should want in a man, he was everything she wanted to be herself. And he had loved her.

No. He had used her. He had never loved her. He loved being with her and meeting all the important people she took for granted because, thanks to her father's company, they had always been part of her life. All the powerful, famous people who could make things happen for an ambitious lawyer with political aspirations. And everyone around her had seen it all along; watched as she let him make a fool out of her—no, as she'd made a fool out of herself.

Cate sat down on the end of the bed, her legs literally giving out under her. Richard might have used her, but she had used him, too. She had wanted to be in love, and when Richard came along she convinced herself that she was. She hadn't loved him any more than he had loved her. What had she been thinking for the past year?

"You know, for an almost genius, Cate Coryell, you're pretty stupid." Just because you could make it through school a few years ahead of everyone else certainly didn't mean you had learned anything about life.

She wouldn't need to straighten her hair or put on makeup or get dressed. She wasn't going out to dinner with Richard tonight.

And she wasn't going to marry him.

She stood up and headed for the kitchen. There was a bottle of some kind of alcohol she had never opened in the cupboard over the refrigerator. Her brother Cody had given it to her on her twenty-first birthday, warning her to be careful with it, but, since she didn't drink, it had languished with the cobwebs for the past three years. Now she deserved a celebration. She was declaring her freedom.

" '*An dram buidheach*,' " she quoted out loud, reading the back of the bottle. " 'The drink that satisfies.' Exactly what I need. A little satisfaction. 'Product of Scotland.' "

She had wanted to visit Scotland since her college Medieval History classes. Such a tragic, turbulent past, and yet so romantic. She had loved those classes, soaking up the history of the times, immersing herself in the lore.

Cate shook her head in disgust, remembering that she had even recommended Scotland for their honeymoon, but Richard was set on Belize, where the senior partner in his law firm liked to vacation.

Well, that isn't a problem anymore.

After struggling to open the dusty bottle, she poured some of the amber liquid into one of her pretty wineglasses and headed back to the bedroom, taking the bottle with her.

"It's time to straighten out a few things in here."

She took a quick sip of the Drambuie and gasped for air, coughing. Cody had been right. She'd need to be careful with this stuff.

First she went to her closet and, climbing on an overturned wooden storage box, brought down an old dress box, tied with an emerald green ribbon. Gently she laid the cardboard box on the bed and untied the ribbon, lifting out an antique ivory lace dress. Her grandmother had worn this when she married her grandfather. Her mother had worn it when she married. To think, she'd almost given up the opportunity to wear it herself.

Never again. Never again would she sacrifice her dreams. Never again would she accept anything less than the real thing. And if she ended up being one of those women for whom there was no true love? Well, so be it. Being without a man would be better than being with the wrong one for the wrong reasons.

She strode firmly to the closet and took out a huge garment bag, unzipping it and tossing its frothy white contents to the floor next to her trash can.

"Without a doubt, the most hideous excuse for a wedding dress ever, regardless of what Richard thinks." It had been vastly expensive, and she had waited three months for the designer to meet with her for a fitting. So what if it had cost a small fortune? It had been her money. She could do what she wanted with the white netted horror.

No doubt some charitable organization would be calling in a few weeks. They always wanted clothes to sell in their thrift stores. This time she could give them something that had never been used.

She congratulated herself on another decision well made by choking down a sip of the Drambuie. It burned a trail down her throat.

Next she pulled a stack of clothing out of her dresser, things she'd bought for her wedding and honeymoon. She dropped her towel and slipped into the white lace bra and panties set. She admired her reflection in the mirror for a moment. This wasn't really her style, not the least bit practical as she normally preferred, but it was so beautiful she was keeping it. A girl deserved a few pretty things. Another sip of the warm liqueur to seal the decision.

Taking the towel off her long damp hair, Cate grabbed the ribbon that had held her grandmother's wedding dress box and tied her auburn curls into a quick ponytail. Then she slipped into the emerald silk pajama set she had thought so sexy when she'd seen it hanging on the mannequin. The elastic waist of the pants hung low, riding on her hips, while the camisole top barely brushed her waistline. She'd hunted a long time for a set to fit like this. At not quite five foot four, she found everything was usually too long for her.

So maybe she could stand to lose another ten pounds like Richard said, but just maybe he should see her like this. Not that he would get to. One more little sip. It went down much more smoothly this time.

Cate turned to the dressing table and searched through her jewelry box, choosing the diamond and yellow gold earrings her father had given her for her college graduation. Normally she never wore anything but her plain silver hoops, but simple diamonds would be appropriate for a wedding. *If there were going to be a wedding. Which there isn't.* Cate was having a difficult time getting the little studs into her ears. Her sense of balance seemed just a bit off.

She glanced at the small emerald eternity band lying on her dresser and placed it on her right hand. It had been a birthday gift from her grandmother. Their shared birthstone. She took just one more little sip and stopped to refill her glass.

Next she reached for the long-sleeved silk Asian-style jacket that went with the pajama set, but stopped as her eyes lit on the bag she'd tossed to the bed when she'd first come home. It held her little treasure, the pendant she'd found in the antiques store today before she'd gone to see Richard.

Nope, not going to think about that scene again.

Instead she'd try on the necklace to see if it looked as good on her as it had lying on the velvet cloth in the store.

Cate held the necklace up and admired it as the light sparkled off the multifaceted emerald. Well, of course it couldn't be a real emerald, even if light did fairly dance off the jewel. Nobody sold those for ten dollars. Still, the gold setting and chain looked ancient. It was so beautiful it had to be the best bargain she'd ever found. It was the perfect "something old" for her wedding. *If I were having a wedding.* Which now, of course, she wasn't.

With some difficulty, Cate fastened the chain around her neck, and stood back to admire her reflection in the mirror.

"Not bad."

The pendant felt unusually warm against her skin, causing a tingling sensation that spread to her neck and shoulders. Or was that the drink?

She pulled the ribbon from her hair, allowing her natural curls to fan out, and lifted her glass in salute to her reflection.

"Here's to you, Richard. Just look what you almost . . ." She stopped suddenly when she noticed an odd green glow behind her reflected in the mirror.

"What the . . . ?"

Cate turned to see a large sphere of emerald green light forming in the middle of her bedroom, pulsing and growing larger. Even more startling than the unusual glow was the man who gradually materialized in the center of the sphere—he was incredible.

Or maybe she was drunk.

Or actually having that nervous breakdown she'd contemplated earlier. *Do drunks having nervous breakdowns suffer from hallucinations about incredibly handsome men showing up in their bedrooms?*

"Oh my God. What are you doing in my . . . who are . . . how did you get in here?" Cate demanded, slamming her full wineglass down onto the dressing table and jerking the chair out in front of her. The little chair wouldn't do much to stop someone his size, but somehow it made her feel better.

He straightened, pausing for a moment, just staring at her before he spoke. "I am Connor MacKiernan. I've crossed time seeking yer assistance, milady. Only you can help me."

He had the most wonderful Scottish brogue. Cate leaned toward him for a moment and then shook her head to clear it.

"Right." Stall for time and this hallucination would probably go away. "Through time." Oh my, he was gorgeous, and with that accent . . . !

But one of them must be crazy.

He was dressed like an ancient Scots warrior, boldly standing there with his legs apart and his hands on his hips, in a bubble of green light, in her bedroom, for crying out loud.

Connor cocked an eyebrow and tilted his head questioningly. "I am no used to begging, but if you require it, I will do so. We've no much time."

"Oh, great. Just great. I have Braveheart-slash-Conan standing in my bedroom, and he's in a big hurry." She blew out her breath in irritation. "What do you want with me? Why am I the only one who can help you . . . to do what?" Cate put her hands on her hips, mirroring his stance. Hadn't someone said you should take the offensive in these situations? She almost laughed out loud when she realized that chances were extremely high no one had ever encountered a situation quite like this one.

"Although some do call me brave, I'm no Conan. I told you, my name is Connor. Connor MacKiernan."

He looked a little annoyed now.

Annoying him might not be such a good thing; he was a really big man. Big and gorgeous.

Is that a knife sticking out of his boot?

"Are you no listening to me, woman? This is important and we hae precious little time." He shouted the last.

While gaping at him, she'd missed part of what he'd said. "Sorry. I'm sorry. I'm not in the habit of having strange men—strange men with weapons, I might add—pop into my bedroom." She stared pointedly at his leg.

That is definitely a knife sticking out of his boot.

"No, you're no the one who needs to apologize." At least he had the good grace to look embarrassed. "I'd no thought of how, or where, I might appear to you." He tilted his head in a slight bow and then, raising his head, he pointed to the emerald necklace she wore. "It's the jewel, milady. It's led me to you as the one to help me save my sister. The Fae magic sent me here to fetch you."

She should be completely freaked out. But he seemed so sincere. *Well, wouldn't all homicidal maniacs, or even simple hallucinations for that matter, seem sincere?*

She could hardly believe it when she heard herself ask, "Save your sister, huh? What exactly does this magic want me to do?"

"You must come home with me, to marry me. Then I'll return you here. No one will even know yer gone."

When Cate laughed, he looked offended.

"Sorry. It's just that, as you can see"—she waved her arm unsteadily around to encompass the disarray in the room—"I've just been dealing with preparations for a wedding." *Is that green circle shrinking around him?* "I still don't get it. Why would you need me to marry you? You don't even know me."

"It's verra complicated."

No mistake, he really did look embarrassed now, and it made him seem much younger, almost vulnerable, as he ducked his head.

"I must marry if I'm to protect my sister. It's no a real marriage. Well, it is, but because it will be in my time, it's no real for you. You'll stay just long enough to marry me and then return to yer own time. Once I hae fulfilled the condition of marriage, I will be free to remain with my family, to protect my sister." He narrowed his eyes. "I will no allow anything to happen to you, lass, if it's fear holding you back."

"I'm not afraid." Well, that was a lie, but it made her feel better to say it. "Where, or should I say when, is your home?" Yes, the nervous breakdown hallucination theory was firming up as the front-runner now.

"Sithean Fardach. Scotland. The year of our Lord, 1272." For the first time, Connor appeared to study his surroundings. "It's a fair distant time for you?"

Cate laughed again. "Actually, 'fair distant' would

pretty much be an understatement." *Now what?* She looked around the room. The glass she had set on the dressing table had fallen over. But instead of spilling, the warm caramel-colored liqueur was suspended in the air, never touching the ground.

"Did you do that? No, wait. Obviously you did. How did you do that?" She pointed at the suspended liquid.

"I canna explain. I dinna understand it all." He shrugged. "It's the Fae magic. Time has stopped here, allowing me to come for you. When you return, no matter how long yer in my time, you will be right here, right now—that's all I ken about it. We must hurry, please."

The green sphere is definitely growing smaller. And he didn't look to her like a man who said *please* often.

What did she have to lose? Chances were, she'd wake up in the morning, probably with a huge headache, and be quite amused by her hallucination.

And if not? If he's real?

Hadn't she just been told today—twice, in fact, by both Richard and her brother—that she needed to be more adventurous? What could be more adventurous than a quick visit to thirteenth-century Scotland? Accompanied by what had to be the most gorgeous man she had ever seen. A man who needed her help.

Connor held out his hand. "We must hurry. Time canna wait forever, no even for the magic."

Cate grabbed her pajama jacket and put it on, jammed her feet into the well-worn woven-grass flip-flops Jesse had brought her from his last trip to Thailand, and started toward Connor. She stopped at the last minute, grabbing her grandmother's wedding dress.

"Can I wear this to be married in?" She held the

dress clutched to her, eyeing him defiantly. If he said no, she wouldn't go.

"You can wear whatever you want, lass, I dinna care, but if yer coming, it must be now."

The sphere was pulsing again.

Making up her mind, she picked up the ribbon she'd pulled from her hair and tied it around the dress to form a small bundle. Taking Connor's hand, she stepped into the glow.

He drew her close, putting both arms around her as the sphere closed in on them. Tingles raced through her body. When he looked down at her, Cate was mesmerized by the intensity in his blue eyes.

"I swear, lass, on my honor, I'll no allow any harm to come to you. I'll protect you with my life. And when it's finished, I'll see you safely returned home."

The strength of his determination radiated from him. She was still captivated by the look in his eyes when he lowered his head toward her, slowly, almost as if against his own will. It took her by surprise when his lips met hers, her own eyes fluttering shut. Electricity arced through Cate's body at the simple touch as a multitude of colored lights lit the world around her.

The feel of his soft lips and strong arms and the look in his eyes as he made his promise were the last things she thought of as the lights winked out.